# Snowed In With A Werewolf

Addison James

Addison James

To everyone starting again. May you find what you're looking for.

# Contents

Series Note      VIII

Content Notes      IX

1. Luc      1

2. Penny      6

3. Luc      13

4. Penny      23

5. Luc      33

6. Penny      40

7. Luc      47

8. Penny      57

9. Luc      64

10. Penny      70

11. Luc      79

12. Penny      90

13. Luc      98

| 14. | Penny | 106 |
| 15. | Luc | 116 |
| 16. | Penny | 126 |
| 17. | Luc | 137 |
| 18. | Penny | 149 |
| 19. | Luc | 158 |
| 20. | Penny | 172 |
| 21. | Luc | 185 |
| 22. | Penny | 195 |
| 23. | Luc | 205 |
| 24. | Penny | 212 |
| 25. | Luc | 222 |
| 26. | Penny | 236 |
| 27. | Luc | 247 |
| 28. | Penny | 258 |
| 29. | Luc | 268 |
| 30. | Penny | 276 |
| 31. | Luc | 285 |
| 32. | Penny | 291 |
| 33. | Luc | 303 |
| 34. | Penny | 312 |

35. Luc                                323

Want More?                             329

Also by Addison James                  330

# Series Note

*Snowed In With A Werewolf* is the third book in the Supernatural Christmas series. While this book does work on its own, you'll be missing the backstory of some of the side characters if you don't read the prior books. Max, Casey, Elise, and Marcus all make appearances in this book.

If you would like to start the series from the beginning, start with *A Werewolf for Christmas*, and then *A Recipe for Love*.

# Content Notes

This book is a steamy holiday romance, but Luc also has some questionable morals. If you know him from the prior books in this series, you'll know that he'll use and manipulate just about anyone, and he's firmly in the morally gray category. With that in mind, here are some content notes, so you can make an informed decision about this book:

*(Light) stalker romance

*Discussions of a prior abusive relationship

*Discussions of a neglectful childhood

*Discussions of a violent childhood (think child soldiers and death cults)

*Feelings of inadequacy

*Fighting and violence, including killing and discussion of torture (not carried out on page)

*Sex scenes, including light bondage and somnophilia

*Adult language

# CHAPTER 1
# Luc

The robbers are expecting a quiet night and an easy score.

I saw a movie like this once, where two robbers were staking out homes of families going away on vacation. No doubt they saw the small family drive away yesterday morning, the harried parents and two kids piling into the dented minivan. Then they saw the lack of lights, the back gate that can be shimmied open even when it's supposedly locked, and the outdated alarm system sign for a company that doesn't exist anymore, and thought they'd have an easy night. It didn't end well for the robbers in the movie, and it won't end well for these two, either.

I listen to them whisper outside the back door as I sit on the staircase, halfway between the woman I came here for and these robbers, waiting for whatever comes next.

So much for my quiet night basking in Penny's proximity. This is only the second night ever that I've had an opportunity to be inside the house, and these morons are going to ruin it for me.

1

When they get the door open, I push to my feet. Nothing good ever lasts.

I meander slowly into the kitchen, leaning my hip against the chipped linoleum counter. The house is so dark that I'm covered by shadow, and I doubt any human could see me. Just the way I like it.

When they finally make it inside, they split directions. One of them goes to the living room, where the old TV and gaming system are practically hidden among the pile of children's toys. The other heads for the stairs.

"I wouldn't." I step up behind him, silent as the grave with two thousand years of practice.

He jumps, turning toward me. "What the—"

"If you wake up my girl, we're going to have a problem," I tell him. "This is your one chance to get out of here unscathed."

I listen for a moment. Judging by the soft breathing, Penny is still asleep upstairs, completely unaware of what's happening in this house. This is the second night I've broken in, and she hasn't so much as twitched as I've walked around. She's always seemed like a heavy sleeper when I watched from a distance. Hopefully, that trend continues tonight.

"Who the fuck—"

"That's not the right question," I scold, stepping closer. "The question is, how smart are you? Because anyone with any brains at all would get out of here right now and save their own sorry skin."

His eyes flick up and down, and I know what he sees. It's the same thing everyone has seen when they've looked at me since I was a child: too scrawny to back up my mouth.

There's a scuff behind me. The other one thinks he's quiet, but my ears are sharp enough that I could hear a pin drop in the house next door. My muscles tense, and I resist the urge to squeeze my hands into fists. I have no doubt I could beat two humans in a fistfight, but that's not the way I win fights.

Not that my usual method will be much help here, either. Poisoning, tricking, and manipulating others into doing my dirty work is a little out of reach at the moment.

But I have a dirty trick I can pull here, and it's a big one.

And what can I say? They interrupted my night with my girl. I don't know how many of these I'm going to get, how many chances I'll have before someone catches on and I have to let this obsession go. I'm just mad enough to think that this is all a good idea.

"Last chance to leave," I tell him. I already know he won't take it. I can see it all, the next three, five, ten steps ahead. Like a chess game, I can envision every move coming down the line.

And I never lose at chess.

He swings. I duck, timing it perfectly so he knocks his friend sneaking up behind me in the face.

There's an echoing crash, one of them falling into the bar cart and knocking over the bottles of cheap liquor. I wince,

3

absently making a plan to replace those while reaching for one of the broken bottles.

Checkmate. It's always good when a weapon falls into my lap. I palm the glass, weighing up my opponents and determining the best place to strike.

When one lunges at me, I hold my position until he steps right into my range, then cut under his arm with my broken booze bottle. It won't kill him, but it'll hurt something awful and bleed a fair amount, which is all I need.

"There're easier pickings somewhere else," I tell them, because I'm not heartless. I really don't give a fuck what most humans do. Crime will never go away entirely, and I'm not going to pretend I can stop it.

But they crossed a line when they picked this house. When they picked this woman.

I can see them turning it over in their heads. The risk versus the reward. The threat that this skinny guy in front of them wearing a suit poses. The bottle in my hand. Whatever they've no doubt already spent the money they hoped to get on.

There's a way to end this quickly. Of course, the most effective way would be to have Max with me, but Max doesn't know about this place. For the first time in our long existence, we're leading semi-separate lives, and I was grateful for that before right now.

Ah, well. Needs must. I force a partial shift, letting the wolf take over my face. Teeth, eyes, and a snout—just enough to make these men practically shit their pants.

I'm dripping sweat under my suit, my muscles starting to ache. It's incredibly hard to hold a partial shift like this. I've practiced thousands of times, but even so I can't hold it long, having to make a decision to shift entirely or to take my human form back. I settle back into my human skin only to see that the would-be robbers have already turned tail and run.

Well, then. Now that that's solved...

There's a footfall behind me, and it's only then I realize the sound changed. The peacefully slumbering breathing from upstairs is gone.

*Shit.*

# Chapter 2

# Penny

The man in Stephanie's living room turns toward me slowly.

I grip the softball bat tighter. It's technically Louise's, but I'm sure no one will mind me borrowing it. It's not like she's using it right now.

The only reason I'm not already swinging is because this man, whoever the hell he is, clearly scared away whoever else was here. I don't know if I just witnessed the robbers turning on each other, or if some sort of vigilante broke into the house, or what. But he doesn't seem like he's here to rob me.

And, I don't exactly know how to take him down. He looks scrawny, but I saw that one of the others was bleeding, and they ran away from this guy like their asses were on fire. Does he have a knife? A gun? Some crazy mixed martial arts skills? If I swing and don't knock him unconscious right away, will that just make it all worse?

"Hi," he says once he's turned fully toward me, like this is a completely normal, casual conversation.

It takes a second to process that I recognize him. That's the governor of New York, the guy who is supposedly going to run for president in a couple of years, and even if I didn't recognize his face from the news, then I'd remember it from the day he did a campaign event at Stephanie and Louise's restaurant and I served him lunch.

In addition to telling one of his staffers that he'd ensure they never worked again if they snapped their fingers to get my attention one more time, he'd tipped two hundred percent. You don't forget a man like that.

Plus, he looks *great* in a suit, and just because I don't touch doesn't mean I can't look.

I pinch my thigh through my sleep pants. This has to be some weird, vivid dream I'm having. Maybe he was on the news last night before I went to sleep or something, so my brain is just plugging his face into this random story it concocted while I sleep.

"So... I suppose I need to explain," he says, still in that same level voice. It's the same voice from when he told his staffer to knock it off. It's the same voice as when he ordered his food. It's the same voice I've heard on the news.

*This is a dream*, I tell myself. *This is a ridiculous, stupid dream that for some reason I can't wake myself up from.*

"*Mreow*?"

Jinx winds between my legs, doing a full figure-eight spin before biting me on my calf. It's her way of showing love, but it also fucking hurts, and that pain is *real*.

I'm awake. The governor is in Stephanie's living room, standing over a broken bar cart, holding a broken bottle, after scaring off some robbers.

"Is that a cat?" he asks, stepping backward.

I look down at Jinx, who's looking right back at me, looking like she's trying to ask *what else would I be*? I feel her. This not-dream is getting weirder.

"Why are you in my house?" I manage to ask, my voice sounding like it comes from someone else entirely.

"Good question. I was in the neighborhood, and I saw the door open, and I was going to close it but then I heard them, so I handled the issue." He says it so matter-of-factly, like he's reporting the weather.

"You were in the neighborhood, checking out people's back doors, at—" I glance at the oven clock, "—two-thirty in the morning?"

"I take due diligence very seriously."

"What business could you *possibly* have in this neighborhood?" I ask, because this is a row of houses with peeling paint and overgrown lawns. Houses with hardworking people, people proud of what they have, but not the type of place I expect to see the governor in his suit and tie at two-thirty in the morning.

"Yeah, I can't tell you that," he says. "Sorry. I'm sure you understand."

I nod, even though I don't really. But he's just so compelling when he says it. I look at that face and his confidence and, sure, he must know what he's talking about. He seems like the kind of guy who knows a lot of things, and I am someone who knows very few things, so sure. He knows what he's talking about.

"Oookay." Only Jinx winding through my legs again assures me this isn't one weird dream.

"I'll replace what I broke," he tells me, like that's my primary issue. I guess it should be up there, though—who knows how much money the booze on that cart was worth? And I'm sure the carpet is wrecked, too, from all the alcohol seeping into it.

"Uh, do we need to call the police?" I ask, feeling stupid that wasn't my first thought. I probably should have done that *before* I even grabbed the softball bat.

"I already took care of everything," he says in a voice so reassuring I couldn't doubt him if I tried. This is a man who takes care of things. It's his whole job, basically. Of course he's already taken care of it. I look at him and I see a man with his shit together, who looks put-together and confident in a way I could never be, and I trust him.

"Alright, then." I have no idea what to do next. What do I say to a guy who broke into my house, but with good intentions? Who apparently frightened away people who wanted to steal my sister's stuff?

I eye him consideringly. I didn't get a good look at those guys, but they were definitely bigger than he is. I've seen videos of small people winning fights, and I know it's sometimes about leverage or smarts or speed or whatever, but still. The governor is not a big man. I'm not even sure if he's taller than I am, and he's certainly skinnier than I am. "Are you okay?" I ask. "They didn't hurt you, did they? I can get the first aid kit. It's mostly for the kids' injuries, but if you need more than that, then I can drive you to the hospital."

Something weird crosses his face, and then he smiles. It makes his whole face softer. "That's sweet of you to worry," he says. "But I'm tougher than I look. I'm not hurt, I promise."

Uh-huh. I don't understand. Did he fight them? Why did they run like that?

"Well, I, uh..." I flounder.

He steps closer. Jinx steps between us, eyeing him up, and I want to bend down and tell her it's alright, that not all men are the same, but I'm paralyzed by his eyes. "You should go back to bed," he says in that soft, hypnotizingly confident voice of his. "Get some sleep. Do you work tomorrow, Penny?"

I mutely shake my head.

"Alright. I'll be by in the morning to replace what I broke. In the meantime, lock the door behind me—but get some shoes first. I don't want you walking through here and cutting your feet." He looks down at Jinx, breaking the connection between us. "And, I don't know, lock the animal upstairs. You wouldn't want it to get hurt."

"Her," I manage to say, sounding firmer than I have on anything all night, but Jinx is my little warrior, and she deserves respect, dammit.

"Her," he echoes. "You have shoes upstairs?"

I nod. All my stuff is upstairs. I rent the room from Stephanie, and I don't like to leave any of my things in their space. It feels intrusive to leave my shit scattered among their family life, even if Stephanie would tell me it's fine.

"Alright, then. Go get them. I'll wait right here."

I scoop up Jinx and carry her upstairs, because he's not wrong about the risks of her stepping in glass. "Sorry, baby," I tell her, depositing her on the bed and slipping my shoes on.

She settles down into the blankets, but when I go back toward the door, she hops up, ready to follow me. I close the door on her, ignoring her howl of protest, and go downstairs.

It's only when I see the governor in his suit that I realize I should have changed. He looks like he's about to walk into a political meeting—or whatever people like him do—and I'm wearing the rattiest pajama pants with a hole in the knee and a sweatshirt that's too big and entirely faded. At least I'm wearing the sweatshirt. The tank top under it barely contains my tits, and that is not something I need to advertise.

"All set?" he asks softly. I nod, so he leads the way to my still propped-open back door. "You'll be safe here," he promises. "I've contacted the authorities, and there'll be extra patrols tonight, alright? And I'll be back around eight. Does that work for you, Penny?"

Well, it's past two-thirty, and being up and dressed and *presentable* for eight will really cut into the amount of sleeping in I get on my rare day off. But I nod, because what else can I say?

He nods too and steps outside, closing the door behind him. I lock it, and I'm halfway back upstairs before I realize he shouldn't have known my name.

# CHAPTER 3

# Luc

I make it back to my car that I parked around the corner before I let my hands start to shake.

*Fuck*. How did everything go so wrong?

She was never supposed to see me anywhere near her house. She was never supposed to know I was there.

Penny Lakes is the lure, the fantasy, the thing keeping me grounded to reality that, at the same time, I can never have. You don't drag a woman like Penny into my world. You don't mar her with the blood and guts I've been wading through since I was a child.

Penny is a hardworking, honest woman who keeps her head down. She lives in a world where someone might not have everything they want, but they respect themselves for what they've earned. She cares about her family. And I'm not like that. I'm the antithesis of that world.

But she smells like fucking heaven. And it only took her looking at me a couple of times that day at the restaurant for my soul to be irrevocably hers.

13

She didn't see the wolf when I shifted tonight. That's the best thing I can say for this clusterfuck—the small comfort that I didn't manage to blow the biggest secret I have. It's a secret I've killed people to protect. I've made laws for my kind, sent my enforcer after people who break them, and here I am, only a lucky few seconds between me and spilling our secret to an innocent human.

Once upon a time, supernatural creatures played fast and loose with the idea of secrecy. We were legends, stories, nightmares that haunted ordinary humans. But when I rose to power and wrestled control of the entire supernatural world, I'd changed that. Humans can't know about us. That is the rule I've set, the one ironclad thing every creature who walks this planet knows not to fuck with me on. We keep our secret. We keep to ourselves. And the humans are never any the wiser.

Call me domineering, but as someone who was born and raised to be sold to human emperors as an enhanced killing machine, I'd wanted them as far out of our business as possible. Humans hadn't made me what I am, and I don't hate them. But it's clear they have no business knowing anything about our world.

*Humans don't have to remain human*, the insidious voice inside me whispers. I squash it. That's the voice that drives me for more, that told me ruling the supernaturals wasn't enough, and I needed power in the human world, too. It's the voice that doesn't let me be satisfied, and it's not used to being ignored.

Penny isn't something to conquer and own, though. Just because she *could* become something like me doesn't mean she should. Who would want that?

That little voice reminds me of Casey, Max's wife. And yes, Casey did choose to become one of us when Max and I found a way to make it happen. And yes, we now know exactly how to make more of us. But that doesn't mean we *should*. I've spent centuries cleaning up the mess of Alexander, the sorcerer who made us in the first place. If I'm going to wade into that water, then I'm going to be fucking careful about it.

Regardless, the thought exercise is doomed before it begins. Max had spent four years convincing Casey he was someone she wanted to be with; Penny doesn't know me at all. I'm a stranger to her who ate in her restaurant once.

And I suppose I can't say I know her either. I didn't even know she had a cat.

I pull my cell phone from the center console where I'd left it earlier, scrolling for a number in my contacts. It's almost three in the morning, but that hardly matters. My people pick up when I call, no matter what.

I don't bother with greetings, just rattle off Penny's address and the repairs that need to be done and tell him to meet me here in five hours. Then I hang up, settle deeper into my seat, and wait.

I've been watching Penny Lakes for just over three years now. It was right after Thanksgiving three years ago that we did a stupid political stunt at the restaurant she works at. We were trying to pass legislation about revitalizing local businesses, and that restaurant has been open for forty-seven years. It's been in the same family, too. It was a prime location.

Needless to say, I hadn't been enthusiastic. No one enjoys spending time on political stunts, and that was what the whole day was. But as soon as the pretty waitress came over to take our drink orders, I forgot everything about that. She'd had a few strands of light-brown hair in her face that must have slipped out of her braids, one on each side of her head, charming me in a way I couldn't quite explain. She'd been wearing scuffed white tennis shoes, dark-wash jeans, and a blue shirt with the restaurant logo on it. She'd smiled so big and bright, and I think more than anything, the fakeness of the smile intrigued me. She faked it with so much enthusiasm, but it had been entirely false.

I know a little something about faking what the outside world sees. Penny and I might have different motivations for manipulating the people around us, but we both do it. Maybe that's what originally drew me to her.

Or maybe it was her scent. My nose is a thousand times better than a human's. Restaurants are busy, overwhelming places to be. But Penny's smell of cinnamon cut through all of it, and I'd followed her scent home without even thinking about it. I'd just ditched my team, doubled back to the restaurant after hours, and followed that scent all the way to this house. She apparently walked to and from work, her scent a well-worn trail over the quarter mile stretch of roads.

And I've spent almost every night here since.

Penny is the first person in my life I've resisted being *me* about. I don't need to control this situation. There's no winning this game. I haven't conducted a background check, haven't had her followed. I haven't asked anyone anything about her. I just sit here every night, catching a glimpse of her through her window, and dream of her.

Every other moment in my life has been about strategy. How to survive, how to *win*. How to seize power and then hold it. How to rule the world and bend it to my will and never be the weakling child I was born as again. But not Penny. I can't win with Penny; she can't be mine. I can sit and dream and take a few hours out of my day to feel something, to think about a world where I don't have to be the way I am. But that's all.

I have to be normal in the morning. I have to act like I know how to be around a pretty woman. I have to act like Lucius Lawson, a guy who has things under control.

I look down at myself. And I probably shouldn't turn back up in the same damn suit.

I'm back outside Penny's house at a quarter of eight. I'm not usually able to be here in the mornings, but on the few I have been she's been up and moving long before now. But she said she doesn't work today. She takes almost no days off. Did she want to sleep in?

I should have said a later time. I should have given her a chance to sleep.

Well, nothing to it now. It'll be worse if I don't show up.

I distract myself by going through a briefing that I've forwarded to my phone. The Christmas holidays are supposed to be a break from work, but government waits for no one sometimes. I'm going to need to make some calls later, but I'll put those off as long as possible. Talking to human politicians can be tedious.

Bartholomew bangs on my window at five minutes of eight. "I got everything you need. Five guys."

"Good."

"What's up with this place?"

"Not your business," I tell him, voice mild, but he's fully aware of the threat behind it. I step out of my car, straighten my suit jacket, and walk toward the door. Bartholomew falls into step next to me, exactly as I knew he would.

"You're in charge here," I tell him. "You have three hours to get it done. The work is finished before we get back. There's no mess in the house. Not even a speck of dust out of place."

Bartholomew nods, but his brow furrows. "Boss, who is this person? Why are you redoing the floors of random housewives?"

"Not a housewife. And consider this your good deed of the day."

He doesn't argue, which is amazing, considering neither of us are exactly known for good deeds. Bartholomew is good for following orders, which is exactly why I called him. He'll keep this quiet, but I can trust him to get it done.

My watch ticks over to eight, and I knock on the front door. I know the rest of the family is still gone, but I worry for a half-second about someone else opening the door, regardless.

I worry about *Penny* opening the door. I'm going to become obsessed with her, and it's going to be so hard to let her go when today is over. I'm selfishly giving myself a few hours. And then I'll somehow convince myself to let go.

I might not be able to come by tonight, or for a while. Maybe never again. I shouldn't have let myself into the house the last few nights; I'd gotten complacent. Maybe a clean break would be best for both of us.

She opens the door wearing another too-big sweatshirt and jeans with a hole in the knee. It's not a trendy hole, either. It's clearly a frayed rip.

19

I had plans to take her to breakfast, but should I take her shopping? We can re-do her entire wardrobe in a few hours. I know the types of places I can take her to get high-end clothes that aren't especially fussy.

*That's crossing a line*, I remind myself. *That's too much. She'll be weirded out.*

I'm not used to having to check my impulses. They've driven me well over the centuries; I wouldn't be where I am today if I didn't chase the things I wanted. But I suppose eventually, I had to run into something I can't have.

"Good morning." I need to remember my fucking manners.

"Hi." She looks around like she expects someone to jump out behind me. Maybe she expects more thieves. "I thought you were bringing replacement booze?"

"I brought more than the booze," I tell her, and snap my fingers so Bartholomew wanders into view. "He's here to supervise replacing that carpet."

"Replacing the... are you serious?" she asks, eyes wide.

"Between the booze and the glass, it should be replaced. I could see the kids' toys here last night, and your cat. And you in general. I don't want you to hurt yourself."

"Jesus Christ," she mutters. "This is too much. *You* stopped us from getting robbed; you don't have to pay through the nose for new carpet."

It's not that expensive, but I know saying that will just dig this hole deeper, so I keep my mouth shut. "He's going to get this work done in the next couple hours. I'm going to buy you breakfast."

Her eyebrow quirks up. There's a scar through the left one; it's not too prominent, but I remember seeing it the first time I met her and again last night. It's somehow adorable. Everything about her is adorable.

"Breakfast?"

"You know, pancakes and bacon and that type of stuff?"

"Don't you have more important things to be doing?"

More important than her? Perish the thought. It's fucking impossible to find something more foundational to my very existence at this point.

And that's the exact type of thing I am *not* supposed to be thinking.

"I got some time. It's almost the holidays, after all."

I know that because Max reminded me no less than a dozen times. Evidently Casey agreeing to marry him on Christmas Eve two years ago makes the day sacred or something, and I shouldn't expect him to work.

"Alright. I—you're sure? I'm not going to—I don't know. Call the newspaper and talk smack about you. You don't have to bribe me."

"It's pancakes, Penny. Not gold bars."

"Alright, then. Let me grab a jacket." I wait patiently in her doorway while she grabs a ratty old coat with frayed sleeves.

She hesitates at the door. "Are we good to just *leave* them here? Alone?"

I resist the urge to ask her what my team would possibly steal.

"Bartholomew will take care of it. Trust me; I wouldn't bring anyone to your house who I don't have faith in."

Asking her to trust me might be a bit much, but she just bites her lip and then nods. "Alright then. Pancakes?"

# Chapter 4
# Penny

This is the second time I've met this man and been convinced I'm dreaming.

The governor shows back up at my house, brings a crew to repair Stephanie's floor, and drives me in his very nice Lexus to get waffles. Sure thing.

The restaurant he picks is one town over, family owned and operated, and has great coffee that I gulp down like it's manna from heaven. The grandmotherly looking woman taking orders promises to bring me an extra-tall stack of waffles and the governor eggs sunny-side up and toast. I don't think she knows who he is, and he doesn't make a thing out of it.

"So, uh... thanks for breakfast." I grab one of the paper napkins and start playing with the edges. It's something to look at that's not him.

"No problem, Penny."

And that reminds me, he knew my name last night too. "How do you know who I am?"

"We met before. Don't you remember?" he asks.

"Of course." Of course *I* do. You remember the day you served the governor steak and all waitstaff remember the man who tipped twice the bill. But the governor doesn't remember his waitress. "There's no way. That was three years ago."

"I don't forget faces. Comes with the job."

"Governor Lawson—"

"Call me Luc. Relax, Penny. This isn't meant to be formal."

I open my mouth and then close it again. I have no idea what to say.

Stephanie says I'm badly socialized, and she's not wrong. Ever since the divorce, I barely see other people. I plaster on a fake smile at work, and I play nice with Stephanie and Louise's two kids, Will and Manny. Other than that, I don't go out. I don't see anyone. I'm practically a hermit and I know it, and I haven't minded it. It felt safe in its own way, and after everything, I've needed safe. But now, my complete lack of experience being around people is biting me in the ass.

"Do you have any plans for the holidays?" he asks over the rim of his coffee cup.

My plan is to *not work* for the first time in ages. The restaurant is closed for the holiday, and Stephanie and Louise went to see her parents with the kids. I have nothing on my schedule. It's a gift all on its own.

Which is great, because it's definitely the only gift I'm going to get.

"Oh, you know. A quiet night I guess," I say, because that sounds better than *being alone*. I rip the edge of the napkin, pushing the little piece of paper around.

"Hm. Me too, probably."

"You?" I blurt. "Don't you have, I don't know, parties to attend or something?"

"I'm not much of a party person. It'll probably be a quiet night, just me in my cabin." His eyes light up a bit as he says it.

The waitress returns with our food and deposits the syrup next to my waffles. I pour what feels like half the jug on, drowning the waffles before I cut them to pieces. "Want a little waffle with that syrup?"

"I like sweet things."

He apparently does not, judging by the stodgy egg breakfast and black coffee.

"You really aren't going to say why you were in my neighborhood last night?"

"I'm really not," he tells me, completely unruffled.

Well, okay then. I frown and eat my waffles.

I don't even know why I agreed to come out with him today. What do I have in common with a governor? This guy is wearing a high-end suit, the second one in two days. And my jeans are five years old and from a department store. I'm pretty sure he went to law school, and I only have my high school diploma. We don't move in the same social circles. What do people like him talk about?

It's not like I needed to come, either. I could have said no. I could have stayed home, curled up in my bed with a book and a cup of coffee and let the guys the governor apparently hired fix the floor and thought no more of it. But he'd just sounded so confident when he said it, like it was a foregone conclusion.

And I'm doing it all over again. I'm letting people who sound confident run right across me.

"Relax, Penny," he says, leaning back in his chair with the coffee mug in one hand. I watch his fingers curling around the mug. They're scarred around the knuckles. That's a weird little thing. Why does this guy who works at a desk and signs laws have scarred knuckles? "This is just breakfast."

"You are aware you're the governor of the entire state, right? And you somehow broke into my house last night, and now you're paying people to replace my sister's floor, and for some reason buying me waffles. It doesn't feel like just breakfast."

He sips the coffee, cool as anything. "First of all, I didn't break in. I followed the people who were breaking in. Second, I'm buying waffles because they're tearing up the floor in part of your house, so it felt like a good time for you not to be home. And third—did you vote for me?"

"Can you even ask people that?"

"You're free to answer or not, Penny."

I'm saved from answering when a man walks slowly by our table. He doesn't say anything, just rolls past like he has all the time in the world, eyes firmly fixed on the two of us. He's a big

26

guy, bulky and broad, with a mean set to his face. The type of guy I try to avoid. When I see them at the restaurant, I know they're going to give me a hard time, probably say something misogynistic, and tip poorly.

I duck my head, not needing to start something with a total stranger, but Luc jumps up when he sees him. "We're leaving," he tells me crisply, and I know better than to protest that I'm only halfway through my waffles.

He throws a stack of bills on the table that more than covers our meal, then grabs my shoulder in a firm grip. He's gentle, and not hurting me, but his grip is insistent.

"Governor?" I ask, trying to keep up with him.

"Luc, please. And we have to go," he says again, aiming for the door.

"Who was that?" I ask, trying to turn my head to see if that man is still there.

"Someone I want nowhere near you," he says simply, not letting up on my arm until we're at the passenger door, when he drops my arm to open it for me.

"Seriously, Governor—Luc—what's going on?"

He pauses, hand on the doorframe. "Don't worry about it," he says quietly. "You're fine, Penny. None of this will affect you in any way."

That's *not* an answer, but he closes the door gently behind me and walks around the car, and I know I'm not going to get one.

He drives me home in silence. When I walk into Stephanie's house, there's a pristine new bar cart that looks identical to the old one, minus the scuffs on the base. The liquor bottles look all the same, like they were never even broken. The only thing wrong is it's in the kitchen, because the ugly old carpet in the hallway is still torn up.

The man Luc let into the house earlier looks up at us. He's wearing a button-down and a tie, but he's still on his knees with the other guys. "We'll be done in thirty minutes."

"What's taking so long?" Luc demands, and I turn to him, eyebrow raised. He sounds impatient, but I'm shocked by all they managed to do in a limited timeframe.

"You didn't give us a lot to work with. I had to send Tim out to buy carpet that matches. Also, you're back way earlier than you said."

"Ran into someone at breakfast," Luc tells him tightly.

"Need me to call Max?"

"No." He says it like it's the end of an entire conversation, like no one ever dares to argue with him.

Maybe they don't. That sounds unbelievable, but considering how I keep going along with whatever he says, maybe it's true.

"Alright then. Give me half an hour." Then he turns back to his task, ignoring us.

Everything about this is so awkward. I shift uncomfortably, but Luc just keeps watching me, not saying anything. I need an out. "I left Jinx locked upstairs. I should go check on her."

"Jinx?"

"My cat?" I say slowly, because who else would it be?

"I've never understood the appeal of pets," he admits.

"You never understood the appeal of having something to come home to at the end of the day that loves you unconditionally?"

He shrugs. "I guess I'm just not an animal person."

The guy on the floor snorts.

"Listen, it was really kind of you to do all this today. I appreciate not having to replace all of that myself or explain the damage to my sister. So, thank you. You're not required to do anything else."

He just raises an eyebrow at me, but I don't want to get into it. It's been a really weird last few hours, and I'd like things to go back to making sense now.

I retreat upstairs, shutting my bedroom door and trying not to listen to the voices downstairs.

My room has more cat furniture than human furniture.

I have a twin bed, a dresser I rescued from a dumpster, a cheap mirror, and a "desk" that's really just an old card table. Jinx has two cat trees, two cat beds, a cat tunnel, and a hammock suction-cupped to the window, not to mention the mice, teasers, and balls littering the floor. Her litter box is in the closet I perpetually leave open, and her food and water dishes are right under the window.

If Jinx is going to spend ninety percent of her time stuck in this room, then I want it to be nice for her.

Sometimes, I feel bad about adopting her. I hadn't known we'd be living like this, that she'd spend most of her day in an eight by eight room. We'd had a nice house once upon a time. Then again, that also wasn't a good place for her. I'll never forget the tiny kitten standing between me and a screaming Greg, her little teeth bared with a hiss. I never should have put an animal in that position.

I'm not a great pet mom, but I love her to death. And I must have done something right, because her favorite place to sit is curled up in my lap, or on my chest, or riding around on my shoulders. She's a fuzzy, purring weighted blanket.

"It's almost Christmas," I tell her, like she gives a single fuck about Christmas. I have a new bag of treats and a selection of toy mice in a bag at the top of the closet for her. I'd debated an ugly Christmas sweater for her, too, but I hadn't wanted my arms scratched to bits. She loves me, but not enough to put up with that nonsense.

"So, we're going to have the run of the house until the twenty-seventh," I tell her. "That's when they get back." Jinx isn't a big fan of the boys. They're not aggressive on purpose, but Will pulled her tail when he was younger, and she never forgave him. With Manny barely toddling around now, I just know we're heading for another tail-pulling incident—or worse—and try to keep her away from the kids.

"Nothing fancy for dinner, but I bought a rotisserie chicken at the store—you can have some, if you want."

"*Mrrup.*" I think she knows the word chicken.

"Mhm. And we can sit downstairs and watch movies on the real TV instead of the laptop." My laptop, a kind of pathetic-looking thing, sits plugged in on the card table. It's plugged in because if I unplug it for more than five minutes, it dies entirely. It's our primary source of entertainment up here, although I admit I put on the YouTube videos of birds and squirrels for Jinx way too often.

"I don't know any cat-themed Christmas movies. Can you think of any?"

She doesn't answer, just rolls onto her back across my lap, batting my sweatshirt strings with her paws. "Why do I bother buying toys, huh?"

I keep babbling at the cat until I can't hear anything downstairs anymore. Then, I distract Jinx with a treat and sneak down the stairs for a peek.

The place is indeed empty, and also spotless. The new carpet matches the old, although not quite as worn. Still, I might get away with not having to explain what happened to Stephanie and Louise. With two little boys under six, they're surely distracted enough that they won't notice that the carpet is a little bit nicer, right?

They cleaned up every inch of the place. The old carpet, the broken bottles, all their tools are completely gone. It's like they were never here in the first place.

# CHAPTER 5

# Luc

I go back to the restaurant as soon as I leave Bartholomew with strict orders to make sure the house is perfect for Penny, but of course by the time I get there, the kid is gone.

I don't know his name. I've never seen him before today. But I know he's a shifter like me, and that means I *should* know him.

Maybe today was a coincidence, except I don't believe in coincidences. People either move with purpose or are moved with purpose by someone else, and in my experience, if I'm not moving them, then that's a bad sign.

Creatures like me—the shifters, the ones who were born human but had damn magic force an animal inside of us—were always designed to be someone else's pawn.

When I was a child, we were made in a disgusting old training camp as a supernaturally enhanced army to sell to the highest bidder. In my case, the highest bidder was a Roman emperor, but Alexander, the sorcerer who made us, sold his armies prolifically and unscrupulously for millennia. We heard reports of new batches of shifter children all the way up until I captured Alexander two years ago.

I know exactly where Alexander is, so I know he's not pulling the kid's strings. But someone is. It's what we were raised for. It's who we are.

I try to follow the scent, but I'm no good as a tracker. I get half a mile down the road before it's lost completely.

Max picks up on the third ring. "It's December twenty-second," he says without any sort of greeting.

"I'm aware."

"Are you also aware I told you not to fucking call me for a week?"

"I'm aware that I have a crisis here."

"Is someone dead?"

"Not yet."

There's a pause, and then Max says, "Understand a dead body isn't necessarily enough to get my attention today. Depends who it is." There's some sort of noise at the other end of the line, then a muffled *"baby,"* and then Max laughs in a way I never in my life heard him laugh before he met Casey. "Alright, alright." He uncovers the phone. "Casey says you can have me for two hours."

"How generous." I could remind Max that, in some ways, I still own his soul. He promised me eternal devotion in exchange for giving him a way to escape Alexander's training camp when we were teenagers. When I'd eventually been willing to let him walk away, he'd found Casey and come back to me right away, looking for a chance to be with her forever. Max will never be free of me.

I don't mention it, though. He'll show up.

I rattle off the address of the restaurant, then turn back and wait in the parking lot. At some point, someone is going to wonder where I am today, and I just have to hope no one spots me here first.

When Max pulls up, he stalks over to my car like he's ready to pick a fight. "What the fuck is it?"

"I was here for breakfast earlier. There was a kid—he's one of us. He watched us, got close, and didn't say anything. I left. By the time I made it back, he was gone. I need you to track him." Max's nose is like a bloodhound. He could track someone across the state without issue. It's just one of his many useful qualities.

"You *left*? And who's *us*?"

Max has gotten shrewder with time. Or maybe he's just so used to peeling through my obfuscations now.

"I was here with a human. Not an ideal situation for confronting a potentially dangerous enemy."

"You think he's one of Alexander's."

"Alexander isn't calling the shots anymore." Alexander is in my basement, wishing he was dead, ruing the day he was ever born. "I think he's whoever took up the mantle after we put Alexander out of play."

A muscle in Max's jaw ticks. "Wasn't aware someone took it up."

"Something always fills the gap, Max." Max has been head-in-the-clouds for two years now, a permanent honeymooner. I can't blame him; he got everything he ever wanted. He has the girl and they have forever, and spilling our secret to her not only didn't scare her off, but it seems to have just made them stronger. Some people have all the luck.

So it's no wonder that he's not thinking logically. But Max is as familiar with the brutality of this world as anyone else, and I need him to find that part of himself for me now.

"Get him for me, Max."

"Kid?" he checks, his eyes getting serious as he locks in on the task at hand.

"Young enough. Late teens, early twenties. White, shorter than you but not by much. Dark hair cropped short. Smells a bit like petrol, honestly."

"I'll find him. I'll call you when I do."

As soon as he turns away, following the scent, I pull out my phone and open the app I use to track my people, following along with Max's little dot.

He calls me shortly after I get to my office. I can't sit in a parking lot all day, and following Max will just give us away. There's a small, insidious part of my brain that wants to park outside Penny's house, but I squash it relatively effectively.

"Well?"

"He was here, and now he's nowhere."

I stand up from my desk, unable to suppress the urge to pace. "What does that mean?"

"It means I made it to a house where the kid undoubtedly went, and now the scent is *gone*. Not just not here. Gone. Like it never was. I can't pick it back up in any direction."

"So, magic then."

"Someone, yeah," Max agrees. He's also pacing on the other end of the call, his heavy footsteps echoing down the line as he stomps his way around. "I don't like this."

Neither do I. Max and I haven't lived this long without having a good sense of when shit is going to get real.

I sit back in my desk chair and put my headset on so I can hear the call and still use my phone. I glance at my tracking app and my lungs squeeze shut.

"Max? What address are you at exactly?" I manage to force myself to ask. Maybe this is just me misreading it. Maybe I'm wrong.

"Like I got here by following street signs? I don't fucking know."

"Max." It's all I can make myself say. I hope it sounds satisfactorily commanding and not like the desperate plea I know it is.

"Hold on." I can hear him stomping around, and then a door opens and shuts. "Street sign says Fletching? House number is 46."

It's two streets over from Penny's house.

"Stay there," I manage to say. "In case they come back." And so someone is close enough to keep an ear out for Penny, even if he doesn't know it.

"They won't come back, Luc. And your two hours are up."

"Stay. There," I say, the command returning to my voice. This is serious. I can't fall apart here.

He's silent for a second, but Max knows when I'm serious, and I am so serious right now. "You explain to my wife why I'm not around for Christmas shopping *again*."

"I'll call her," I snap, and I will. From the car, on my way to Penny's house.

By the time I get there, I talk myself down from my more extreme plans. I'm not going to kidnap her out of her home and drag her somewhere safe. I'm not going to barge in and stand right next to her until the threat has passed.

I park my car diagonally across the street from Penny's house. A lot of people park on the street around here, so I imagine every neighbor simply thinks I'm someone else's car. It's what I've banked on the other hundreds of times I've parked near here.

According to my tracking app, Max hasn't left that house. He's not going to find anything, and I'd be better served by sending him out searching or bringing him here to regroup or even letting him go home so I don't completely lose him to resentment. But for once, the logical option loses out.

I'm not leaving this fucking spot. Max is going to be kept nearby in case I need him, and if we're lucky, I don't ever have to tell anyone else about Penny.

The house is quiet. There's a light on in the upstairs window, the one I sometimes get lucky and can glimpse Penny through. I don't see her today, though, but I can scent her, her soft, cinnamon scent calming my nerves slightly.

I alternate between watching Max's little dot on my phone and watching the house, but as the day gets later and the sun gets lower, nothing's happened.

I'll have to think of an endpoint, the time where I pull Max off this fake job and send him on his way, either releasing him to go home to his wife or finding a legitimate task for him.

I have to decide when that point is, but until then, I sink lower in my seat and watch the house.

# CHAPTER 6
# Penny

Something wakes me. I don't know what it is for a moment, but my heart is racing as I stare at my ceiling, and then I hear it again. A crash downstairs.

"Not fucking again," I groan, because seriously—what are the chances that someone attempts to rob us two nights in a row? I know this isn't the nicest neighborhood, but nothing like this has ever happened before. Some of my neighbors don't even lock their doors half the time, but somehow it's *my* house that keeps getting targeted?

Well, I'm unlikely to get saved by a mysteriously wandering governor again, so I pick up my cell phone and dial.

"Nine-one-one, what's your emergency?"

"Someone broke into my house," I whisper, wincing at the sound. The house is so still that I worry they'll hear me.

"Broke into your house? Ma'am?"

The third step from the top creaks. It has for as long as I've lived here, and tonight that creak is as loud as a cracking whip.

I mutter my address into the phone, then frantically look for a place to hide.

Why me? What the hell makes this house so damn appealing to criminals?

Jinx has woken up and realized something is wrong, but the poor baby is meowing her head off, because she believes she's an intimidating lion instead of a tiny little cat who is liable to get hurt when whoever this is finds their way in here. I scoop her up and try to hush her, looking around frantically for somewhere to go.

There's no place to hide. I don't really have anything to give them. My ancient laptop surely isn't worth anything. I wasn't allowed to keep any jewelry when my marriage ended, and I have a single twenty dollar bill in my wallet. Something tells me that won't satisfy these robbers.

A crash echoes through the hallway, subtlety apparently completely forgotten, and then a loud growling sound. Is there an *animal* in my house?

Jinx moves from meowing to yowling. She sounds like she's in actual distress, and I try to soothe her. She protests, biting my arm, but I get her to settle against my chest.

What do I do? I can't go out the window; it's a fifteen-foot fall to the ground with nothing I could hope to climb. There's *something* happening in the hallway. Is this the safest spot for me? Do I hide here until the police come?

How long will that take?

I'm pacing now, and then my bare foot hits something. Louise's softball bat. I never put it away last night, too weirded out to let the weapon go. I deposit Jinx on the bed and scoop it up, choking up on the bat like I'm about to hit a grand slam.

Maybe they don't know I'm here. Surely they targeted this house because they assumed it would be empty. So if I can just get the element of surprise, then maybe...

I force myself to take a deep breath, steadying myself so I can swing this bat with full strength.

I swing open my door and step out, bat raised, some sort of primal yell dying in my throat when I take in the sight before me.

There's a giant wolf in the hallway, pacing back and forth with a bloody muzzle. It's dark so I can't be sure, but I'm pretty positive there's a significant amount of blood on the floor. What the *fuck*?

Last night someone tried to rob me. Tonight an *animal* breaks in? Two animals? Where did all the blood come from?

How'd it get in? I know I locked the door. I checked four times.

And then the craziest thing happens–the wolf turns into a man. It happens quickly, but I can see each step of the process as his body bends and re-shapes. The fur fades, the snout shortens, and then there's a man on two legs in front of me. I blink at it, trying to take it in.

It's the governor again, only this time, he's completely naked.

"Oh, I'm dreaming again," I whisper to myself, dropping the bat slightly so I can pinch myself again. Didn't I have this dream last night?

But then he turns toward me, murmuring, "Penny," and I know I'm not dreaming. I know I'm not because that's exactly how he said my name earlier, and I could never dream that up. The soft way he says it, like he's caressing every letter, like it's worth something—I couldn't imagine that on my own.

This is... real?

Or it's a hallucination, I reason. Sure, the governor is here—*again*—somehow, but I hallucinated the turning into an animal thing. And the blood too, probably. And for some reason, I'm imagining him naked. Well, I can probably guess the reason. It feels inappropriate to look, but I can't help myself.

I don't remember what I ate before I went to bed, but it had to be laced with something.

I'm swaying. I don't realize it until the world starts to actually shake, and then there are hands on me, stronger than I expected from a small guy, holding me steady. "Penny?" he asks, and it must be my imagination, but I think his thumb is stroking over my bare arm. "You okay?"

"Am I *okay*?" I demand. "No, I think I'm high."

His thumb stops for a second. "Did you take something?"

"I'm assuming my dinner was somehow laced. Or I, I don't know, swallowed cleaning chemicals or something. That's the only thing that explains all of this."

He huffs. "Alright. Let's get you sitting down, then." That seems like the most logical thing to do, given my situation, so I nod and let him lead me over to my bed.

Jinx jumps up and rubs against my side, and I automatically reach out to pet her. Her soft fur grounds me, and I let my eyes slide closed. Alright. I'm going to be alright.

Only I'm not, because the governor is sitting next to me, using my blanket to cover his lap and leaving just a few inches between us, and now he's on the phone with someone. It's rude to listen to someone else's phone calls, but I don't really think there's a way around it right now. His voice is all I can hear.

"—Tagged two of them," he murmurs, turning slightly away from me. "They ran." A pause again. "Well, I had to prioritize..." He trails off, then darts a look at me. "Never mind. Listen. This isn't safe anymore. I have to get her out of here."

He listens for a minute, then says, "No. Her safety is my priority. And there's only one place—I know it's safe because if they could find it, they would have. I need you to beat us there and take care of the trash." He hangs up the phone without saying goodbye. "Alright, Penny? We need to leave. Now."

"I called the police," I tell him. "They'll be here any second, they'll keep us safe..."

"You *what*?" he demands, and he sounds mad enough that I flinch back. His voice instantly softens. "No, of course you did, of course, I'm glad you protected yourself—I'll take care of it." He picks his phone up again and starts texting. "Alright. My guys will take care of it."

"What, do you have *spies* in the police department?" I ask. It sounds ridiculous as I say it, but he doesn't laugh.

I'm not sure he can laugh. He always has such a serious face.

"I have spies everywhere. It's kind of what I do."

I'm stuck on what he *does*, whatever that means, but he's already moving, once again walking through my room naked like he doesn't even notice. "Alright, this is simple. Do you have a bag?"

"A bag?"

"A duffle bag, an overnight bag—a damned trash bag? Something?" He looks down at himself like he just realized his condition, and asks, "And maybe a towel? A pair of sweat-pants?"

There's a duffle bag in the hall closet. I have no idea why I'm willing to listen to this man—maybe it's the lingering authority of knowing he's literally the governor, or maybe it's just the confident way he talks—but I get up and retrieve it. When I turn away from the closet, he's right there, mere inches away. I didn't even hear him approach.

There's definitely blood on his face. His hair is matted to one side, not quite the same clean and neat look he had earlier today.

"Got it?"

"Did you not trust me to walk alone?" I try to keep my eyes on his face.

He looks slightly guilty, eyes darting to the side. "You almost passed out a few minutes ago, Penny. I know this is shocking."

"I don't even know what *this* is." I move back into my bedroom, moving for my dresser so I can give him a pair of my sweatpants. He takes them when I hand them over, pulling them on without taking his eyes off of me.

"We can discuss that on the road."

"The *road*?"

"Yes. We need to leave, Penny. I have a safe place to take you. And we're leaving in five minutes, so let's pack. What do you absolutely need for the next few days?"

"My cat."

"I said *need*."

"My. Cat," I repeat. "She needs me. I need her. I'm not leaving her."

His brow furrows. "You know what? Fine. Whatever gets you out of here faster. And if you forget underwear or something because you're too busy packing cat toys, that's on you."

"Think about my underwear a lot?" I ask him.

He huffs, then walks away. "I'll cover this up," he mutters, gesturing to the damage in the hallway that I'm still very much trying not to think about. "You pack. Five minutes."

# CHAPTER 7
# Luc

Twenty minutes later, we're in my car with a full duffle bag and the damned cat shut into a cat carrier in the back seat. It had taken me less than thirty seconds to change into the spare set of clothes I keep in my trunk; every other second was dedicated to Penny's "essentials."

Between us, we carried out the cat, her bag, cat food, and an empty litter box and a fresh carton of litter to re-fill it with. And through all that, I can confirm she remembered her underwear.

I never knew that Penny liked thongs that much. I never would have guessed from looking at her, and now I feel like this forbidden knowledge is going to destroy my limited grasp on my self control. Watching her pack nearly gave me a heart attack.

I'm not going to survive long enough for Penny's underwear to be what does me in though, because I am already barreling toward the edge. None of this is me. None of this is collected and in control.

I gave up Alexander. The man I hunted for more than a thousand years, that I dreamed of torturing and tormenting for centuries, and I let my revenge be cut off at only two years; I won't even be the one to kill him. I suppose Max also deserves the right, but that's not the point. For Penny, I gave him up in a heartbeat. Max will have him dead and gone from the cabin's basement long before we arrive, and Penny will never need to know the safe place I'm bringing her was once used to torture a man.

It's nice enough, if you don't go into the basement. It'll be a perfect place to convince her she wants to be with me.

Because Penny saw me tonight, and when a human sees us, there are very few options. Sometimes magical intervention is possible, making them forget. Sometimes we have to kill them.

Or—I could bring her into my world. I could make her like us. And that means I can make her *mine*.

Yes. This isn't what I planned originally, but plans change, and I need to think on my feet. Penny's stuck in my world now, and there's no going back. And that means so many possibilities for our future just opened up.

"Alright, I think it's time you tell me what the fuck is going on," Penny says, voice wavering slightly. She's looking straight ahead like she's the one who needs to be watching the road. But I can't keep my eyes off her.

She's still wearing pajamas. I don't even know if she realizes that, but she didn't bother to change back at the house. Maybe it was the shock she was clearly suffering through, maybe it was not wanting to change around me, maybe she's just comfortable. But she's wearing the same pajamas as last night, the sweatshirt too big for her and falling over her hands.

She wasn't wearing the sweatshirt earlier. The tiny little shirt she has on under it, clinging to the curve of her breasts—No. I'm not letting my mind go down that path. It'll just drive me insane when I can't touch her yet.

"I think you have some guesses." I manage to look away to check the road. So far, no one is following us. I doubt anyone will—as Max has complained to me dozens of times, modern cars are the bane of any tracker's existence—but it can't hurt to be careful right now. I'm carrying precious cargo, after all.

"I think you should tell me before I tuck and roll out of this car."

"You won't, because I have your cat."

She actually *growls* at me, a sound so bizarrely cute from someone who is definitely not meant to be growling. In my world, growls mean danger. Here, it's adorable.

I don't say that. I've been enough of an asshole to her, and the last thing I need to say is that I don't take her seriously. Of course I do. She's just *soft* in a way I'm not used to. Breakable and fragile, and I don't mean that in a bad way.

Where I came from, everyone assumed I'd die young. I was the weak link, the runt of the litter. Surviving meant I made myself hard in a world that was already brutal; I had to be more savage, more ruthless, than everyone else. There could be no room for weakness.

Penny showing her frustration when she doesn't have the fight to back it up is a breath of fresh air. I'm not sure the world has always been kind to this woman, but at least it didn't make her like me.

"You know what you saw, Penny," I tell her, tapping my thumb against the wheel. "I know you did. Tell me."

"It's ridiculous."

"It's not."

"I was tripping on something." Even she doesn't sound like she believes herself.

"You know you weren't. C'mon. Things have been weird since I showed up yesterday. Talk through it; you'll feel better."

She growls again, apparently not responding great to being told what to do. I think she's going to go silent, try to out-stubborn me, but then she starts talking.

"There was so much blood on that floor. And your *face*."

"Yes." It's still on my face. I can feel it drying now, starting to itch and flake. I should have washed my face before we left her house, but I'd been too distracted watching her open her fucking underwear drawer, like some kind of sexual predator.

"Did you stab whoever it was or something?"

"C'mon, Penny. You know what I did. Say it." I'm straddling a fine line, needing to get her to believe this without breaking her mind, but the sooner she accepts this, the easier things will be for the both of us.

She's silent for another few seconds, then the words get dragged out of her. "You were an animal."

"Mhm." Better to just confirm it now and not let her doubt herself any longer. "A wolf, actually, if we're being specific."

I'm sure there's a more delicate way to drop the truth into someone's lap, but I don't know it. I've never had to tell a human before. I know Max was forced to show Casey when Alexander and his guards attacked their home in the middle of a dinner party. The dragon Marcus, who Max is in regular contact with for some unfathomable reason, apparently told his human mate when she was attacked by a demon. Maybe there is no gentle way to enter our world.

"What are you?" she asks softly.

"You know, Penny. Put it all together now."

She huffs. "Condescending asshole," she mutters, and I can't help but smile slightly. So this hasn't broken her entirely, then. Good. "You're a... werewolf?"

"Werewolf, shifter, whatever you want to call us. I am."

"How is that fucking possible?" she demands. "You are—leaving aside *biology* and *science* and whatever the fuck else, how? You have to be one of the more watched people in the country. Your name comes up as a future president practically every time I watch the news."

"It's not as hard as you think. Practice, mostly. And I don't turn into the wolf randomly—I have control." If only she knew how much control, exactly. But I don't think she's quite ready

51

to hear about the intricacies of ruling the supernatural creatures that secretly surround her every day.

"Okay, back to science. How is this *possible*? Are there more of you? Is this like a secret mutation, and you're born this way?"

Penny inadvertently stumbled on the big question already. "Not born this way," I say shortly. "But made. Through magic, not science. There are creatures that were born supernatural, though—not that they're relevant right now. And I was turned probably within an hour or so of being born, so I've never known anything else."

Not born this way. Not accepted by the supernatural creatures because we weren't like them, weren't a species of creatures they recognized. Certainly not accepted by the humans, who lost their damn minds at best and saw an economic boondoggle at worst when they looked at us. It had taken the better part of a thousand years to make the supernatural creatures see me—and, by extension, my people—as genuine, real threats, thereby forcing them to acknowledge us. It had taken another thousand years to get the humans to respect me too.

I know people around me think I'm power hungry to the extreme, that my greed makes me do things with no payoff. And it's true it's often thankless and difficult to rule the hidden supernatural world, and I really have next to no interest in the humans. But no one can say I'm not a player now. No one can see me as disposable again.

Of course, Penny doesn't know what she's stumbled on with her comment. She will one day, because if Penny is going to be in this world then I'm going to make her *mine*. There just isn't another viable path forward, now that she knows the truth.

My mate, the same way Max has Casey. He went soft after meeting her, and I don't think I can ever be soft. But the idea of having someone like that, someone who is a safe harbor, someone I can tell everything to, someone who knows me like that—I want it.

But only with Penny.

For now, I have to get her over the hump of accepting what she saw tonight. "Who was in my house?" she asks softly.

"Good question." She's thinking logically, then. She's not going to be one of those humans who loses their shit when they find out the truth. "I don't have exact details. I can tell you last night really were just two humans who wanted to rob you and picked the wrong house. They probably thought everyone had left town and were hoping to get lucky before the holiday. They weren't any special threat—you probably could have scared them off with that baseball bat of yours. But tonight, it was shifters like me. One was a wolf, the other turned tail before I ever saw him transform, so I couldn't tell you. And *them* having an interest in you is why we're leaving town."

She's quiet again. Penny's quiet a lot, and I can practically feel her brain turning ideas over, processing this all. I struggle for the patience I normally have so easily; I can't rush her on this. "Why were they interested in me? I'm nobody."

"You're not nobody." *You're mine,* I want to snarl. I feel it bubbling in my chest, this possessive need to claim. I take one hand off the wheel to rub at my chest, like I can somehow work the need out.

I went from thinking she could never be mine, not really, to being ready to claim her publicly so quickly. But no, that's not quite right. Penny's always been mine, even when I didn't think it was safe to admit it.

"I'm a waitress. I'm a thirty-year-old divorcee. I have no idea why I'd ever be appealing to some werewolf; that is so far above my head." She turns toward me. "Unless... please tell me you're not going to say my ex-husband was one of you, too?"

I didn't even know she had an ex-husband before this very second, and this is what I get for not doing a background check, for being a sentimental idiot and deciding that Penny was the one situation I didn't need to control.

I'll rectify that as soon as I have a moment. I'll do the background check, learn the ex's name and why they divorced. If he hurt her, then I'll have him killed.

"Not that I know of," I manage to say. "It might be my fault. We didn't talk, obviously, but my assumption is they were looking for me. But I'm hard to pin down, and they must've picked up my scent at your house."

"My house, that you just so happened to be walking by last night and just coincidentally saw the open back door."

I squeeze the steering wheel, forcing myself to take a deep breath. She's getting there. "Ask your question, Penny."

"You told me it was official business. Like it was classified or something. What were you doing there? Was it related to this?" She says *this* like it tastes weird, gesturing to me as she does like she can see the furry wolf beneath my human skin.

"In a way."

"What way? Why my house?" she demands, turning in her seat now.

"Because you live there." I'm not being helpful and I know it, but I'm fighting for every second I can get with the progress we've made, before I tell her the truth and no doubt set us back. Perhaps sets us irrevocably back.

No. I won't allow that. She might freak out. She might hate me. But surely some light stalking—and really, emphasis on the *light*, because I didn't even do a background check, didn't go through her underwear drawer, didn't put cameras in her house—isn't more alarming than the fact that I turn into a literal werewolf. If she can handle that, she can handle anything.

"I was there for you."

She hits the center console suddenly enough that the cat, who's been remarkably quiet, yowls in protest. She ignores the thing, which I suspect is a rare occurrence. "You said it had nothing to do with me. Give me a straight fucking answer."

"I've been there for you. Multiple nights. I don't just re-member your face from when I saw you that one time—I see you all the time. And even on the nights where I don't get there until it's way too late, long after you've gone to sleep, I like knowing you're breathing and nearby."

She's dead silent, the fight gone out of her. I risk looking over at her, and she's sitting perfectly still. I'd think she was a statue if I didn't know better. After a couple of minutes of this, I ask her, "Would holding the cat help you feel better?" Surely that's why people have the things, right?

"If we let her out of the carrier, she'll get underfoot and that's unsafe." She says it so mechanically, and while I want to argue that I think my literally predator-sharp instincts can handle a nuisance cat, I know that's not the point.

"Alright. What can I do for you, then?" There has to be something.

"You... you've been stalking me?" She still isn't moving. I need her to give me some sort of reaction, some sign that things will be alright.

"If you want to call it that."

"And what're you calling it?"

Well, shit. She's not wrong; I don't really have a better word. "Okay, it's stalking. Light stalking, though."

I can feel her eyes boring holes in me even as I refuse to turn and look. Finally, she asks, "Why?" and her total confusion drives a spike through my heart.

# CHAPTER 8
# Penny

The governor who will one day be president, who is also a werewolf with *blood* on his face, who might be kidnapping me to an unknown location, has been *stalking* me. Alright.

It's like my brain and body disconnect. I'm still sitting here, can feel the rumble of this very nice car's engine, the leather of the seats, the heater blowing on my feet, but it's all distant, miles and miles away from where I really am. My brain is a spinning mess outside of this all, looking for anything it can latch onto to make this world make sense.

I want to go back to when I thought I somehow accidentally drugged myself. That was a lot easier than this. Sadly, I'm beginning to think this is somehow real, which means I have a dangerous stalker that I have to deal with.

A stalker who saved my life *twice*, some part of me reminds myself. And he tipped two hundred percent when I'd been his waitress. And he wanted to get out of that house fast, but he'd let me take the time to bring my cat. And the worst part of it all is, even knowing what I now know, I still feel safe here. He might be kidnapping me, but I can't convince myself he'll actually hurt me.

Even so, I still need to know *why*.

"Can't you guess?" he asks, hands tight on the steering wheel.

"Were you hunting me? Do you guys, I don't know, eat humans?" It sounds stupid even as I say it.

"No, we don't eat humans. I eat exactly the same things you do, Penny. You've seen me eat."

"Then why?"

"Because you're *you*," he says, which doesn't clarify anything.

"Exactly. You can see my confusion." My heart starts beating faster again, but this isn't like when I saw the wolf.

He shakes his head. "Penny, you were wearing dark wash jeans and a t-shirt with the restaurant logo on the front the day we met. You had your hair in two braids. You smelled like cinnamon—you always smell like cinnamon—and when you looked me in the eye, something inside me changed. Believe me, I have big things on my mind, but it was like none of them mattered anymore. When I'm near you, everything else gets a little quieter." He looks over at me for a second. "When I'm with you like this—it's like my brain is silent for the first time in two thousand years."

"Two thousand years?" But no—that's something to deal with later. It's big, it's mind-boggling, but there's somehow

58

something bigger to contend with. "So you've been following me because you're, what, obsessed with me?"

He shrugs. "*Obsessed* puts it lightly. And following puts it too strong. I don't spend my days following you around. But I hung around outside the restaurant sometimes. I park near your house as many nights as I can get away with." He flicks a glance at me again. "If it helps, I haven't had anyone else follow you. I haven't taken pictures of you or anything. And this week was the first time I'd been in your house."

Somehow, it *does* help. It shouldn't, but it does. He just has a way of talking where I trust everything he says. Something about it makes my breath fluttery and weak.

I need to shake myself out of this. I knew someone like that once, someone who was just trustworthy. It resulted in my marriage, then my legal troubles, and finally my divorce. I won't fall for that again.

"So, your *business* in my neighborhood…"

"Was you," he confirms. "Was feeling some rest for the first time in days, and getting a moment to relax because I was near you." He squeezes the wheel so tight I hear it creak. Luc doesn't look strong enough to do that, but maybe this is a case where looks can be deceiving. "And I led them right to you."

"You couldn't have known." I can't believe I said it, that I'm reassuring the werewolf who stalked me and put me in danger, but the words just slip out. He looks sad, and some part of me doesn't want him looking like that.

"I should have. It doesn't matter if I knew about an active threat, just the fact that I'm *me*—" He cuts himself off, taking a deep breath. "I'll do better in the future. I'll work out a security plan for you."

"Security plan? Future?"

His mouth ghosts into a smirk. "Penny, one thing you should know—I always get my way. I thought you were something I could only have from a distance. But now that you fell into my lap? I'll never let you go."

I rock back at that. It should feel just as much like a threat as everything else that's happened tonight, but it doesn't. No, it feels like something I don't want to think too hard about, but definitely not a threat. "Don't I get a say in this?"

"Trust me, Penny—I can be very persuasive."

I can't dig into that right now. He can try all he likes to persuade me; it's not like I can leave. As he already pointed out, I'm not going to tuck and roll out of his car without Jinx, and once he gets me wherever we're going—

That reminds me. "Where are you taking me?"

"A cabin I own. It'll be safe. No one knows about it, and it's secure both physically and magically. Plus, my head of security will be there to help me create a strategy for protecting you. The cabin is comfortable, which is good because you might be there a while."

"I have work in a few days."

"Penny, given the circumstances, I think you should quit."

Okay, now we've hit something that actually sends my blood racing. It's not that I love my job, because I don't. It's a job and it pays, and it has the bonus of helping out my family. But who the hell is he to tell me I should quit? "Am I your prisoner, Luc? Gonna keep me hostage?"

He squeezes the wheel again, and maybe the darkness causes me to imagine it, but I swear there are indents left behind from his fingers. "Penny, to keep you safe? You can't imagine what I would do." *Fuck*. I'm torn here, half ready to fight him—and half ready to collapse under the heavy reassurance of his words. It shouldn't feel good; it sounds more like a threat than anything else. But I can't help it.

He looks over at me, and I have to hope that he can't read what I'm feeling on my face. "No more questions for a bit. I think you're overwhelmed. You can ask all you want when we get there. In the meantime, we have another two hours. You should sleep."

I scoff. "There's no way I can sleep right now."

"I think if I stop talking for two minutes, you'll be out cold, actually."

"Is that some sort of werewolf mind control? Some magical trick?"

"No. I can't do anything like that." His voice softens. "You're scared and overwhelmed and tired, Penny—I can hear it in your voice, smell it on your skin. You need a rest; you'll feel better after. Give it a try."

I want to argue, but he goes completely silent, just letting the hum of the engine and the rushing road fill the car and, much to my consternation, I'm asleep within minutes.

When I wake up, I'm being carried. I think the transition from the warm car to the frigid outdoors is what woke me; I crack my eyes open to see Luc is the one holding me, and another man, this one significantly larger, hanging around.

"—Get her things," Luc tells him. "Be careful with the cat."

"You let her bring her cat? You know animals hate us." Oh. Is *that* why Luc had been resistant to Jinx?

"Tough it out."

The man moves without arguing, and I get my first good look at him. He's built like a mountain, and if yesterday you told me this man was a werewolf, I probably would have had an easy enough time believing you.

Luc looks down at me, and when we make eye contact for the first time, I get trapped in his dark eyes. They're bottomless—like staring down into a deep cave, like staring into an abyss. History and violence and so many memories are all swirled up there.

"You're okay," he whispers to me, so quiet I don't think the other man is supposed to hear. This is just for me.

I nod because I know I'm okay. It's foolish and stupid, and I've now been brought to a secondary location that looks like a remote rustic cabin with nothing around. This should be my worst nightmare. I should fear death and dismemberment and all sorts of horrible, awful futures.

But I don't. Instead, I close my eyes and let myself be soothed by the gentle rhythm of his steps. His feet crack on the hardwood porch, then a door swings open and we're inside.

The first thing I register is that the room is warm. The second is the sound of a crackling fire. It is a rustic cabin, but much more like a Christmas movie than a horror movie, only without any decorations.

He keeps moving, and soon he lays me down in a bed with the softest mattress I've felt since my divorce. My muscles collapse completely into the bed.

He chuckles. "Sleep a little longer," he says, pulling a thick quilt over me, and I'm asleep again before he even leaves the room.

# CHAPTER 9

# Luc

M ax is waiting for me in the tiny kitchen, holding the carrier with the stupid cat like it might explode.

"Just release the thing," I tell him.

"Set up the litter box first. Unless you want it shitting in your house."

Max has seen what was in my basement, so he knows a little animal shit really isn't the worst thing that's been here. But I suffer the indignity of filling a litter box—because I am apparently now a servant to a cat—and put out a bowl of water so Max can release the animal.

She hisses at us and then slinks away, keeping an eye on us while she retreats toward the bedroom Penny is sleeping in.

"You're welcome, fucker," I mutter.

Max snorts. "So, who is she and why are you letting her slow you up for a cat?"

I almost tell him to fuck off, but I stop myself, considering. I'm going to need to tell Max. For one, I need to use him to protect Penny right now, and he'll work better if he understands the stakes. For another, Penny is going to be at my side forever, so it's only a matter of time until he finds out. She might not believe that this relationship is permanent yet—she might even disagree—but I know it, and I can be convincing.

"She's my wife," I tell him. "Or she will be, anyway."

He stares at me, completely still. I have a feeling the roof could fall in and he wouldn't move. "You told me two years ago, when I wanted Alexander and the spell to make Casey like us—you said I wasn't the only one who had someone. Her?"

"Her," I agree.

"Does she know yet?" he asks.

"Not yet."

He's silent for a second. "You've been following her?" There's no judgement in his voice; I know he also stalked Casey a little bit, although he only followed her for a matter of weeks before he asked her out.

"Yeah."

"You'll convince her," he says confidently.

I want to brush it off, to say *of course I will* and move on. But instead I tell him, "I had to tell her about us today. She saw."

He shrugs. "Casey took it okay. So did Marcus' wife, Elise."

"You both knew her first. She'd already fallen in love with you; of course she took it okay. She was ready to promise wedding vows. Being a werewolf probably fits right into *for better or worse*. But Penny doesn't trust me an inch yet." I start pacing the small kitchen, a weakness I rarely let myself show. We're all like this; wolves pace when stressed. I usually hide it better, but I can't help it right now.

Somehow this thing with Penny feels like the biggest, most important thing I've ever done. Two thousand years, countless coups and battles and all-out fights to the death, but getting this woman to fall in love with me matters more than any of that.

"I don't know. She came with you. She let you carry her in. That's not a bad start."

I want to know when Max became such a damned optimist—probably around the time Casey said *I do*—but I can't fight him on it because I'm desperately clinging to the idea. A chance. All I need is a chance.

I glance around the cabin. What once was a convenient place to hurt people will serve perfectly fine as a place to convince Penny to fall for me. It's not like she can leave on her own, and it's so cozy. Cute, almost—or I hope she'll think so, anyway. And there is only one bedroom. Not that I'll force my way into her bed—I've slept plenty worse places than a couch—but maybe it'll help.

"What'd you do with Alexander?" I ask abruptly, needing a change of topic before I march into the bedroom and bury myself under that quilt with her.

"Killed him quickly. Didn't exactly put up much of a fight." There's no judgment in his voice, although I know we both know how I brutalized that man. Alexander couldn't put up a fight because he could barely breathe on his own. I'd slowly and methodically ripped him apart over the last two years. "Burned the body, buried the remains."

That's the thing about Max. He's a cold-blooded killer when I need him to be, but he's never been cruel. Honestly, despite being the toughest, most capable little monster in our litter, he might have also been the kindest. Not that we had many opportunities to be kind back then, but Max had always had it in him.

And then there's me, who spread the torture out for two whole years, and could have happily gone another ten before I felt vindicated. I wanted to snap every bone in his body, just for them to heal so I could do it again. I wanted to remove pieces slowly, and I wanted him to feel every second of it. It only feels fair, considering the number of children that man turned into soldiers—and that's only the ones who survived. I wouldn't have given him such a kind burial either; I probably would have let my wolf out and pissed on the bones.

But I need to control that, because that is a side of me Penny absolutely cannot see.

"Was he here the whole time?" Max asks.

"I bought this place to hold people like him. Came up here when I could get away." I close my eyes, remembering the visceral joy of entering the basement and seeing Alexander there, trussed up in chains and looking wrecked. He never could quite recover from the damage I did to him. "I got your secret to immortality from him here."

"Going to use that on your girl?"

There's no question about it. I didn't want Penny dragged into my world, but that ship has sailed. And there's simply no way I'll let her go now, and that means being together forever.

"Some day." I'll convince her. Hopefully sooner rather than later; I'm acutely aware of the threats out there now. It'd be reassuring to know that she had razor-sharp teeth and claws to protect herself with.

"Well, good luck to you," he says, clapping me on the shoulder. "Listen. If your girl was attacked tonight, we have bigger problems. And I get why you wanted me to take out the trash before she got here, but I could be much more useful hunting down whoever is after you."

I rake a hand through my hair. "Go find what you can. I wounded one of them; there's plenty of blood at Penny's house."

"Whatever fucking spell they were using to hide themselves from us will probably get in the way, but I'll get what I can." He glances at the clock on the microwave, then mutters a curse. "It's fucking December twenty-third. We better end this quickly."

"What, you suddenly religious now?"

"If by *religious*, you mean worshipping my gorgeous wife, who agreed to marry me two years ago tomorrow—I'm a fucking altar boy."

I snort, the tension alleviated slightly. "Alright. Let's end this quickly, then."

"And you can try to make some progress while I'm gone. You should feed her."

*Shit.* "Is there any food here?" There's some canned goods, I know that; I stocked this place up for emergencies just like this one. But while I can eat beans from a can if needed, it's not exactly a romantic meal.

I didn't prepare this place for a seduction, but I should have.

"You're welcome." Max clasps my shoulder again. "It isn't much, and I'll bring more back for you two. Maybe you can have a romantic little Christmas of your own, huh? But for now, there're my leftovers. Put it on a plate and it won't even look that bad. And hey; try to get that cat to like you. Maybe she'll like that." Then he walks out the door, letting the cold in again.

It's almost five in the morning now. I doubt Penny wants a sandwich at this hour, and I should let her sleep as much as possible. They say everything looks better in the morning, and I don't know if that's true, but at this point, I'll take all the help I can get.

# CHAPTER 10

# Penny

I wake up with a cat on my head, biting my scalp gently to wake me.

Once I get Jinx to move enough that I can breathe, I take in the room I'm in. I didn't get a good look when Luc brought me in last night. To tell the truth, I half-thought I dreamed it all. But this room, with mellow wood paneling and a rough wooden bed frame that looks like someone actually went outside, chopped down a tree, and carved it by hand, it all *screams* some cozy winter cabin.

I force myself to sit upright. This is a nice bed. It dominates most of the space in this small room, which means it's perfectly lined up with the window looking over a forest.

I close my eyes. Right. Because I followed a werewolf who's been stalking me into the middle of a forest with nothing around for miles. I make *great* life decisions.

The bedroom door pushes open, and I spin to see Luc standing in the doorway. He leans casually against the frame, eyeing me.

He's wearing the same clothes as last night, but he's washed the blood off his face and out of his hair, looking much more put together. Everything about him looks collected and in control, and I pull the blanket up further to hide under it even as I can't stop watching him.

"Good morning," he says. "Or afternoon, really."

I wince. "I slept that long?"

"You were exhausted, and had good reason to be. Sleep was good for you."

"I never sleep this much. I'm usually up by six." I pause, looking him over. "But you probably knew that, didn't you?"

"I'm not usually there in the morning." He doesn't even have the grace to look embarrassed. No, he's as calm and collected as he always is, eyeing me like I'm something to study. "As much as I want to be. But I look forward to learning all about how you like your mornings."

"Coffee," I say, because really, that's the only thing I want right now, although I wouldn't say no to more waffles.

He winces. "Yeah, about that. We don't have much in the way of food. Max will be back later with more. But for now, coffee is off the table."

Jesus Christ. Surviving without coffee even for a few hours sounds miserable, but I'm not really in a position to complain. I mean, I've begun to process that this man probably saved my life last night.

And that he's also the reason it was in danger in the first place. It's complicated.

"Alright. I'll survive," I manage to say.

He frowns and steps further into the room. He's not a big guy, but he just seems to take up so much space. Maybe it's that the room is already tight and I'm sitting while he stands. Somehow, I doubt that that's it. It's getting hotter in here just from his presence, and I barely resist fanning myself.

Jinx headbutts me in the back, reminding me I've committed the sin of being awake for five whole minutes and not feeding her. It's practically a crime against humanity in her eyes, so I scratch her between the ears and climb out of bed.

Luc just *stares* at me. It's like he's frozen on the spot, eyes completely captivated. I look down to make sure I hadn't accidentally stripped naked in my sleep, but nope. Still in the same ratty sweatshirt and worn pajama pants. It's definitely *not* a look that makes people stop in their tracks.

Well, unless they're always well-dressed and probably rich as hell like Luc, in which case maybe he's just offended by the eyesore and can't believe someone would bring it into his house.

"Uhm, I'm going to get dressed," I tell him, fidgeting slightly now. Not that my day clothes are much better, but it's the best I can do right now. Then I realize what my hair probably looks like. "And could I get a shower?"

His eyes slip closed, breaking the spell. He takes a long second to answer me, then says roughly, "First door on the left leaving this room."

I nod, scurrying to grab my bag. He steps out of the way, giving me space to pass, and I leave the room before a tail whips me in the leg. "I should feed her."

"I fed her when we got here," he says.

"You... did?"

"Yeah." He shrugs. "I have to do something to get her to like me."

Judging by how Jinx is standing behind my legs, she hasn't decided she likes him yet. "Well... thanks," I mutter, then allow the cat to follow me into the bathroom as I scurry away.

This man kidnapped me, but he also looks at me like that after having ensured a cat he clearly doesn't like got fed. It's a little confusing.

The bathroom is small but functional. The products in the bathroom are simple, but I can't complain; I barely remembered to bring my toothbrush, never mind shampoo. I'll take what I can get.

The water pressure is better than I have at home, so I take an extra minute in the shower, letting the bathroom steam up around me. By the time my hair is clean, the mirror is completely fogged over, and the air's thick enough to choke me. I pull on clean clothes from my bag, pet the weirded-out cat, and take a deep breath before opening the door.

It's warm in the living room, the fire roaring, but that's not what catches my attention. No, what makes me stare is Luc, carefully plating sandwiches at the kitchen table.

He turns when I enter. "Lunch?" He looks back at the plate, something complicated crossing his face. "It's better than nothing, but I'll have something better for you tonight."

I look over the table, then choose to sit in the chair at the furthest end from Luc. He looks for a moment like he might say something, but then closes his mouth and just nods, sitting at the opposite end and gently pushing one of the plates with sandwiches across the table to me.

It looks like I got the better end of the deal. At least my sandwich doesn't have a bite clearly taken out of it. I somehow doubt that's his.

"Do you like this?" Luc asks, looking at the plates between us, something like worry creasing his brow. "I should have asked first. I don't even know if you eat meat."

"But don't you know everything about me?" I ask him, head tilted as I take in the nervous look on his face. "Isn't that the whole point of stalking someone?"

He shakes his head. "No, Penny," he says, voice seemingly deeper now. "That's not, as you put it, the point." His hand squeezes into a fist on the table before releasing. "What I did—what I wanted—it wasn't like that. I just needed to be near you. I know nothing about you that I can't see through a window. And frankly, most of the time, I was lucky to get a glimpse of you walking by."

He pauses, gaze steady on me, and I somehow feel like he can see right through me. "I know you have the sweetest—*fuck*, the most captivating scent I've ever smelled. I know hearing your voice lights up my entire day. Everything else—I still need to learn."

I gulp, flushing under the intensity of his gaze. I was never particularly outgoing, and this much scrutiny feels like being under stage lights in front of a crowd of thousands. Only worse, because I don't know what show to put on.

He's obsessed with me and doesn't even know anything about me. He doesn't know about Greg, the divorce, and the legal issues. He doesn't know about my parents. About how perilously close I've come to financial ruin in the last six years—and how Stephanie and Louise have kept me from falling right over that edge.

I can't decide if I should tell him and get it over with, ruin whatever image he's built in his head so this can be over, or if I should let it go on a little bit longer. Someone looking at me like I'm the star they orbit around makes my heart race.

Perhaps I could blame the kidnapping for why I feel all fluttery, but I don't think so. I can't convince my body that this man will hurt me, despite the fact that I know he turns into a giant wolf with lethal teeth. This isn't fear; I don't know what it is, exactly, but it's definitely not that.

I shouldn't want it, because what's the point of him feeling like this if it isn't even real? If it's all going to crumble like a house of cards the minute he learns any of the truth about my past?

Like he's a mind-reader, Luc leans a little closer, making eye-contact with me before he says, voice careful and precise, "I'm ready to spend the rest of my existence learning everything about you. And before you get in your head—nothing, absolutely *nothing*, you could tell me would scare me away."

I squirm, looking away. "I thought you said you *didn't* know anything about me."

He chuckles for a second. "I don't. But I can read your face, Penny. And whatever you're worried about, don't be. If you did something you're afraid of me finding out—trust me, I've done worse. If you've been hurt and you don't want to share—I'm not a patient man, but I'll wait for you to feel comfortable. And then I'll kill whoever did it."

I swallow, my throat suddenly tight. *Jesus.* I grip the arms of my chair, trying to keep my hands from shaking.

"Eat your food, Penny," he commands quietly. Luc's commands aren't exceptionally demanding, and they're definitely not loud. He just speaks in a way that he expects to be obeyed, and I bet it never fails him. "You look like you could use it. Unless you want to get started telling me things now?"

I pick up the sandwich with shaking fingers and take a large bite. If he's disappointed I didn't take the second option, he doesn't show it, instead just watching me eat like it's a fascinating piece of art.

The fluttery feeling is back.

After I take a second bite, Luc leans back in his chair, still watching but more relaxed now. "I had this place built to be highly secure," he says, matter-of-fact now when a minute ago he was talking about *killing someone* for me. "Nothing can get to you here. No one knows where we are, and there're both magical and mortal protections on this place. Barring putting you on the opposite side of the planet from me, this is as safe as I can make you."

"I won't go to the opposite side of the planet," I tell him. "My family is here."

"I wouldn't let you go," he admits. "Because at least here, I know where you are. Can make sure you're okay. This place is safe, Penny. You don't have anything to worry about."

"Except you?" I dare to ask him.

If I expected that to upset him, then I'd be disappointed. He doesn't even react, just shaking his head, his face as carefully neutral as before. "Not me. I hurt other people, love. But not you."

*Love* sends a shiver down my spine that I can't suppress, and he notices. "Oh, love," he says again, not putting any extra emphasis on the word, just watching me tremble as he says it. "I'll treat you right, I promise."

I have no idea what to say to that. I want to hear him say it again. It's a crazy thing to want. I want to hear more, want him to tell me what *treating me right* means. I want—

I gulp, trying to get my breathing right. It's a losing battle, and Luc just waits me out. When I'm at last feeling like a functioning human again, he says, "Here's what we're going to do today. You're going to eat your lunch, and then we have the whole day before Max will be back. You can relax; you had a shock yesterday. And you can ask me any of the questions that I'm sure are brewing in your head. Nothing's off-limits, love. Not for you."

I reach for my sandwich again, needing something to do while my brain frantically spins and tries to come up with questions.

# CHAPTER 11
# Luc

I watch her eat the rest of the sandwich in silence. It's only when she gets to the last few bites that I remember I have my own food. Of course Max would take a bite and then stick it back in the fridge. Marriage seemingly hasn't fully domesticated him yet.

I take a half-hearted bite, not particularly interested in dry roast beef. But Penny's shoulders relax when I do it. I don't know if it's seeing me doing something she considers normal and even human, or if she thinks my attention is off of her now. It never is, of course. I could be fighting a hundred armed enemies and my attention would still be on her; a sandwich certainly won't get in the way. But if she feels better, I'm not going to correct her.

There will be a day where the attention I pay to her will make her feel good. We might even already be partially there. Maybe it's wishful thinking, but I don't think the squirming she's doing is from discomfort. She might wish she wasn't interested in what I'm offering her, but I know I have her attention.

I will make this woman the center of my world. She'll come to crave it, know that she can always look to me for safety and comfort and praise and a listening ear. Someday, she'll know I'm *hers* when I've known for so long that she's mine.

"You're really two thousand years old?" she asks me, pushing her plate with only crumbs left away from her.

"Give or take. We didn't do a good job at keeping count back then."

"Good lord. Doesn't life get boring?"

"There are things to keep it interesting." *Like you*, I don't say. Always new wars, new enemies, new challenges to conquer. But never a person, never someone to walk beside and make this life worthwhile—until now. Until her. I want to do it all over with her, show her all the best things I've seen, travel the world, and give her everything she could ever dream of.

Her brow is creased, and I ache to ask what she's thinking. But I told her she could ask whatever she wants, so I keep my mouth shut; this time is for her, not for me.

"How does that... work?" she asks, stumbling over the word, but I get the gist.

I shrug. "There was a sorcerer who realized if he raised boys that no one cared about and trained us like animals, we'd be stronger, faster, more vicious than the average man—and that was profitable. We called ourselves a litter, because we were literally raised like dogs. I think half of us died before we were ten." She's getting a little paler now, so I rapidly move on. She doesn't need to hear all the terrible pieces of my past. "Anyway, I made a plan and got away. Max was with me, too."

"What happened to the sorcerer?" she asks, her voice quiet.

I really need to think before I speak to her. I might make a conscious effort not to terrify humans in my day-to-day life, but I never soften my words to make them feel better. But for Penny, I need to find out how to balance telling her the truth with not overwhelming her.

"He's dead now. That all was a long time ago." I surreptitiously look at the clock on the microwave. He's been dead for about ten hours, if that, but she doesn't need to know that.

"So, not all of your kind are immortal, then."

I bristle at being lumped in with Alexander. He's not *my kind*; I don't claim him. But that's neither here nor there. "We are. Alexander didn't meet a natural end, Penny." I sincerely hope Max made it painful, in fact.

I should have reminded him on the phone that Alexander attempted to kill Casey to teach Max a lesson. That would have riled him up.

"So, you're all immortal. Then, why me? I'm going to die someday, Luc."

Like *hell* she will. Penny is going to have an incredibly long life.

"There are ways to become one of us. Not all of them are as brutal as what Alexander did to us."

She stares at me like she's trying to read my soul and struggling. I wish I could lay it out and bare it all for her, but I don't know how to give someone that. I'll try for her, though. "And that's what you want for me?" she asks.

The answer is obviously *yes, of course*. The answer is I would change her right now if I thought I could get away with it. She'd be safer that way.

That's not the answer to give her, though. "If you ever want it," I say as diplomatically as I can.

"Because you really do such a good job selling it." She rolls her eyes as she says it, and I fight a smile. Good. She's scared and unsure, but she's still got the attitude. She's going to be okay.

It's a good point, though. "I promise you not every story is a horror story. And you can take it as a good sign, maybe; I know how bad it can get. I'd never let you go through that, Penny."

She processes that slowly. I know she's still resistant to hearing how I feel about her, and that's fine; we can work on that more later. But I'm hoping it sinks in, nonetheless. I'll never let anything hurt her. "And after going through that, what made you think, *wow, I really want to go into politics?*"

I snort. "That's not quite how it went." I've never had to explain this before, though. Either people are too scared of me to ask, or else they've been there the entire time like Max has, and therefore don't need any sort of explanation for why I am the way that I am. But Penny deserves the truth.

"I'm small," I admit to her like it's something she somehow wouldn't have noticed.

"I think you're about average height, actually," she says.

No, unfortunately I'm not anymore. For a long time I was perhaps average for a human, but small for a supposedly lethal, killing machine of a werewolf. But humans keep getting taller as the centuries go on, and I stopped growing a long time ago.

"Well, I wasn't what they envisioned when they were raising us to be soldiers. I was the runt and everyone thought I'd be one of the first to die. Then we escaped, and we found creatures that we thought were like us to help—but they weren't like us, because they saw some stupid distinction between being born like this or made like this. They didn't help us. I don't respond well to being looked over, love. I couldn't stand it. So I ensured that it wouldn't happen again."

"So you went into politics?" She's skeptical now, but she's also *paying attention to me*, and I can't resist; it's like a drug, and I need more of it.

"Love, I conquered the world. Supernatural creatures much older than me know to fear my name. When I give an order, it's obeyed. When I tell them there are rules to living in my world, they follow them. I set the terms of our world and no one is ever going to tell me I don't belong there again. After all that, it only made sense to continue." Humans are easier to rule, although following all the finicky rules of running for office had been annoying. With supernatural creatures, sending Max to tear someone's head off is a valid governing strategy; with humans, it doesn't quite work the same. I had to learn charm, a skill I'm still not sure I fully mastered.

"That will make you a queen," I point out.

She shakes her head. "Don't do that."

"Do what?"

"Tell me these stories of the future you imagine like they're already true. Just—give me a few minutes to get my head around this."

That's not a *stop*, so I'll happily give her a few minutes if that's what it takes to get through to her. "Alright, love. Whatever you need."

She doesn't seem to hear me though, pushing back from the table to walk over to the window, staring out into the woods. I watch her, hoping this isn't a longing to escape. I can't let her go, and not just for my own selfish ends—there are things out there dangerous to her health and safety, and I can't keep her safe if she's away from me.

It's starting to snow outside, fat flakes landing on the trees, turning them white. I remember what Max said about us having a romantic little Christmas here. Could I give her that? A pretty view, a warm fire, and hopefully better food—I could make something nice for her.

I'm seconds away from texting Max to buy the ingredients for a Christmas dinner and hot chocolate mix and a damn tree when she speaks again. "If you need someone by your side who can do all that for you politically—who can be a queen and, fuck, an actual for-real First Lady someday, then it's not me."

"Why not?" I demand. I don't see the disconnect here, but whatever thought is plaguing her right now, I'll defeat it. I'll make her see how wonderful she is.

I can see a murky reflection of her in the glass, and her lip quirks up in a sardonic little smirk that makes my stomach swoop. "You should have been a better stalker," she says. "Should have run the background check. If you had, you'd know that I have a record, Luc. And that's pretty disqualifying."

A *record?* What does a creature like me care about some petty human crime? I've probably committed far worse crimes by accident. "No one gives a shit in my world, love. I promise you that."

She growls again, and there's something wrong with me, because that stupid little sound makes my cock jump. "You are a *governor*. You are supposedly running for president in a few years. You don't just live in your world, Luc. And I might not be a political expert, but even I know that voters frown on First Ladies with records." She shakes her head, looking down. "Why am I even talking about this like it's serious?"

I'm moving before I can talk myself out of it, stepping right into her space and wrapping my arm around her shoulders. She tenses for a second, but then, inch by inch, she relaxes and leans into me.

It's a victory, but I fight the urge to preen. This only works because she thinks I don't notice; the calmer I stay, the more relaxed she'll be.

"You're talking about this like it's serious because you know it is," I tell her, keeping my voice low and even to hopefully reduce spooking her. She needs to hear it, but I know it's a lot for her right now. "I know you haven't had as much time as I have to come to terms with this, so I'll be patient. But love, this *is* serious. And I don't care about any petty little crimes you committed. Whatever parking ticket you have doesn't mean shit."

She laughs, the sound broken and sharp. "You think I got a parking ticket?"

No, that doesn't seem to match how anxious she is right now. I can't imagine what she would have done that has her so worried, though. "I don't think you've killed anyone."

"I tried," she admits, shocking me enough that I tighten my grip on her.

"Are they alive?" I demand, barely leashing the monster baying in my chest. I can feel the wolf pushing to be released, but I hold back. Penny wouldn't appreciate that.

She rolls her eyes. "Yes, you can rest assured I failed."

"I won't," I vow to her. "Just give me a name, love."

"You have no idea why I tried to kill them. Maybe I have a past as a mugger. Maybe I used to assault little old ladies."

And maybe I'll take up sheep farming. Some things aren't even worth contemplating. "Penny, if you tried to kill someone, you had a good reason. They harmed you, and I'll ensure it doesn't happen again."

She huffs. "It's done. I did what I did, and he's in prison and I have a record but I'm *not* in prison. I'm free of him now."

"Give. Me. A. Name," I bite out, losing the battle of control slightly.

"Greg. Greg Patton. What does it matter? It's over."

It matters because now I can find him. I'll get her to tell me what he did to her, but I don't need to wait for that; he no doubt had it coming and more, and I'll simply finish what Penny started.

I debate if I should tell her that or not. Somehow, I doubt offering to slaughter her enemies is the romantic gift I think it is. And anyway, I'm not doing this for praise; the world needs to learn that crossing Penny is a death sentence.

"He's not the point," she continues. "The point is that I tried to kill a man, and that's not even the whole thing. All of that would come out in *five minutes* if a reporter looked into me. I can't be by your side, so whatever little fantasy you've spun—it's over, Luc. It can't be."

Like fuck it can't. There are a dozen different ways to handle this, and not a single one involves letting Penny go. I have her now; I'd sooner let my wolf go than I would her.

"What happened, love?" I ask. "Tell me what he did." We can deal with her belief about her place at my side later, when I have all the facts.

"Why do you think he *did* something?" she asks again. "Maybe it was all on me."

"Penny," I say as patiently as I can muster, "I know you. No, listen—I don't need to have learned your social security number to know who you are, deep down. And you're good. You wouldn't attempt to kill someone who didn't deserve it. You're the type who hesitates, and that means he pushed you to it. So, I'll ask again: what happened?"

She squirms out of my grip, and I force myself to let her go. I don't want her to feel caged, even while at the same time I want nothing more than to cage her. Especially right now, when I have a feeling she's about to tell me something terrible.

She's here in my well-protected cabin, in arm's reach, under my constant gaze. Nothing will happen to her, I remind myself, forcing deep breaths as I turn to follow her movement.

She picks up her discarded lunch plate and walks it into the kitchen, beginning to wash the dish and refusing to look at me. But I have more practice waiting people out than she does, so I just lean against the counter about five feet away from her, waiting. Watching.

When she's washed the dish for so long I'm half worried she's going to scrub a hole through it, she flicks a glance my way. Whatever she sees on my face must break down her last barriers, because she mutters, speaking to the sink and not me, "He was my husband."

I clutch the counter tight enough that it cracks, but keep my face neutral, willing her to feel safe enough to tell me this story.

# CHAPTER 12
# Penny

I'm wishing he ran a damned background check. I'm wishing he was a more thorough stalker. Maybe he would have left me alone, which doesn't make me feel as good as it probably should. At the very least, I wouldn't have to tell him this story.

"I got married young," I tell him. "I was nineteen. He was twenty-six. As you can imagine, it was a shitty idea."

He doesn't say a word, but when I dart a glance his way, he's watching with eyes focused on me like lasers. I doubt a nuclear explosion could take his attention off of me.

I set the clean plate in the drying rack. Then, needing something to do, I wet a paper towel and go to the table, ready to wipe up the crumbs. I can feel the heat of him behind me, leaving a scant few inches between us. I bet he wants to be even closer, and this is his version of restraint.

There's a part of me that wishes he wouldn't restrain himself. I've never had to tell this whole story before, and I could use some comfort right about now.

"Anyway, Stephanie and I grew up with nothing. Mom left when I was eleven, which I don't really blame her for, but she never came back for us. Dad forgot we existed half the time, so I spent a lot of time learning to keep us both afloat. Big sister things, you know? I basically became her mom at eleven, and it was a lot."

"No child should go through that," he rumbles. My throat tightens as I keep scrubbing the table.

This man told me he spent his childhood in a death cult where half of the kids died before ten, where people assumed he'd die first, but he still sounds sincere.

I shrug. "It is what it is. But at eighteen, I was hustling hard. Completely unqualified, but I needed money. I wanted a place for us both. I wanted Stephanie to go to college even if I wouldn't. I was never going to get that making minimum wage at a coffee shop, but I was killing myself doing it, trying my absolute best. And Greg—his office was down the street. He came in all the time. It started with him learning my name. Then there was flirting. And then he asked me out. And then—it went fast. We were engaged four months later, and married two months after that. Too fast, and I was too young, but he paid our father's mortgage and promised to help me send Stephanie to college and, I admit, I was blinded by it all. Designer clothes and food I couldn't even pronounce, a house so big that four of my childhood home could fit inside. He'd take me places, show me things. I was enamored with the life."

"But not the man," Luc surmises.

"At first I was. I thought it was—well, eighteen year olds are dramatic. He was my Prince Charming. My knight in shining armor. But things got weird."

"Weird how?" Luc asks. He's even closer to me now, and he could reach out and touch me if he just moved an inch.

The table is spotless now. I move to throw away the paper towel, and Luc lets me walk past him, falling in step right behind me. I wet another paper towel, then wipe down the kitchen counters as I talk.

"I wasn't delusional. I knew Greg liked me because I was pretty, and probably because I was young. I could deal with that. I could be arm candy if that's what it took. But he got demanding. And I'd try to live up to his demands, but I could never make him happy. All the flirting from when we first met was gone. It was all criticism, and yelling, and then ignoring me. And then—Greg had a lot of money, and it all went over my head. I trusted that the money was there and would continue to be there. Only turns out, he was also money laundering as a side business. I didn't know, couldn't know. And then he kept giving me papers to sign, telling me it was this or that—health care proxies, insurance paperwork, whatever. I was an idiot and didn't understand any of it and I signed, and when the feds came knocking, it was my name on a lot of those accounts."

I don't have to look at him to know he's radiating fury. The wolf feels closer to the surface, the room hotter, the air thicker.

It should make me nervous, but it doesn't even break my stride. He's not angry with me.

"I didn't sign up to go to prison for him. I turned on him immediately, told them everything I knew, even if it wasn't much. And then I went home to pack my things, whatever I thought I could get away with. I was going to go to Stephanie's; she and Louise had just gotten married, but I knew she'd take me in even if it was massively inconvenient." I trail off. My baby sister had turned out to be the savior between the two of us.

Luc clears his throat. "You didn't explain the attempted murder yet," he says, tone gentler than I think he's used to.

"When I was packing, he came home early. I couldn't hide what I was doing and hadn't thought of a lie in advance, so it all came out. I confronted him. Demanded to know how he could do that to me. He got in my face, screamed at me for betraying him. Grabbed me, shook me, put his hands around my throat—" I can still feel them there, clammy and squeezing while I filled with the raw certainty that I would die "—and I had one of those stupid stiletto shoes he'd bought me on the bed. I picked it up and swung it for his throat. The heel got him and ripped a hole in him."

He makes a noise that is distinctly canine, a pleased sort of rumble that warms me up from the inside out. "Fierce," he praises. "You didn't finish him off, though?"

"In the end, I didn't have it in me. I called 911 and waited for the police to arrive. We were both arrested. They told me if

I pled guilty to the assault, they'd cut me a deal if I gave them information about the money laundering. I'd stabbed Greg, after all, and the only proof he'd hurt me first were bruises, and those fade. I never served time because of that deal. I was on probation for two years, and it'll never be off my record. Greg's serving fifteen years. Nine years left." I look up to stare out the window, not liking to think about that. He's going to get out someday, and I'll spend every day looking over my shoulder when that happens.

Men like Greg see their wives as property, I've since learned. My betrayal had been unfathomable to him, and I just bet he'll spend fifteen years in prison dreaming about how to punish me for it.

Except maybe it won't be an issue, because Luc says, "You're a merciful woman, love, but I've never had mercy. I'll take care of him for you."

I try to muster up some sort of feelings. Regret, maybe, or revulsion. Nothing comes. If anything, I just feel even warmer, like Luc's threats are a soft blanket he's wrapping me in.

I stop washing the already-clean counter and finally look at him. "That story will come out in five minutes if you tell people we're in a relationship. Which we're not, by the way, but hypothetically. You need to know that."

He holds up two fingers. "One, we are absolutely in a relationship. I am yours and you are mine and this thing is forever. I'll be patient until you feel it too, but I know it's going to happen. And two," he says, folding down one finger, "I don't give a fuck what people say. You think I can't fight through it? I've fought harder battles than the human press."

"You'll drag it all out there," I mutter. "It'll be in the news again. My name, my face—and now Stephanie has a family, and she and Louise run the restaurant—she doesn't deserve that. You'll ruin me and my family for this infatuation, and I—"

Luc wraps his arms around me, holding me so my back is to his chest, rocking me slightly. It's only then that I realize I've started to hyperventilate, lungs working too hard for too little air while the thoughts of what could happen crash together in my head.

"Easy, love," he murmurs, his voice cutting through the buzzing in my ears. "Okay, I hear you. We don't have to talk about this right now. It's okay. You're okay." And then, like I weigh nothing, he picks me up under the knees and walks us both to the couch, sitting down with me in his lap.

And I let him. I collapse into it, soaking up his warmth and strong arms and chest. He's steady. The world isn't going to break while he holds me.

Jinx jumps up on the couch, then settles right into my lap, so we're stacked three high.

Luc chuckles slightly. "That's the closest she's gotten to me," he says. "You have a loyal cat, love."

I pet her back, and her fur under my fingers steadies me a bit. With Luc's warmth at my back and hers on my lap, my heart rate slows and I can think again.

This is embarrassing. But Luc inadvertently hit all the worst thoughts I've had at once—Greg getting out, and then the idea that everyone will *know,* will see it all over again. The only way it could be worse is if we somehow brought up hurting Stephanie in the conversation.

He must be able to tell that my heart rate is slowed; everything I've seen so far tells me he has some crazy senses. But he doesn't let go, doesn't change our position in any way.

Finally I ask, "Last night, do I remember your friend saying animals don't like you all?"

The arm he has banded around my middle tightens and he strokes my hand. "You heard right," he murmurs. "They can sense a predator in us and tend to stay clear. We're not great with household pets, much to Max's wife's consternation. But your cat is brave, Penny. She's willing to risk me to comfort you. That's amazing."

"She stood between me and Greg a few times," I admit. "When he yelled. She was so little then, but she'd plant her little body between us and hiss and spit at him. She's a trooper."

"I'll have to invest in some luxury cat treats, then. She deserves them."

"Good idea. Maybe if you feed her the good stuff, she'll warm up to you. She's food motivated." Between the warmth and the gentle, rhythmic movements of his fingers and the soft purring of a Jinx, my eyes slip closed.

"Good to know," he whispers, and I swear I feel his lips ghost over the crown of my head. "You can sleep, love. It's okay."

And like his permission is all I need, I do.

# CHAPTER 13

# Luc

S he's so fragile in my arms. Strong, but breakable.

I don't dare to move a muscle. I make my breaths more shallow, worried the movement of my chest will cause her to stir, and I can't have that. I need every blissful second of soaking up this contact.

And I'm not entirely selfish. She had a panic attack, but I helped her calm down. My presence, my touch did that. I'm going to keep holding her and let her reset her mind and body.

She needed someone and she turned to me. She might not recognize it that way, but that's what happened.

She'd be more comfortable in the bed, but I don't move her. There's probably a big difference between waking up in my arms on the couch and waking up in my arms in bed, at least in her mind. And her waking up without me holding her isn't an option, so on the couch we stay.

The cat eyes me balefully, but when I don't move, she gives up and settles down, purring in Penny's lap. Brave cat.

I need to call Max. I need an update on whatever he's found, but I also need to give him a new task. Greg Patton is going to die.

Would Penny like that? It's going to happen either way—no one lays a finger on her and survives—but is it something she wants to know about, or something she's better off remaining in the dark about?

Either way is fine. I can take care of the gruesome side of the world for both of us. Penny doesn't need to do anything but survive and be happy.

I pause, fingers absently stroking her hand. What will make her happy? I have no idea. That seems like something I should know. I'm already failing her.

Does she like it here, in a quiet life? Does she want an expensive house and designer shoes, like she had when she was married? Would she be content as a future First Lady if she didn't worry about what people would say about her?

She likes her cat. She seems to appreciate her sister and her sister's family. That's the entire extent of what I can say for sure about what matters to her.

That's my to-do list, then. Order Patton's death, then learn what will make my wife-to-be happy. No, wait. And order expensive cat treats. If I can somehow bribe the cat into liking me, then that'll make Penny happy.

Her breathing shifts. She's waking up, and she didn't sleep long. Does she need more sleep? It dawns on me that I have no idea how long humans should sleep for. I'll add it to the list of things I need to learn.

She takes a minute before she opens her eyes, but she snuggles back into me at the same time. My heart might combust with how cute she is.

"Give me your hand," she says, voice raspy with sleep.

I don't even bother to ask why, just running my hand along hers until our fingers are entangled. This is new, but I'm not going to question it. Is she seeking comfort? Does she just want to touch me as badly as I want to touch her?

She runs our linked fingers over the back of the cat. More of Penny is touching the animal than I am, but I can still feel the soft fur. I shudder, trying to think of the last time I touched a still-living animal. I don't think my own fur is this soft.

Jinx picks her head up, but seems reassured that her human is still here and settles right back down.

"See?" she says, still sleepy. "She likes you. You're not that scary."

My breath catches in my throat, realizing what she's given me. I was separated from her because her precious pet would never like me. Now, she's broken that barrier and invited me in.

"I'm plenty scary," I assure her, my voice a little choked up. "But not to you. And not to her, by extension."

"And not to my family," she adds.

I really couldn't give less of a fuck about her sister and sister-in-law, so I just nod. "Them too," I agree. "I'll protect all of you."

She keeps stroking the cat, my hand in hers, and she turns our hands until I'm touching the cat more than she is. Between the dying fire and the snow coming down outside the window and the warmth of her in my lap, I can't think of a more perfect scene.

I hate to break it, but now that she's awake, I need to ask her, "Does that happen often?" It's not a problem if it does; I'll learn whatever I need to make her life easier.

She doesn't pretend she doesn't know what I'm talking about, which I appreciate. I can help her, but only if she's honest with me. "Only when I think about all that," she tells me, voice concise and clear, like she's reporting statistics that have nothing to do with her personally. "When I think about Greg getting out, or having to endure everyone looking at me about that again—that sets me off."

She says it so matter of factly, but I still have her in my arms, and her body tenses just at the thought. I kiss her temple. "You never have to worry about Greg coming after you," I tell her. She never has to worry about him getting out at all. "And as for having everyone know—I hear you, love. You don't need to worry about that."

"Someday, you'll get tired of this," she tells me, still using that same matter-of-fact tone.

"No, I won't. Penny, I met you three years ago, and I haven't let my mind stray since. I've lurked outside your window for a glimpse of you." I debate how much to tell her, but decide to just go for it. "Penny, I did something two years ago. Something I probably shouldn't explain to you, because I doubt you'd still think I was a good man. And I did it to help a friend, but also, it could help us. It gave us a chance at a future. I found a way to make people like us that's not torture. Even when I didn't think I could ever use it, I still wanted it. But we're here, and I need you to understand I've been planning for our future this whole time. I'm not going to suddenly change my mind."

She shrugs. "I was easier then, Luc."

"I hunted down an ancient evil and extracted a two millennium old secret from him. What on Earth do you mean by *easy*?" I ask, agitated now. Why can't she accept this? How desperate and pathetic do I have to become for her to realize I'm obsessed and that's not changing?

"I mean you didn't actually have to factor in me as a person," she says. "I didn't have feelings yet. I was just this *thing* you could project on."

Fuck that. I move my hand from around her middle to gripping her waist, then I pick her up and flip her onto the couch. The cat falls off her lap with an indignant hiss, and I suppose I should feel bad about that, but I can't bring myself to worry about the cat's feelings when Penny has such a fundamental misunderstanding. She runs off toward the bedroom, howling the whole way.

I hover over Penny. Everything in me says to pin her in place, to grab her wrists and straddle her hips and make sure she can't get away. I resist the urge, if just barely.

Penny's eyes are wide, darting around to take me in. I stare back, needing her to know how serious I am. "It sounds," I begin, voice kept level by the skin of my teeth, "like you think I could be someone like your ex-husband. That I could just want you as a possession, and then I'll discard you when you don't live up to my expectations. And I need to convince you that that's not true."

Penny squirms. "Nothing can do that except time," she murmurs, an interesting but unexplainable look crossing her face.

"I have so much time," I tell her. "And so do you, but that's neither here nor there. I will know you from the inside out, love, and I will adore every inch of you. The good, the bad, the ugly—every precious inch. You're my future, Penny."

"You have a future," she points out. "And I don't fit in it."

I growl, and her eyes go even wider. There's a whiff of fear there now, radiating through her pores, and I consciously fight to master myself. Not like this. I won't scare her like this.

"There is no future that you won't fit into," I vow to her. "There is no world where I don't want you. Don't adore you. I will give you everything you can dream of, and you just have to give me enough time to learn what that is. But I will learn. And I will woo you."

"What if what I want is privacy?" She challenges. "To not end up on the six o'clock news? No, I've done that before. Even worse—to end up in the celebrity gossip magazines. I won't be the punchline of a late night TV joke, Luc."

When she says my name like that, nothing else in the world matters. She wants privacy? Done. I'll resign tomorrow, leave the humans to their own devices, and buy us a private island. I'll have to make appearances in the supernatural world, because they're a lot harder to just let go, but they also won't give a fuck about her and her human crimes. They'll respect her because I tell them to, and she'll know I love her above all else.

"If being your man means I can't have the campaign, then fine. It's done. I'll step back. I don't *care* about that, Penny. I care about us." Her eyes are wide again, and I shift my weight so I can grip her chin with my right hand, forcing her to look at me so she can see how serious I am. "You are it. You don't like something? Say the word. It's done." I'll make a phone call right now. I have reporters who I talk to when necessary, and I'm positive I could get one on the phone. I could have the story out there that I'm not running in an hour. If that's what it takes for Penny to see it—

Penny grabs my wrist, and I think for a second she's trying to push me away, but then she uses it as leverage, leaning up until her cinnamon scent encompasses my entire world, and then her lips are on mine.

I blink, but then sink into it. When the universe gives you everything you've ever wanted, you don't ask questions; you just kiss her greedily and pray there will be more.

# CHAPTER 14

# Penny

Luc kisses like a man who's been starving for a long time, desperate and all-consuming. It's infectious, this desperation, because it fills my entire being.

I met this man not even two days ago, I distantly remind myself. He turned into a giant wolf and also kidnapped me, the little voice says. I ignore it all. I haven't had something that feels this good in so long.

His body is warm, and while he won't put his weight completely on me, I ache to feel him on me. I bet being under him like that feels safe, like the entire world is just Luc and his kiss.

Luc seems to be studying as he kisses me, looking for what draws a reaction. When one hand brushes my breast and I arch up against him, nearly unbalancing us both, he pulls away, nips at my bottom lip, and rasps, "How far can I take this, Penny? What can I do to make you feel good?"

The amount of attention he's paying to me makes me shiver, makes me feel seen. Greg wasn't like this. Even at the beginning, he knew he could rely on my inexperience to cover up his many faults. He was selfish and I honestly think half the time he could have gotten off with a blow up doll, for all the attention he paid me. But Luc—Luc looks at me like he sees nothing else. Like there's nothing else in the world but the two of us, right here.

"Love? Tell me what you want," he prompts, stroking his thumb down my cheek. I shiver, captivated by those dark eyes.

Had I thought they looked cold? No, they're warmth. The deepest night, the heaviest blanket, wrapping around me and keeping me warm.

What I *want* is a bit more of a complicated question, though, and now might not be the time to think about that. "Just let me—" I murmur, reaching for his belt.

He pulls away, physically moving his whole body out of my reach until he's on his knees between my spread legs, looking down at me. I mourn the sudden loss of his warmth, the light pressure of what little weight he rested on me now gone. "No," he says firmly, and I shiver at the command in his voice. "I didn't ask what you could do for me. I asked what *you* like."

"Maybe I like sucking dick," I say, just to be contrary, maybe shock him a bit.

He quirks an eyebrow, utterly unphased and entirely too attractive for it. "Do you?"

Who knows? I imagine doing it because I want to, as opposed to as an expectation, would feel different. I imagine Luc in all his obsessive, over-the-top glory, growling praises as I suck his cock. Yeah. I think I could like that.

He's still waiting for an answer, and we both know that he's not really asking if I like sucking dick. Not that I think he'd be uninterested in that information, but I can tell Luc is used to having his questions answered, and I've already been ignoring one.

"I like... not having to make the decisions for a little bit. Knowing that my partner is going to take care of me, and that doing so is their favorite thing." I manage to look him in the eyes, jutting my chin out a bit with the challenge.

I know what I like because after Greg was sentenced, Stephanie kept pushing me to get out there again, to find someone better. And it turned out that I had no idea what would be *better* for me. All I knew was I kept failing at finding it, and it made me feel like shit.

So I'd done a lot of reading. A lot of romance books, yes, but also a lot of blogs and embarrassing "sex tips" articles in magazines. It was humiliating to learn what I liked that way, but probably understandable enough considering how many normal developmental milestones I missed. My teenage years were filled with hungry nights and trying to make Stephanie's now too-short hand-me-downs last a little longer. Then I'd been working, and then I'd met Greg. I'd never done any of the normal exploration.

So far, all my imagining has been pretty faceless. Confident guys with strong hands and growly voices, but no specific features. Would Luc do that? Could he do that?

If I expected him to look put-off, then I'd be disappointed, because the way he's looking at me can only be described as *wonder.* "You were made just for me, weren't you?" he rasps. "You need someone to be obsessed with you the same way I need to obsess. You're *mine*, love, precious and perfect. Say you understand that."

I shiver. In a few sentences, Luc has hit more of what I need to hear than every failed date since my marriage ended.

Because yes, I am his, aren't I? He dragged me into this world, explaining how he's been *stalking* me because he's obsessed, and I could barely muster any anger. I should have been furious, but really, my heart's been opening to him the whole time. When he admitted he was obsessed enough to lurk outside my window for three years, my brain went *who, me?* and my heart melted into a puddle.

"Say it," he says, voice firmer now but still quiet and level. I bet Luc never shouts, and that alone is a turn-on.

I'm in so deep here.

Deep enough to agree with him, any rate. "Made for you," I say, reaching out to touch him again. This time he lets me, leaning a little closer so I can touch his face, trailing my fingertips along his jawline. His eyes flutter closed for a second.

He's perfectly still. It's like touching a statue, and then he springs into action, sliding his hands over my wrists and pinning them above my head in a grip that's gentle but undeniable. His thumb traces the delicate skin of my wrists as he leans closer, watching me with single-minded focus. "You like this?"

"Uh-huh," I nod, mind already a little soft at the edges. When was the last time another person got me wet? And he hasn't even properly touched me yet. I want him to pin me here and ravish me. I want him to let my arms go so he can slide his fingers into my panties. I'm dripping for him, and I want *more*.

"Good girl," he murmurs, and I shiver. He smirks, clearly noting my reaction. Luc is going to catalogue every squirm, every breath, every time I arch closer, and he's going to take merciless advantage, and I don't even mind, because I know he's going to use it to make me come harder than I have in my life.

I've never trusted someone to take control and have my best interests at heart before. But Luc wants my pleasure more than he wants his own, and that's a heady feeling. I give into it, letting him pin me down and arching up for another kiss.

He gives it to me, kissing me so long that I half wonder if werewolves even need oxygen. When he breaks the kiss, he nips at my jaw, then kisses down my neck, across my collarbones, and back up the other side. He pauses there, asking, "How do you feel about marks?"

We should have had this conversation before we ever got this far, but I don't want to stop now. "Mark me," I demand, because I *want* it. This man, this obsessive, dominant man, wanting me so bad, being so passionate about *me* that he can't help but leave marks? I feel like my panties might combust.

The sting of his teeth in my neck pulls a noise out of me I didn't even know I could make, long and low and so, so desperate. I want him, I need him, and I can't wait any longer.

"Luc, please—"

He nips at my neck again, this time right above the last bite, licking the spot when he's done. "No need to beg, love," he says. His voice has dropped lower, reaching a rumbly register I didn't even know was real. "I'll get you there, I promise. In the meantime, though—let me enjoy you. You're fucking perfect, Penny, and I'm going to touch every inch of you."

My impatience dies away, a swift death like it was never there. He wants to look, to touch, because he wants me? He can have all day.

"I'm going to strip you naked, kiss every inch of your body, touch you until you scream, and then fuck you until you can't walk straight," he tells me, and only the erection I can feel pressing against my stomach gives away that this is more than a matter-of-fact conversation. "I'll move you where I want you, pin you where it'll best please us both, and I'll make you come until your eyes cross. I'll talk to you exactly like I have been, love, because you're fucking perfect, my waking fantasy, and I need you to know it. That's it for today, nothing else, nothing we haven't talked about—and what do you say if you need me to stop?"

It takes a second for my brain to parse that I've even been asked a question; I'm drowning in waves of lust, swept under

111

by his words. But when he just stops and waits, not moving or speaking, I process that he's waiting for some sort of safe word. "I'll tell you to stop," I tell him, too punch-drunk to think of anything more creative, "and you will, right?"

He leans down and kisses me. "I always will, love. This is about what makes your perfect body happy. If it hurts, or is uncomfortable, or you change your mind—you say stop." That's an order, so I nod, languid and slow, slipping deeper as his fingers start stroking the inside of my wrists again.

"I could tear these clothes right off you," he growls, eyeing my no doubt heaving breasts as he talks. "Could rip them apart to get to you."

Oh, *fuck*. "Do it," I demand, immensely impractical given the limited amount of clothing I have here, but I couldn't care less. His hands are on my wrists still, but his grip loosens, no doubt ready to touch me somewhere else, to help me get naked for his ravenous gaze. I need him, need his hands, need his desperation and hunger and—

The seam of my sweatshirt tears, ripping from the bottom all the way to the neckline. I blink. "Jesus, you're strong."

"Mhm," he agrees, pulling the fabric off me entirely until I'm left in my bra. He slices through that too, and it's only then I realize he's using claws.

It's a mind trip to see someone I'm having sex with have *claws*, but I don't have time to process it before his mouth is on me. He's sucking at my nipples, holding my ribs in place with gentle pressure so I don't arch right off the couch. And then he's nipping around the areola, and he's going to leave so many marks. I'll wake up tomorrow and see his teeth marks all over my chest, see the indisputable proof that he wants me, that I'm desirable like this.

I whine, more needy than I've ever sounded in my life, but Luc doesn't even look up, just continuing to mark up my tits while his thumbs stroke my ribs. I thrash and push against him, begging for more. I need him lower, need him inside me, need to feel him, full and hard against me.

He takes an infuriatingly long time. I'm just about ready to complain, but, like he's a mind reader, he murmurs into my skin, "You are so goddamn perfect, Penny. I need to taste every bit of you. Need to be all over you, every inch. Be patient for me."

I can be patient.

When he's done marking my tits and stomach, he finally reaches the waistband of my jeans. "Do you know how many nights I've dreamed of how your ass looked in your jeans the first day we met?" he asks, and there's a level of reverence that makes me shiver. "You've haunted me, love."

My jeans are gone before I can even process that, and I have no idea if he tore through them or just pulled them down, but I'm down to my thong while he remains fully dressed above me, taking in every inch of my body.

"And these," he groans, snapping the band to make his point clear. "Haven't stopped thinking about them since last night."

"Pervert," I manage to say, sounding like myself again for a moment. "Spying on my underwear drawer."

He growls, leaning down to nip yet another mark into my skin, this time right at my hip bone. "I'm going to get to know your underwear drawer very well, love. Going to pick them out and dress you up for the day, then rip them off you the moment I get you alone. Get used to it."

*Fuck*. All clever retorts are gone now. I've never been this turned on, this desperate for someone. I need him.

"Luc, I need you to—"

He pulls my thong down my legs, more careful with it than I expected, and then tucks it away in his pants' pocket. "You need me to fuck you good and hard? Fill you up and show you what you do to me?"

I pout, completely naked in front of him as he takes in my body. "I can't actually see what I do to you, you know," I tell him, eyeing the bulge in his pants that is infuriatingly still hidden from me.

Being naked while my partner is still clothed should come with a little bit of humiliation probably, but I don't feel it at all here. All I feel is Luc's desperate, starving hunger for me, and it just unspools my control more, sending me even higher.

I think I like this, having him look at me like this, having him dressed and solely focused on me. But for our first time, I really want to see him.

"We can't have that," he agrees, putting enough distance between us so he can pull off his clothes. I hate the distance, apparently as desperate and obsessed as he is already, but I don't complain as each piece of clothing gets carelessly tossed aside.

I remember him saying "I'm small" earlier like a confession. If I remember correctly through my sleep-induced haze, his friend from last night is the size of a small tree, so if that's the standard Luc compares himself to, then yes, he is small. But for me, he's on the shorter side of average, absolutely starving for me, and clearly well aware of what to do with his hands.

And probably the rest of his body too. My eyes land on his cock, proud and hard and *fuck*. Maybe I do want to experiment with sucking cock sooner rather than later.

He's staring at me again, taking me in just like I'm taking him in. We are so fucked, the two of us caught in this feedback loop, this desperate *need*. It's only been two days, and I have to keep reminding myself of that.

Two days too long. I need him. I part my thighs slightly for him, giving him a glimpse that draws his whole attention and makes his breathing speed up. "Luc..." I say, half a plea and half an offer, and he's on me in a second, taking it.

# CHAPTER 15

# Luc

She says my name like a little breathless moan, and I'm gone. For the rest of our lives, I'll be powerless to resist that voice.

I'm on top of her, pressing her wrists into the couch cushion once more, noting the way her eyes get heavy and desperate when I do. Every inch of this woman is perfect. I'm going to learn everything that makes her body sing, and I'm going to show her pleasure she never thought she could have.

There's a lingering thought about the ex-husband, and if he fucked her like this. I hate the way it makes me feel, but it doesn't matter. He'll be dead soon, and I'll be the one making Penny feel pleasure for the rest of eternity.

He didn't give her anything I can't. Money? I have scads of it by now. Designer clothes and vacations and nice houses, and yes, looking after her family too—whatever she wants. And I'll never betray her trust. Every day will be about making her happy, and every night will end with me fucking her until she sees stars.

My fingers flex around her wrists and she moans, the sound ripped out of her as if against her will. "That's it, love," I tell her, voice lower than I'm used to. I've had plenty of sex before, but no one has ever gotten me quite this needy. "Let me make you feel good."

She's covered in red marks left by my teeth. They'll bruise tomorrow, and I'd feel bad except I could feel how much each and every one turned her on. My Penny needs the proof of my obsession written into her skin, and I'll refresh the bruises every morning and night if that's what it takes.

I move my leg slowly, until my thigh is pressed against her cunt. She's soaked, and her hot, slick heat on my leg makes my eyes flutter for a second. "Such a good fucking girl," I tell her, experimenting with moving my thigh against her until she moans again. "Letting me make you feel good. Letting me prove to you how much I want you."

I promised her to keep it simple today, to not cross any lines we haven't already discussed, but my mind spins endless possibilities for the future. Would she let me tie her up, bring her to the edge again and again and again just so I can watch how beautiful she is while she teeters on the edge, desperate to come? Will she let me touch her in public, just because I'm desperate to have her?

She bends her knee, repositioning her leg and moans, high and needy, when the new angle gets her exactly what she needs.

"That's it, love," I rasp. "Ride my thigh. Make yourself feel good."

She does, grinding against me, but I can tell that she needs me to take back over, so I do. I transfer both wrists to one hand. "I'm going to fuck you," I tell her, looking into her eyes, watching her watch me. "Going to fill you up, love. I'll go slow." Penny hasn't spent a single night not at her home since I started following her, and I like to believe that means it's been a while for her. I don't want to hurt her, and I watch her face for any signs of uncertainty. I don't see any, just her nodding enthusiastically, clearly ready for me.

I don't wait around; we both need this. I push inside her, staying true to my word and going slow, murmuring sweet praises as I carefully watch her face, inching into her until I'm at last bottomed out, surrounded and strangled by her tight heat.

"So fucking perfect, love," I tell her, squeezing her wrists lightly, guessing it'll make her whine, and immediately being proven right. "I got you. I'm going to make you feel so good, yeah? You're going to be your beautiful, sexy self and I'll get us both what we need."

I'm heroically resisting the urge to come immediately. Nothing has ever felt this good before, and I want this to last forever. I want to *live* inside her.

That should sound crazy, but with Penny, I somehow think she wants that too.

I rock my hips into her, her tight walls barely letting me move. "So *fucking* tight," I groan, and I'm ready to tell her more, to expound on her virtues for hours, when a soft *mreow* interrupts us.

Penny rocks against my grip, the haze clearing from her eyes in a heartbeat. I look up and frown at the little beast that's decided to be brave today. She's watching us from the back of the couch, and I don't think I imagine the judgment in her little eyes.

"Jinx!" Penny cries and I release her wrists and help her sit up, mourning when I slip out of her. How can a place be home after only a few moments?

"Shoo," I tell the cat, waving a hand at it. That gets me an unimpressed look from both Penny *and* the cat, so I shut up and watch Penny when she grabs her cat off the back of the couch and gently places her on the ground.

"You shouldn't see me like that," she scolds the cat. Then she looks at me. "Maybe we should move to the bedroom? So we can shut the door?"

I'm so relieved that the cat hasn't entirely ruined the moment that it takes me a second to process what she said, but that's the best idea I've heard all day, so I nod and scoop her up. She yelps, clinging to me in an extremely gratifying way.

"Put me down!" she insists. "I'm too big for you to carry like this."

I snarl and nip at her neck in punishment. That only makes her groan, so perhaps not an effective punishment, but it's a sound I appreciate regardless. "Penny, I could lift your fucking car," I growl.

She has the gall to roll her eyes at me. "I just mean—*fuck*—" I move, one hand supporting her weight and the other creeping down to palm that glorious ass. "I just mean that I weigh a hundred eighty pounds, asshole, and I know I'm not light."

I think she thought I was exaggerating when I said I could lift a car. "Change of plans," I rasp, hoisting her a little higher. "Can't wait to get you to the bedroom. Going to fuck you right against that window." I'm going to hold her up, press her against the glass and show her exactly how strong her man is.

I have the presence of mind to pause for a second, asking her, "Is that alright? There's no one around for a good twenty miles, but I understand if you don't—"

She squirms and shoves a hand between us, and I don't know what she's up to for a split second. Then her hand, soaked in her own wetness, is in front of my face, and she just drove me over the edge of sanity without saying a single word.

I suck at her fingers while I slam her against the window, only barely mindful of my strength. She gasps when the cold glass touches her back, and I moan around her fingers when she arches her tits toward me.

I release her fingers to give them a few more bite marks, but I can't escape the feeling that we're being watched. Not from something unknown outside the window though. No, it's the fuzzy, four-legged creature that my future wife insists is important to her. "Fuck off," I tell the cat, then bare my teeth at it until it scurries back into the bedroom.

"Be nice to her," Penny scolds, voice a little breathless. "You're going to have to get along to live together."

I thrust back inside her before she can second-guess that thought, and I know I'm going to be buying luxury cat food to make this up to the stupid animal later, but then Penny's sweet cunt drives all thoughts of cats and food and the entire damn world out of my head.

*"Fuck,"* I groan into the silky soft skin of her neck, digging my fingers into her hips so I can bounce her up and down on my cock. I force myself to pull back enough so I can look at her, watching her head thrown back against the glass, her long neck and beautifully fucked-out face on display. "You're a fucking masterpiece," I tell her. "A painting. Look at you here, beautiful like some angel, all the snow falling around you. You're so fucking perfect, love."

I pull her down particularly hard, grinding inside her, and her orgasm sweeps through her, pulling a gasp from her like even she didn't expect it. I hold her there, rocking her through every tremor, every delicious squeeze around my cock. "Such a good girl," I tell her, in awe of her beauty. There's a flush trailing down her chest now, mixing deliciously with the redness from my bites. She's glowing, radiant and wrecked, and I need *more*.

121

"Give me another," I tell her as soon as she comes down. "Let me see you come again, love."

She's panting, still rocking on my cock as I move her, but she says, "I can't. I never come more than once."

Of *course* she can. I bet she's basing that off talentless, selfish wastes of space like her ex. But I'm not here to be selfish—I'm here to worship her like she deserves. I'm absolutely sure I can get her there, but I don't know her body like that yet. I don't want her to feel bad if I'm wrong and she can't give me another one. Not yet, but soon, I'll know her body better than anyone, better than even she does. I'll know every note I can play on it, every reaction I can pull from her. For now, I'm going to learn her. "We'll see," I tell her softly, gently rocking her hips for her. "But we're damn well going to try, love. If you trust me with your body, then I'll show you pleasure like you've never known."

It takes her a long second, but she gives me a hesitant nod, so I lean in to steal a kiss, sealing our mouths together in a way that feels like sealing our souls.

The window has served us well, and I'm definitely going to remember how beautiful she looks being fucked like this, but I need a better angle, so I deposit her on the table, drawing her ass right to the edge, then part her pretty thighs and drop to my knees.

The taste of her on her fingers earlier was both a tease and not nearly enough. I inhale deeply, filling my lungs with the scent of her. *Fuck*. My gorgeous fucking woman, smelling so sweet and needy for me. Her cinnamon scent is even stronger like this, sharp and intoxicating.

I spread her thighs further, then put her feet up on my shoulders. "Going to buy you a pretty little anklet," I tell her, pressing a kiss to her calf. "So every time you see it, you think of your legs around my head when I eat you out."

She gasps at that, which turns into a long moan when I lean forward and lick a broad stripe through her folds. Her hands shoot out to grab at my hair. It's short enough that she struggles to grip it, but I let her try. I let her struggle for a moment before I gently take her wrists in both hands and pin them to her side on the table. My love *likes* it when I restrain her, when I make her unable to do anything but take the pleasure I give her. And I'm going to give her so much fucking pleasure.

Her clit pulses under my tongue, and her breathy little moans fill the entire cabin. *This* is music, and I want to hear it every damn moment of every day.

She squirms in my grip, twitching and pulling, but not fighting me. She hasn't said stop, hasn't even implied it, and she's rolling her hips against my face. Penny is going to come again, just like I knew she could, and she's getting close.

"That's it," I murmur into her thigh. "You're so good for me, aren't you, love? Getting right to that edge again, letting me watch you come—so fucking pretty, Penny. Come for me." I turn my attention back to her clit, nipping lightly when I suck on it, and she crashes right over that edge with a gasp, riding out her pleasure against my face.

I release her wrists, surreptitiously checking that I didn't accidentally bruise them. I'm all for marking her, and she clearly likes it, but there's a world of difference between marks I leave on purpose and hurting her in an accident. Until she's stronger like me, I'll have to keep myself in check.

She's staring at me like she saw a ghost. "Are you alright, love?" I ask, pushing upright so I'm standing between her thighs. "Didn't hurt you, did I?"

"I didn't know I could do that," she murmurs, eyes a little glazed but voice clear. I run the backs of my fingers across her face, down her jaw, then tilt her chin so I can kiss her.

"I'm going to teach you all sorts of things you didn't know," I promise against her lips. "Trust me."

"I do trust you," she agrees, voice matter-of-fact while she says something that makes my heart practically beat right out of my chest. She trusts *me*. I went from stalker to trusted lover in thirty-six hours, and my Penny wants me as much as I want her.

She frowns and reaches for me, her hand landing on my bare chest. Her fingertips exert only the lightest pressure, but each one feels like a brand. "You didn't come," she says.

I didn't, and that's secondary to Penny and her pleasure, but I study her face carefully, looking for any sign that she's done.

This could be all for today—I could have already pushed her far enough.

But I don't see that in her eyes. No, I see a woman who's opened a door in her mind somewhere. Who's gone from what sounds like a truly terrible sex life to something that makes her hungry for more.

"I know you might not believe it, love, but you're not done yet." I pinch her nipple, making her groan and arch toward me. "Your body has so much more to show you. Are you ready for it?"

"Uh-huh," she agrees, head bobbing while her eyes glaze over again, hot and sparking with her pleasure.

I grin, scooping her up and encouraging her to wrap her legs around my hips, and walk us back over to the couch so I can prove to her exactly what her body can do.

# Chapter 16
# Penny

Luc is balls-deep inside me, guiding me as I bounce on his lap, when his phone rings from the pile of discarded clothes.

We both stare at the spot for a long moment, then Luc grounds out a low, "*fuck,*" and maneuvers us enough that he can reach his pants without pulling out of me.

"Be quiet for me, love," he says, like he's not currently *inside* me. "I don't want to share your pretty noises with anyone."

"Luc—" I begin, and he waits a second. But I don't know what else to say. I'm not saying *stop.*

When that thought becomes clear to both of us, he accepts the call and raises the phone to his ear, using his free hand to press against my belly, holding me in place while he grinds inside me. I bite my lip, remembering what he said about not wanting anyone else to hear. If that's another werewolf on the other end of the call, then they probably have above-average hearing, so I need to somehow not shout how good Luc is making me feel.

"Max," he says crisply, and I hate him for a second, hate how he can sound perfectly put together when he still hasn't fucking come. He's been edging himself for—I don't even know how long it's been. Too damn long. And yet he sounds like he's ready for a press conference here.

I squeeze my pussy around him, just to see what he'll do.

The hand on my stomach tightens, fingers digging into my skin, but I can't tell if he's scolding me or holding me steady for more. I don't really care, either. I don't know if supernatural orgasm control is part of his shifter powers, but right now it seems like it is, and I want to see exactly how far that goes.

"They can't have disappeared," Luc says, then leans over and nips at my neck. I can hear something through the phone, but he has the sound low enough that I can't really make out any words.

"Alright, come back. We'll re-group and make a plan." He listens for a minute, then says, "No. This isn't negotiable, Max. My wife's life is on the line." His voice is lower than I've ever heard, deep and threatening. That should be scary, but somehow instead it's a turn on.

He'd never use that voice on me, I know, and that's what makes the difference.

"As soon as possible," he clips, then ends the call and throws the phone to the side. Both arms wrap around me again, squeezing me even tighter this time, and he leans in to growl directly in my ear, "My wife doesn't play fair, hm?"

"That's the second time you've called me your wife in the last five minutes," I point out, my voice getting high and breathy at the end when he fucks up into me.

"You just tell me the time and place, love, and I'll be there, marriage license in hand. The second you're ready, I'll put the ring of your dreams on your finger."

I look down at my left hand, clutching his arm like a lifeline. I've been ring-free for six years, and the last one had been... something. Flashy and too big for normal, every-day living. I won't go back to that.

"What if I don't want a big wedding?"

"Name the time and place," he repeats. "I want to be where you are; that's my only wedding requirement."

He grinds into me, and I sigh, body going lax all over again. There's no way I can come a third time. No way—

*Fuck*, that feels good.

Not good enough to derail my train of thought, though. Maybe it's the two orgasms already under my belt, but I'm more clear-headed than I was earlier. "This is crazy," I murmur. "We're talking marriage. This is the first time we've ever had sex."

He starts moving me with a little more purpose, dragging his cock in and out of my sore body. "You've been handling this remarkably well so far," he murmurs, voice unfairly level. "So I should have expected to hit a wall at some point. Penny, love—I would marry you right this minute. You and I, we're forever. Trust me; nothing will change that."

I consider that, and definitely don't hate it. "So, should I call you my husband?" I ask.

Luc freezes for a second, and then he's coming, growling my name before he bites into my neck. I gasp at the sudden shock of it, then the hot, claiming come filling me.

*Jesus.* I've apparently found the secret weapon to break Luc's impressive self-control.

His tongue laps over the new mark on my neck, then he kisses it, pulling away and mumbling something that sounds like my name—if my name were some sort of fervent, devoted prayer.

"You are a dangerous woman," he accuses me, and I've never heard a man sound so happy to be in danger. "Now, one more time, love. I'm going to make you come for me one more time."

"There's no way I can—"

"You can," he interrupts, smooth confidence returning to his voice. "I'm going to make you come, and then we're going to get cleaned up and find what's left to eat in this house before Max shows up. I'm going to savor every last second I have with you before he interrupts us."

Apparently, he's said enough and believes his word will be obeyed—and really, he's not wrong about that. He knows I'm going to listen to him at this point.

Luc trails one hand between my thighs, finding my sore, swollen clit and tracing it lightly with just the tip of his finger. I groan and buck into his touch.

"Fuck," he mutters, and I'm pleased to have shaken his control, even just the tiniest bit. "Your tight cunt—the way you squeeze me—I can't—fuck."

He kisses my neck again, trailing his lips from my collarbone up behind my ear and then back down, sucking little bruises into my skin as he goes.

His friend Max is going to arrive and find me looking like I've been mauled by a bear—and right now, I couldn't care less. Luc has one hand on my stomach, one on my pussy, his lips on my neck, and he is driving me toward my third orgasm of the day. Somehow, this man has control over my body that I've never had.

"Come for me, Penny," he growls into my ear. "Show your husband how fucking beautiful you are when you come."

Apparently, the magic word works for me too, because I can't hold out any longer. My third orgasm overtakes me like a sneak attack, clobbering me over the head until my vision whites out, and the only thing tethering me to earth is Luc and his hands.

After what seems like a difficult deliberation, Luc lets me shower alone, mumbling something about needing to make sure I'm fed. He doesn't seem thrilled about any distance between us, but I'm half-worried that if we end up in the shower together, I'll have my first proper experience of shower sex—and I'm not sure my body can handle another round.

I let the hot water pulse over my sore muscles, offering some much-needed relief. It feels like I just finished a workout—one I haven't done in six years, or maybe ever, if I'm being honest. Greg certainly never made me feel like this. He barely ever made me come—never mind three times in one afternoon.

It's an excuse to check in with Jinx, too, to pet her and love on her and assure her that nothing is wrong, that she's safe here. Luc scares her, but my sweet girl still soaks up my affection even though I must smell like him by now.

Luc is frowning at a few cans sitting unopened on the counter when I emerge, but his eyes dart right to me the second I step out of the bathroom. "Hello, gorgeous," he rasps, taking every inch of me in. "Have a nice shower?"

"Excellent water pressure, thanks," I agree, finishing toweling off my hair. "So, do we have a washer here, or...?"

"Yeah. It seemed useful," he says, something about his tone striking me as a little odd. "I'll deal with it later. It's downstairs."

"This place has a downstairs?" I ask, leaving the towel draped over the doorknob and making my way over to him.

He freezes. "Mhm. Unfinished basement, kind of dangerous. Don't go down there." His eyes flick to a door off the kitchen I just assumed was a coat closet. His voice is definitely weird now, but I'm not going to dig. Not yet.

I'm suddenly reminded that this isn't a vacation cabin. He's explicitly described it as a safe house, somewhere entirely unknown. I have absolutely no desire to know why Luc needs a safe house. Not right now, at least.

Maybe someday. If this isn't a fever dream, if this is more than just some sex-induced haze, then we're going to be together for a long time, and I'm done with being kept in the dark by people who supposedly love me. But this feels like something to tread carefully around.

"What's for dinner?" I ask, pausing to check the time on the microwave. Jesus, we were fucking for a long time.

"Come see," he invites, and I walk over only for him to pull me into his arms as soon as I get close. One hand goes around my chest, the other landing on my stomach, pulling me back into him. He makes this sexy little growling noise, one that seems practically subconscious and makes my pussy make a valiant try at getting wet for him all over again, and then runs his nose along my neck. "You look fucking beautiful with my marks, love."

I can't deny it; I saw them in the bathroom mirror, after all. I won't be forgetting what we just did for days, although I have a feeling that Luc is the type of man to refresh the marks before they fade entirely. I'll probably never be without them again.

And while that sends a delicious pulse through my core, I need to be practical for a moment. "Any chance you have a scarf somewhere? So we don't advertise what we just did to your friend."

He chuckles. "Penny, you can't hide that from him. Max's nose is sharper than a bloodhound."

I smooth my hands down my shirt, self-conscious. Luc catches my hands, holding both of them over my stomach. "I showered!"

"My scent will be on your skin for days, even with the shower. And your scent is on me. Besides—this whole place smells like sex."

Oh, right. I look surreptitiously around, eyeing the couch, the window, the table, all places we've fucked in the last few hours. "Should we open a window? Air it out?"

"The windows don't open, and all that would do is let the cold in. Max's sense of smell is strong." When he can tell I'm not satisfied with that answer, he kisses the crown of my head. "Don't worry. I've been to his home. I've listened to him wax poetic about his wife for years now. Call this payback and it'll be fine. He's not a judgmental person."

I sigh, accepting my fate that the first time I met this man, I was practically unconscious, and the second I'll be advertising how much sex I've had today. "Fine. So, dinner?"

"I have canned black beans and canned chickpeas. Thoughts?"

"Neither of those is a meal." I consider. "I could make really shitty veggie burger patties, maybe."

"Sorry, love. Max did say he'd bring food back before he left."

I look out the window, unable to see anything but a wall of white. "Jesus, it's really coming down out there. You sure he can even make it here?"

"He'll be here." He says it so confidently, but I'm still not sure. And even if he does get here, I doubt he stopped for takeout. Veggie patties might really be the best I can do.

"Ever heard of frozen dinners?"

"I'll stock up before the next time we get stranded while hiding out." He kisses the crown of my head again, then lets me go, and I pretend it doesn't make me feel practically naked not to have his arms around me. "There's also not a first aid kit here. Didn't ever expect to have humans, although I really should have planned better once I found you. You're not too sore, are you?"

"I'm sore," I admit, because I get the feeling that lying to Luc is like lying to a lie detector. "But not too sore. It feels okay."

"Good. Let me know if there's something I can do." And then his hand cups my pussy like he's patting it, possessive and a touch domineering and somehow also sweet. "You wearing another one of those pretty thongs for me, Penny?" he asks, reminding me that he still hasn't returned the thong he took off me earlier.

I don't know why he's so obsessed with them. It's not like they're fancy; they come in a damn plastic pack. I just don't like panty lines. But he's made multiple comments about my underwear, and it doesn't take a genius to see how he feels. "Wouldn't you like to know?" Just to turn the tables on him, I remove his hand carefully and walk closer to the counter. He lets me go, although I can feel his hot gaze biting into my back. "If you behave, you'll maybe find out tonight."

"Tell me what *behaving* looks like then, so I make sure I meet your standard." His voice is low, husky, like I promised him way more than I thought I did. "What rules do you have for me, love?" he prods, stepping closer, boxing me in against the counter. "What will make you happy?"

Jinx *meows* from the bedroom doorway, and Luc actually growls. I laugh, swatting at him. "For starters, stop that. Get along with my cat."

He sighs, but then steals a kiss that has me pushing closer. "Anything for you," he agrees. "I'll feed the beast, who apparently is going to eat better than us tonight."

Jinx winds around my legs while Luc gets the food out. I bend down to pet her, trying to ignore the twinge in my thigh muscles. "Hey, baby," I murmur. "You were so good for me today; thank you."

She butts her head against my hand, and I stay crouched down, scratching behind her ears while Luc mutters to himself, preparing the cat food.

He stops suddenly, head perking up. "Max is here," he says. I don't hear anything, but then Jinx reacts too, stepping closer to me, tail puffing up, so there's clearly another werewolf in our midst.

# Chapter 17

# Luc

I quickly finish feeding the damned cat, not wanting to give Max something to comment on when he gets in, then stand by the counter, waiting.

Penny can finally hear him when he reaches the porch, and I spare half a second to marvel at how unobservant humans are. It's not their fault of course, but it does mean I'll need to be extra vigilant on Penny's behalf.

Max opens the door without knocking, shaking snow off of himself in my entryway like the dog he is. He is holding a few grocery bags though, so I'll forgive him.

"We're stuck here for a bit," he announces, kicking off his boots by the door and setting the grocery bags on the table. I watch him as he does; I can practically still see Penny sitting on the edge, beautiful as she comes for me. If he notices, he pretends not to.

"Stuck?" I ask.

"It's coming down bad," he informs us like we possibly didn't notice. "I slid the car into a ditch a half mile or so back.

This road is shit, Luc, and when you add the snow and ice... we're stuck here until we can dig the car out."

Well, that's inconvenient, but not the end of the world. My car is just fine, after all, parked underneath the ramshackle car park next to the cabin. It probably doesn't even have snow on it.

Now, if the tires will hold up to this kind of snow is a whole other question.

Penny gasps in concern. "Are you alright?" she demands, and I fight the urge to pull her back to me as she walks over to Max.

He looks bemused, clearly never expecting anyone to worry about him over a minor car accident. But this is all new for Penny, and she probably hasn't put together that it's really just an annoyance to us.

Because what Max didn't say is that the car wouldn't be enough to keep us here. He and I could make it out of here just fine; if we transform to our wolf forms, the trip would be a walk in the park. Wolves are particularly adept at trekking through the snow and cold. Needing a car is more for Penny than anything.

"You must be Penny," Max says instead of answering her. "Nice to meet you."

She steps back, looking shy now. I step up behind her, touching her hip. "Hey," she says. Then, "I know you're helping. So, thank you."

Max's whole face softens. "Of course," he says, then looks at me. "Although I'd like to be home tomorrow. Since it's important to Casey and I and all."

"If I remember right, she didn't agree to marry you until, what, eight at night?" I ask. "So technically, the morning doesn't mean anything special. Actually, if memory serves, you were with me that morning. So, this'll be fitting."

Max looks the both of us over, no doubt taking in Penny's bruises and the scent of sex I didn't even try to wash off. "I'm going to remind you you said that someday," he says. "When you two are married."

Penny blushes a furious red, completely unexpected from the woman who made me come by calling me her husband. "Max..." I growl in warning.

But he just shrugs, turning away from us. "I brought food. Let me use your bathroom and I'll get out of your hair."

"What, you're just going to go back out there?" Penny demands.

"Won't hurt me, I promise."

"Stay. At least for dinner." I want to tell her no, tell Max to ignore her and get lost. I want every second I can get with just Penny and I. But contradicting her will just set us back, so I keep my mouth shut and brace myself for having Max intrude.

Max grins, the shit-stirrer, looking between the two of us. "Sounds good," he agrees, and then he walks off toward the bathroom, dripping water on my floor as he goes.

Penny turns the meager groceries into a halfway decent meal, cooking up chicken cutlets and rice and having three servings on the table in record time. "Do you work in the kitchen, too?" I ask, looking over her meal.

She snorts. "Do you think this meets restaurant quality standards? No. I can feed myself enough to stay alive, and that's it."

I consider what she's saying. Max has long since returned from the bathroom, but he's being decent enough to pretend he's not watching us. Honestly, he's texting on his phone, presumably with his wife, so he might genuinely be ignoring us. "What do you enjoy doing, then?" I ask her, stepping closer. "Do you enjoy your job?"

She exhales slowly, her shoulders rising. I want to grab them and rub out the stress, give her a little massage and get her to calm down again, but I keep my hands to myself. "I guess. A job is a job. I like that it helps out my family." She pauses for a second, head tilting to one side. "I have no idea, Luc. I've never had any time to decide what I enjoy."

I consider that. It's a familiar enough story; both Max and I can relate to a childhood focused entirely on survival at the exclusion of all else. Hell, I don't think Max and I stopped to really think about what we like until we met Casey and Penny.

"We have plenty of time to figure it out," I offer, then snap my fingers in Max's direction. "Dinner is ready."

He stands smoothly, crossing to the table and sitting at the seat on the far end. I take the opportunity to slide my chair even closer to Penny's. "Thanks for dinner, Penny," Max says before I'm forced to prompt him to say it.

"You're welcome," she murmurs, cutting her chicken. She looks over at me. "This is a pretty well supplied kitchen for you to keep no food here."

Max catches my eye across the table, head tilted. Two thousand years between us means we can talk without words most of the time, and I know he's wondering just how much I've told her. I stare back unblinking, warning him against telling Penny more than she needs to know right now.

It's not that I want to keep secrets from her, and I fully plan to tell her everything someday soon. Penny will be my closest confidant, and she'll know more than anyone. I have no real secrets from her. But I can't afford for her to freak out right now, not when things are so new and her safety depends on her trusting us.

Max blinks, accepting my order, and says, "That's your boyfriend there. Buys the nicest of everything even if he never plans to use it."

Aside from not loving the word boyfriend—it seems too simple for what we are, especially when she's already called me *husband*—his answer is as good as any, and I nod.

Penny considers it and then nods, and I'm not sure if she believes him or not. I wish I knew. I want to press her, to ask her, to learn every inch of her beautiful mind. But now isn't the time.

"So, do either of you want to explain to me what's going on?" Penny asks, pushing her food around her plate.

Max looks at me like he wants me to moderate, but I look at him, because I also need an explanation of whatever he's found. He sighs, dropping his fork. "How much do you already know?" he asks her, voice matter-of-fact but not unkind.

"I know that someone is apparently trying to come after me because of Luc," she says. "And that's pretty much it."

"Yeah, that's a good start," he agrees. "Basically, Luc noticed an unknown shifter when he was getting breakfast—I'm presuming you were there, since he didn't deal with it then. He sent me to hunt them down, and it seems like they've hooked up with a strong sorcerer who's cloaking their location pretty powerfully. We don't like either of those things, and after they tried to kill you, I went to sort it out."

"And what'd you find?" I demand at the same time Penny asks, "What's wrong with other shifters?"

Max's eyes dart between the two of us, clearly trying to decide who he's meant to answer first. I wait for him to decide, because truthfully I don't know either. I'm used to being answered immediately, but if Penny is going to be my queen, she should be put above all others.

Max apparently comes to the same conclusion, because he nods and turns his attention fully toward Penny. "Shifters like us aren't born naturally."

"Luc said. But he said you were turned basically right after birth, so what does it matter?"

"Because without fail, every shifter we've met was turned by a sorcerer with evil intent. They're either with us, or someone else is pulling their strings. And if these ones aren't with us..."

"Someone is pulling their strings," Penny finishes. "Who?"

"That," Max says, tapping the table emphatically, "is the question. And unfortunately, I don't have a better answer. Whoever it is, their magic is strong. It's like the shifter's scent completely drops off the map. I tried circling around, looking for any sort of weak spot, but nothing."

That's shit news, but not entirely unexpected. "We're as safe as we can be here," I tell Penny. "They don't know where we are."

"They shouldn't have known where I lived, either," she points out.

"I wasn't as careful as I should be when I went to your house." It physically hurts to admit failure like that, but she's owed the truth. "I didn't think—well, I just didn't think." I was blinded by want. Penny was separate from my world. I could

143

never touch her, so I let myself believe my world couldn't touch her, either. It was stupid and I owe her better. "This place isn't like that. I've never been anything but careful here. This is the place where I go when I have something to hide, love. There's enough protection in this place to stop most anyone dead in their tracks."

"Most anyone," Penny says quietly.

I study her carefully. Her stiff shoulders and tight grip on her fork tell me all I need to know, all I should have realized earlier—Penny is scared out of her mind.

And who could blame her? I thrust her into this world that's so far beyond anything she ever thought possible. What's worse, I did it with violence. She knows someone is trying to kill her simply for having the misfortune of being mine. I've ripped her away from her home, her routine—the only thing she still has is the damned cat, and right now she's cowering in the bedroom, wisely avoiding the two full-grown werewolves in the kitchen.

I distracted her pretty thoroughly with the sex, and as much as I'd like to return to that plan, we can't go on that way forever. I have to ease her mind in a way that doesn't involve orgasms.

"Penny," I say firmly, leaning closer so I can tilt her chin up, forcing her to look at me. "You are looking at two of the fiercest, most feared creatures to ever exist. Entire armies tremble before me and Max. They have for two thousand years. Nothing, absolutely nothing, is getting past us to touch you."

I can see Max open his mouth out of the corner of my eye, but he's wise enough not to say anything. We can talk later, in private, but right now, I need to focus on Penny and give her peace of mind.

She swallows, then nods slowly, not breaking eye contact with me the entire time. "Alright," she whispers, then clears her throat. "I—I trust you two. I believe I'm safe here. But what about my home? My sister and her family are coming back in a few days. They're going to re-open the restaurant. The kids are going back to daycare."

"I'll take care of it," Max says. Protection details aren't our usual cup of tea—we're typically more focused on threats and executions, truth be told—but if Max says he'll take care of it, then I have complete faith that he will. "We have people on our team I trust. I'll get them on your family, and your family will never know they're there."

I want to reassure her and say that no one would go after her family, not when they hold such little value to me, but I can't say it honestly. For one, I can never predict what rogue shifters will do. And for another, while I don't give a fuck about her family, I'm beginning to worry what I'd do to keep them safe just because Penny cares about them. Surely someone else, watching from the shadows, could make that same calculation.

"Can I talk to them?" she asks.

"Not about this." That, I have to be firm on. She can't go spilling the secret. "But if you just want to talk, as long as you think you can hide this, then yes. Feel free. I don't want to take your family from you."

Do I care about them? No. Do I understand what it means to have a family? Also no. But I can see when something is important to Penny, and I want her to have everything that makes her even remotely happy.

Penny nods again, and I can feel the trust she's placing in us like a physical weight. I vow to do everything I can to deserve it.

"Is this going to be forever?" she asks. "You told me to quit my job, Luc. Are we going to be hiding here forever? How's that going to work? Surely someone will miss you soon. Explaining why I'm not home when Stephanie gets back will be hard."

Someone is probably already missing me, but I'm relying on the confusion of the Christmas holiday and the intelligence of my senior team to cover this up for me. The internet is a fantastic invention, and I'll at least be able to keep up a minimal presence from here. "It's not forever, love. Just until we figure this out. We'll get this cleaned up, and then we can talk about what's next. I promise you, Penny. We'll take care of it."

Max clears his throat. "I'm going to check the perimeter." His eyes dart between Penny and me, and I know what he's asking without asking; he needs me to separate from her for a minute.

"You okay if I join him?" I ask her quietly.

She puts on a brave face and nods. "This place is safe, right?"

"It is. And nothing will get past us," I promise her.

"Alright. I'll clean up. And it'll give Jinx a break."

I make a mental note to prioritize trying to make peace with the damned cat, since she's clearly so important to Penny. I'm not even sure it's possible, considering I can't really explain to the animal that I don't mean her any harm. But maybe I can win her over with food and treating her mother right. Maybe there can be a truce at least.

But right now, I need to know whatever Max doesn't want to say in front of Penny. I kiss her forehead, then follow Max out the door.

The snow is knee deep and coming down in sheets. "You rolled the car into a ditch?" I ask him.

He jerks his chin down the road. "Half a mile in that direction. You can't blame me—this road is shit and I couldn't see anything."

And Max isn't as good a driver as he thinks he is, but I don't bring it up.

He's a shitty driver but he's perfectly capable of lifting a car. As soon as the roads are passable again, he can get it set to rights.

Not that I think we're going anywhere. I can put on a good front for Penny, but we're going to be here for a while. Max, my best hunter, couldn't find the threat. I'm not exposing her to risk, which means here is the only safe place.

Max is silent for a moment, starting to trudge through the snow, soaking his pants that barely started to dry during dinner. I follow him.

"I think this is Alexander," Max says.

I stop. "Alexander is dead. You told me you burned his corpse."

"I did. And you know full well he hasn't been capable of doing anything like this in the last few years. But before the scent was lost, I recognized one of them. Do you remember, two years ago, when I found Alexander—there was a shifter kid?"

"I remember." Max, a softie deep down, had been unable to kill the kid. We'd known Alexander had been making more of us, but, other than the ones Max killed when they attacked his home, we'd never found any of that last batch.

"I wondered if Alexander killed him, because he was a weak link. But he was in Penny's house last night, I'm sure of it. He'd be about nineteen now, I'd guess, maybe twenty. And I don't know who is pulling his strings, but last time I saw him, he was with Alexander."

The cold doesn't truly bother Max and I, but in that moment I feel it. It's like a ghost passing through me. Alexander's ghost, back to haunt us already. "We never knew—we always thought about the shifters. But what if Alexander had other sorcerers with him too?"

Max nods grimly. "My thoughts exactly. Think it's an apprentice?"

I look out into the woods to where I imagine Alexander's bones are buried. "Not an apprentice anymore. Just a threat."

# CHAPTER 18

# Penny

As soon as they're gone, Jinx comes back out, creeping low to the floor while she checks all the corners.

"You were so brave about Luc earlier," I tell her, crouching down and extending a hand to tempt her closer. "Did both of them scare you?"

I don't really blame her; Max could definitely squash her flat and not even notice he stepped on her. But we're going to have to do something to get her used to Luc.

She lets me pet her, and when I sit on the floor, she crawls directly into my lap, turning twice and settling down on my crossed legs, purring like a buzz saw. "I know, baby," I murmur, stroking her back. "It's all okay, though. I know you're scared, but you're safe here."

I can hear myself repeating what Luc told me. The difference is the cat can't even understand me, and all she needs is for me to pet her and she'll feel nice and safe.

Then again... Luc petting me would probably make me feel safer, too.

"I need to wash dishes," I tell her softly. "Do you want to come?"

I end up washing up with a cat draped over my shoulders like I'm a rich lady with a fur stole that sometimes bites me if I move too fast. I'm almost done with the dishes, hands starting to prune from hot water, when the door creaks open. I panic for half a second, but Luc walks in, Max right behind him, both of them soaking wet.

"Jesus, it's really coming down out there, huh?" I ask as they both shed their boots by the door.

"Not going anywhere," Max agrees. He stares at Jinx, but doesn't step closer. Jinx tenses up, little claws digging into my shoulders, but when neither of the men make a move, she relaxes slightly.

"So, what's there to do around here?" I ask. "Board games? TV?"

I'm practically advertising to Max that I didn't explore the cabin after I woke up, but Luc already assured me that we can't hide how much time we spent fucking from him, so I'm letting it go. He hasn't made any comments yet, and I'm assuming he's not going to start now.

"No TV, sorry," Luc says, stepping closer to me. Jinx tenses but doesn't move, her claws digging into my shoulders again. She's going to leave little pinpricks through my shirt. "No board games either."

"Who has a secret safe house with nothing to do?" I complain.

Max snorts, but Luc just puts his hand on the small of my back, murmuring, "I have something you can do."

I open my mouth to tell him off, trying to decide how I feel about him saying that when Max is around, but Max interrupts to say, "I'm going to call my wife," and stomps back outside.

Well, okay then. Now that we're alone, the air seems charged between us, like an electrical current is running between his fingers and my skin.

"Done?" he asks quietly.

"Yup." I drain the sink, setting the last dish in the dish drainer. Jinx chirps, clearly not liking the movement, and I turn to kiss her head before pulling her off me and setting her on the floor. I have a feeling that she shouldn't see what's going to happen next.

Like all cats, she pretends this is exactly what she wanted, sauntering off to her food bowl with her tail held high.

"Come to bed with me." He says it matter-of-factly, simple and straightforward, like he's already assumed I'll say yes.

And I will, I realize. I don't even care that Max will be coming back in the house at some point, and that he'll presumably be able to hear us. The cabin isn't that big.

But it is *Luc's* cabin, and I'll take full advantage of that.

"Yes." It comes out more as a breath than a word, but Luc gets my meaning, and he's carrying me again, scooping me up so fast I don't even know what happened until I'm halfway to the bedroom.

Something tells me I should get used to being carried around.

When we're in the bedroom, Luc kicks the door shut with a sense of finality, like he can close out the rest of the world. Then he looks around the bedroom like he's never seen it before.

The bedroom doesn't feel much like Luc, I realize, taking it in properly for the first time. It's simple and a little rustic, clean and impersonal. I know Luc has told me this cabin is just a safe house, so it makes sense.

What does his bedroom look like? What does his house look like?

Fuck, he lives in some sort of governor's mansion, doesn't he? I think I heard that once. There's no *way* I can visit him there and escape scrutiny.

How much time does he have left in his term? I try to do the math on election years.

"What're you thinking about?" His voice startles me out of my thoughts, breaking my concentration. I turn to him, cradled in his arms as he sits on the edge of the bed.

"Is it going to be like sneaking out to see your mistress for the next year or so?" I ask, then decide not to voice the bigger fear; that he'll have me, and decide I'm not worth giving up his aspirations for.

To his credit, he doesn't ask me to explain how my thoughts arrived here. He just stops, holding me tighter as he says, "No. Never."

"I told you I won't be in the spotlight." I feel like I'm holding my breath. This is the line I won't cross. Will he meet me where I'm at, or is this asking too much?

He shakes his head. "And I won't ask you to. One thing you'll learn about me, love, is that I listen. And then I plan. I'll resign after the holiday."

I gape at him. He talked about giving up his presidential bid, but this is too much. "You can't do that."

"Why not? My lieutenant governor is perfectly capable. Honestly, she's doing more for the great state of New York this weekend than I am. I can't do anything so special for the humans that I need to stay. And you come first."

He says that so simply that I feel my entire brain reset. It's like he pulled the plug and plugged me back in, giving me a fresh start.

And he seems to see it on my face. "My pretty girl needs a reminder that she's always first, hm?" he asks. He looks around the room, then back to my face. "Are you sore, love?"

"A little." I haven't had sex in six years, then had a marathon of it. I feel like being sore is expected, but I definitely don't regret anything.

He seems to contemplate that, then nods like we had a conversation. He gently pushes me off his lap, depositing me on the edge of the bed. "Earlier, your only job was to feel good, to feel how obsessed with you I am." I shiver, still remembering that feeling; the way he touched me, the raw intensity burning in his eyes. "Now I need you to do two jobs."

"Two?" Jobs? Like having sex with him is somehow work?

He nods. "Feel good. Feel how obsessed I am with you. And—watch."

And he drops to his knees between my thighs, and it's only then that I realize he positioned me so I'm facing the full length mirror in the corner of the room.

*Oh, fuck.*

I'm staring at myself, not yet fully caught up to what's going on, when Luc tugs lightly at my pants, working them down my legs, much more careful than he was earlier. Every movement is slow, precise, controlled, until he has me completely naked, thighs spread in front of the mirror.

He turns so he can see the both of us for a second, then looks back at me with a grin. "There she is," he murmurs, voice dripping sin. "My perfect Penny. How you think I could pick anything else above you—how you think I could ever stand to hide you away—is beyond me." He doesn't give me time to answer, kissing my clit and pushing my thighs wider, licking my core with a single-minded determination.

I look down at him, taking in his strong posture, the firm way he holds my thighs, the way he takes charge and looks so damn good doing it. But he must have a sixth sense, because

154

even without looking up, he pulls back enough to bite my thigh, scolding me and saying, "No, love. Your job is to watch yourself, remember? See how fucking beautiful you are when I make you feel good. See what makes me so damn obsessed. So—watch."

He refuses to start again until my eyes are on the mirror, staring at my own wrecked face. The fact that he can unwind me so quickly makes my head spin; the fact that I'm already close to coming just from watching myself is unbelievable.

But he can, because I can see the pleasure in my own eyes, the longing on my own face, and I don't know if I see what Luc sees, what makes him so obsessed, but I know I'm not going to question it. I'm not going to let it go.

"Come for me, love," he murmurs. "Come on my tongue, let me taste you."

I can't resist his command, not in that deep, self-assured voice, the one that tells me he already knows my body better than I do after a single day.

Unable to disobey Luc and take my eyes off the mirror, I watch myself come hard, watch the pleasure overwhelm me as Luc insists on wringing out every single drop of pleasure. Once he's convinced I can give no more, once I'm red and flushed and hazy with it, he stands, crawling up the bed and pushing me onto my back, kissing me and making me taste myself.

"You get it now." It's not a question, but I nod anyway. "I won't give you up, Penny. I won't do this in half measures. You're mine, and I am all in. That means building a life together as soon as possible. When it's safe to leave here, I'll resign, and you and I can go anywhere in the world you want."

I should have protests—I have family, a job, I can't just up and leave—but my brain is too scrambled to form any of them into thoughts.

So I kiss him again. His kiss is languid, slow, content even when I know he can't be. He hasn't come.

"Do you want to..." I trail off, trying to reach for his pants.

"I can go to the bathroom, love. Whatever you want."

I don't want that. No, he told me to watch, and I'm in the mood to *watch*.

"Will you show me how you like it?" I ask him. "Let me watch?"

"I'll let you have anything you want," he says, already tugging at his own clothes. Once he's fully naked, he takes his cock in hand, keeping eye contact with me the entire time. "This is what you do to me, Penny," he says, and I can't figure out how he sounds so calm when his cock is so hard it looks like it hurts. He starts stroking himself off, grip tight, twisting a little at the head, and groans. "Keep those pretty thighs spread for me. That's it, love. Don't look away. Nothing can feel better than your eyes on me—*fuck.*"

He's already close, leaking and rocking his hips into his fist, and I couldn't take my eyes off of him if the world was ending.

He comes, groaning my name, eyes slipping closed with the pleasure of it. "I fucking love you," he mutters as soon as he comes down from his high, leaning over to kiss me. "I love you, I love you. I *adore* you. Mine."

"Yours," I agree, a bubbling like champagne in my body as I say it, giddy with the thought. "Yours."

"Mhm." He kisses me one more time, a definitive peck, and says, "I'll be right back." Then, without a stitch of clothing on, he walks out of the room, presumably to go to the bathroom.

He walks back in a minute later, warm washcloth in hand, and he cleans both of us up before tucking the blankets in around me, sliding behind me and holding me close. "You look tired. It's been a long day; you should sleep."

"You're not tired?"

He kisses the back of my head. "I need less sleep than you do. One of the side effects of being this way."

"Mhm," I agree, keeping that in mind as my eyes start to droop. He's not wrong; I'm exhausted.

And maybe I can blame that exhaustion for what I say next, my filters low and my mouth spouting off the first thing that comes to mind. "Hey, Luc?"

He kisses my head again. "Yes, love?"

"If you want more of that, in the middle of the night... you could wake me up that way. Fuck me while I'm still sleeping. I think I'd like that," I murmur, then drift off to sleep while his arms squeeze me even tighter.

# CHAPTER 19

# Luc

*F*uck. Me.

Penny drifting off while muttering that I could fuck her in her sleep might be the single hottest thing I've ever heard.

I won't, not tonight—she said she's sore, and I'm not convinced half-asleep mumbling counts as proper consent—but if we talk about it and she still wants it? I'll wake her up that way every damn day.

I listen closely for a minute, but I don't hear anything, not even Max back in the house. He's outside somewhere, and perhaps I should feel bad, but I definitely don't. Showing Penny how I feel was way more important.

When Penny's been asleep for half an hour, my phone starts buzzing. I groan but slip quietly out of bed, keeping an eye on Penny as I check my messages coming through.

It's three news alerts, pushed to my phone by Calliope, one of the people who scans for this type of thing for me. A savage coyote attack just an hour from here. I frown, looking it over.

"Max," I say while stepping into the main room, knowing he can no doubt hear me. He opens the front door a moment later, grabbing my coat by the door to hold over his naked crotch. So he's been curled up outside in his wolf form, then, giving us some privacy.

"What?"

I show him the news stories. A man leaving a store got into a shoving match with a stranger when the stranger apparently swore at him. And all of a sudden, a coyote appeared as if from nowhere, savaged the man to death, and ran off, along with the other participant in the fight.

"Shifters?" Max asks dubiously, watching the gory video footage someone captured. "In broad daylight? That bold?"

I shrug. "You think a sorcerer is pulling their strings, and I'm inclined to agree. Why this would benefit him, I haven't worked out yet. But they're clearly following someone else's laws."

"Want me to find them?" he asks seriously.

"And eliminate them." No one saw the shifters transform, so we can count our lucky stars. Damage control when humans see something they shouldn't is always tedious. But these shifters don't get a free pass just because the worst didn't happen.

I consider for a moment. "Unless you think they have information about this sorcerer. Then beat it out of them first."

"Want me to drag them back here? You seem to have quite the set-up downstairs."

"Penny's here. No one comes here," I snarl, temporarily losing my cool.

He raises an eyebrow. "Alright, noted. I'll take care of it." He turns toward the door, and then he's gone again, leaving my coat on the porch as he turns back into a wolf and bounds out into the blinding snow.

After I slip back into bed, I get up only twice, once to build the fire in the main room back up, and another time to patrol the interior perimeter of the house, the restless wolf under my skin driving me to secure my mate's den. Between those times, awash in Penny's cinnamon scent, I'm able to sleep.

True to her word from yesterday, Penny wakes with the sun. She stretches much like her cat, going still when she realizes there's another person in bed with her.

I'm still operating under the assumption that Penny hasn't shared a bed with anyone since her ex-husband, and I quickly move to head off any worries. "Good morning." I kiss the crown of her head, my fingers holding her belly tighter, pulling her back into me.

Much to my gratification, she relaxes instantly. "Kinda thought I'd wake up with you already inside me," she says.

"Disappointed?"

She goes still. "Was it weird? Did I... I'm sorry."

I roll her until she's under me, pinning her wrists above her head again since that worked out so well for us yesterday. "Let's get one thing straight—you can ask me for anything you like, and if it's at all possible, I'll give it to you. There is no weird, or too much. Ask for anything." I lean down and kiss her to emphasize my point. "I just didn't consider half-asleep mumbling to be actual consent. But if you want it—"

"I do," she quickly agrees, eyes dilating and breathing a little heavier now.

"Then you'll have it."

"Would *you* like it?" she presses.

"I like everything about having you," I tell her, easing up on her wrists slightly so we can talk. I sit back, and I don't miss the way her mouth opens, her body subconsciously chasing mine. "I'm possessive, a little selfish—obsessed with you, Penny. Fuck yes, I love the idea of fucking you while you sleep, because I just can't get enough of you."

She shivers, pupils dilating even further. I can smell her getting wet, her sweet scent cloying the air, and I want to drown in it.

"Tell me what else you like," I press her, trying to keep us on track. I could fuck her right now, and she'd easily let me, but we should have had this conversation yesterday.

She shifts, posture becoming more serious as she sits up in bed. My eyes trail over her naked form as the blanket pools around her hips, taking in her soft belly, the swell of her breasts, and then back to her face. "I like knowing I'm the center of someone's world," she admits shyly, not looking directly at me. I want to make her look, make her see how everything she says just makes me hungrier for her, but I restrain myself. "I didn't have that. With Greg, I mean. I was at best an accessory that he didn't care about any more than he would his watch or shoes or whatever. At worst, I couldn't do anything right and he yelled. And I just—"

"You want a partner who reassures you that you're fucking *perfect*," I finish, silently planning crueler and crueler ways to murder Greg. I think my basement would be a perfect place for him.

"You don't think that's selfish, right? I know it is a little, but I just—"

"You're not selfish to want someone who puts you first," I tell her. "To want someone who fucking loves being with you, who treasures you. And I swear, Penny, I'll give that to you."

She's silent for a moment, cheeks flushing, but then she says, talking more to the blanket than me, "I can't feel unwanted, or replaceable. If I could just be any other stranger in your bed, in this relationship—I can't do it. It sends me back there and I don't like who I am like that."

"You know from experience." It's not a question, but Penny nods anyway.

"Stephanie kept encouraging me to try dating again, but first dates—well, by their very definition, you're disposable to that person, right? You're basically auditioning, and they haven't decided if they like you or not yet. It's not their fault, and they're allowed to decide that I'm not for them—but that process hurt, and I couldn't get past it."

And here I was, stalking her, revering her existence, hungry for her before we even met properly. We were literally meant to be.

I lean forward so I can pinch her chin, making her look up at me. "You won't go on a first date ever again," I say assuredly, then pause. "Except I haven't taken you on a proper date yet, so you'll go on one last one. But you can rest assured that I'm already sold on you, love. I'm head over heels, obsessed to my core. You are the center of my universe. This isn't an audition; you already got the part, and no one else was even considered."

She's looking at me with a kind of hunger that I recognize intimately, because it's what I feel when I look at her. I kiss her, unable to help myself, then lean back. She pouts, chasing my lips, but I use my hold on her chin to keep her in place. "Tell me what else you like," I order softly, bringing us back to my earlier question.

"I liked when you held me down," she says, eyes watching my mouth. "I like the things you say to me. I like how you can pick me up and move me around wherever you like."

"Would you like it if I tied you down? With ropes? Gentle ones, nothing that would hurt."

She considers it. "Depends. Not if you leave me like that. Not if you ignore me."

"Like I could ever ignore you. I don't think there's a force on this planet that can keep me away from you. No, I want to tie you down so there's nothing you can do but take what I give you while I devote myself entirely to knowing your body."

She shivers, biting her lip. "Then... yes."

"If I wanted to tease you, get you to the edge again and again and again, but not let you go over, just because you look so goddamn beautiful when you're about to come?"

"Uh-huh," she nods, voice a little weaker now, eyes hungry. She pauses for a second, then asks, "But you'd let me come eventually, right?"

"Of course, love. I wouldn't be able to resist. And what if I wanted to see you come again, and again, and again? Let you feel what I do to you, make you come until you can't see straight, until you can't walk, and don't remember your name anymore?"

"I—yes. Please."

My perfect fucking woman. "Good girl," I murmur, because she said she likes the way I talk to her, then pause. "You know you can tell me *no*, say *stop*, and you'll still be good, right? You're always my good girl. My perfect love."

She's soaking the sheet between her legs right now, and I'm not much better, hard enough that I'm worried about blood flow to my brain just from thinking about her like this.

"What if I want to sit you on my cock, not to fuck you, just to keep you close, keep us connected? What if I want to hold you and not let there be any space between us at all, because I can't stand to be separated from you?"

She nods again, shaky and a little disoriented. I decide to stop there before I overwhelm her; that's plenty enough information to start with, and I can already see a thousand ways to make the both of us very happy. Just when I'm about to ask her which fantasy she wants to start with, the front door slams open. Max stomps inside, and shouts, "Stop stinking up the place, love birds!"

His words break the spell. Penny wrenches away from me, hiding her face in her hands, clearly mortified. For my part, I'm torn between relief—there's a threat coming for us and I shouldn't let myself get so distracted that Max can sneak straight into my house without me noticing—and pure, blinding rage that he'd take this moment from me.

"We should... we probably need to... fuck, he heard everything, didn't he?" she whimpers.

Yes, he almost certainly did, but I refuse to be embarrassed if he doesn't know how to mind his business. "He was outside the whole time," I reassure her, carefully dodging the question.

She seems mollified, at least, and to my immense displeasure climbs out of bed. "We should probably go out there. Make breakfast, at least. I want coffee."

I'm about to offer to bring her breakfast in bed, but she's already pulling clothes out of her bag, so I sigh and pick up my clothes from last night because I'll follow her anywhere.

When we emerge, Max is in a stare-off with the cat, both of them on opposite sides of the open space. Jinx is on the back of the couch, puffed up like a cotton ball while watching Max in the kitchen. And Max, despite being six and a half feet tall, looks like he thinks the cat might lunge at him.

"I don't know what you feed cats," he tells us, not looking away from the fluff ball.

"Cat food," I tell him, because stupid questions deserve stupid answers. Penny picks up the cat, which looks like a safety risk considering how keyed up she is, but Jinx relaxes in Penny's arms.

"Good morning," Penny murmurs to her. "No one here is going to hurt you. Everyone here is fine."

Max finally looks away to share a look with me. We both know we've hurt plenty of animals before; we've spent too many years surviving on the fringes of society, and letting our wolfish

166

sides out to hunt was the most consistent way to assure we were fed.

I make my way into the kitchen to set out the cat food, because I can use all the goodwill from Jinx I can get. "You can take your shower, love," I tell her. "Coffee will be ready when you're done."

She leans in and kisses my cheek, and I make a mental note to make her coffee every morning.

As soon as she closes the bathroom door, Max steps up beside me while I fiddle with the coffee maker. "Well?"

"Same thing. There's a trail, and then it's just... gone. Like they vanished into thin air. And not like when someone gets in a car, because then you can at least catch a clue—it's *gone*. Like it never existed at all."

That's what I was afraid of. "They're getting bolder."

"Is this really about Penny?" Max asks. "I mean, she seems nice, but she's a human. What could they want with her?"

"Me," I say heavily. "I'd die for her, Max. I'd give them whatever they want if they had her." I've never had a weakness someone could exploit before. You win at chess when you never even let them get to your side of the board, and for centuries, I'd dominated the game. Now I have a glaring hole in my defenses.

And I wouldn't trade Penny for the world. I'll just need to play a better game.

There are options. I don't know how to fight a threat we can't locate, but the world is only so big, and I own all of it. I can smoke them out, but it'll take time and patience. I've always had both in spades, but I'm not sure it'll work that way this time.

They'll slip up. They always do. I have to believe that.

"You can't give them Alexander," Max points out.

"They don't know that."

"What's next?"

"We wait." Unfortunately, it's perhaps all we can do right now.

The coffee maker makes a great, heaving sigh, like a dying animal on its last breath, and I stare at it. A nicer coffee maker. I add it to my list of things to get.

Well that, and a house to put it in. I'll be out of the governor's mansion in a few weeks, and as comfortable as Penny's seemed here, I refuse to have us live full time over a torture chamber. I need to find a place to live for the both of us.

That draws me up short. What kind of house would Penny like? I know Greg apparently had a large house, and her sister's house seems tight for five people. Neither of those places are necessarily homes Penny picked for herself.

Well, now she's going to get to pick. She can have literally anything she wants, wherever she wants it. The world is hers now.

Penny emerges from the bathroom, hair wet and hanging loose around her shoulders, skin flushed pink from the hot water. Her eyes are bright as she follows the scent of the coffee, and it's like her presence chases all my tension away.

"I brought eggs," Max says, interrupting my fantasies of buying Penny a home and carrying her over the threshold. "Wasn't sure what you liked, sorry."

"Eggs are fine," Penny says, looking down into the fridge to find them. "Coffee is what I really wanted, so—thank you for bringing some."

I bite my lip to stop myself from saying something, because my irrational jealousy hates that she has anything to thank him for. *I* should be the one bringing her things she likes.

I need to get a grip.

Penny pops out with the eggs and some shredded cheese Max apparently brought. "Scrambled eggs?" she asks, looking around at both of us.

I'd literally eat rocks if she handed them to me, so I nod.

I bring Penny a mug of coffee, sliding it next to her hand on the counter while she heats up the pan. The smile she gives me rivals the sun.

"We don't have sugar," I apologize, remembering how she drowned her waffles in maple syrup the other day.

"I'll take caffeine any way I can get it at this point. An IV would work just as well."

She picks it up with the hand not holding a spatula and takes a long sip, eyes slipping closed in a way I didn't realize she did when she isn't about to come. She holds it there for a long moment, then sets the mug down. "Thank you," she murmurs, and I'm pretty positive I could take on an army single-handedly if she'd say *thank you* like that.

I kiss her forehead instead of saying that, because I don't need to seem any more unbalanced than I already do in front of Max. He was remarkably calm about the whole stalking thing—it's probably one of those things where those in glass houses can't throw stones—but I know there's a fine line here.

Max and I might consider ourselves friends. It took a long time and a lot of years denying it to get here, but I can't deny I'm closer to Max than anyone on the planet. We were raised together, fought together, escaped and survived together. He's been my right hand since I offered him a way out of Alexander's clutches.

But therein lies the problem—I'm his friend, yes, but also his commanding officer. In the pseudo-military structure we were raised in, commanding officers who looked weak were killed quickly. And while I doubt Max would do that, considering how much we've been through together, there's always a risk he won't follow me anymore.

People fear my name, but Max is the monster under the bed that other monsters warn their children about. He might need me to direct him, but I need him to keep the world in line.

But when Penny asks him how much cheese he likes in his eggs, he smiles gently at her, and something inside me eases. We're going to pretend this is normal, then, and that the three of us being here, in a house built over a torture chamber, snowed in and eating eggs and ignoring how the whole house smells like sex, is just another day for us.

# CHAPTER 20

# Penny

C offee. Sweet, life-giving coffee. I drink it greedily as I cook, but I barely have time to register it's gone before another mug is pressed into my hands.

I look at Luc, eyebrow raised. "You know too much caffeine is bad for humans, right? You're an enabler."

"You didn't get a cup yesterday," he says, like that's a perfectly logical conclusion.

I make Max's eggs first, considering he's the one who bought the food and also had to stand outside in the cold while Luc made me come my brains out last night. Then I make a plate for Luc, but he doesn't touch it until I've finished mine too, with extra cheese and yet another top-off of coffee. He carries both of our plates to the table, setting my plate down right where my ass was yesterday afternoon while he ate me out, smirking devilishly at me as he does.

I make a mental note not to get between these two and a meal as I watch them shovel their food down. The table is silent except for chewing and forks clinking on plates for several minutes, but I'm only partway through my eggs when they're both finished, pushing their plates away from them.

Max moves like he's going to stand, but Luc glares at him until he sits. "You don't have to wait for me," I say to both of them, but Luc ignores it like he suddenly can't hear me, and Max just shrugs.

"Nothing better to do out here," he says. "So, Penny—how're you handling all this?"

I raise an eyebrow, not expecting to be psychoanalyzed over eggs at seven-thirty in the morning. "Fine, I guess," I say. "I mean, if I don't think about it. Here is… small. Okay. Nothing weird here, right? But then I think about what's out there, and I—well, I try not to think about it."

Both of them exchange a look too complicated for me to read.

"You're going to be perfectly safe," Luc tells me, reaching over to squeeze my hand. "They might be stupid enough to try, but nothing is going to get past the two of us."

Max nods. "Everything they know, we learned two thousand years before they did. We've had a lot of time to perfect it. Absolutely nothing they'll do will surprise us."

That's all well and good, but a militaristic view of the situation isn't helping me. I know they're both trying, and I guess it's relieving to know I'm not going to die today. But this is bigger than that.

The world has changed. Things I never expected are out there, and some of them are unfathomably after me.

I shift. "Do you think that, now that they've realized I'm protected, they've given up? If they just thought I'd be an easy way to hurt Luc..."

"It's more complicated than that," Luc says. "Max confirmed who they are last night, or at least as close as we can get. They want something specific from me, something I can't give them anymore. I'm sure they think you're leverage."

I'm now in a world where the life of another human being is considered *leverage*. I swallow, hands shaking as I drop my fork. "What do they want?" I whisper, even while wondering if I really want to hear it.

Luc seems to be thinking the same thing. "I'll tell you anything you want to know," he says, voice even, "but you have to be sure you really want that. Once you know something, you can't unknow it."

I thought letting him fuck me was the crossroads. I thought taking his talk about the future seriously was what would cement this. But now, I see that those were mere stops along the way—this moment here is what will define us. Either I'm part of his world now, or I'm not, and my answer will decide that forever.

"Tell me," I say, hands still shaking as I try to make my voice sound firm. I can't have him thinking I'm unsure, because I'm not; I need to know. I need to be a part of this.

Max and Luc look at each other again, but only for a short second. "You know how we're made?" Max asks.

I nod. "The basics."

"A sorcerer made us like this. Bred kids to turn into shifters and sold us to the highest bidder once we were trained, and that training was something no one should endure, never mind kids." I nod, because I've heard this part of the story before, but it doesn't get any less terrible.

"I told you his name was Alexander," Luc carries on, picking up the story. "And two years ago, Max caught him. After two thousand years, he was finally mine."

The way he says *mine* is the antithesis of when he says it to me. I feel cherished, possessed in all the best ways when he says it to me; for Alexander, I can't imagine it ended well for him.

The thing is, Luc already told me this. And he implied that Alexander was long dead. But—no, he didn't. He'd just said it all happened a long time ago, didn't he? "Okay. So you killed him?" I guess, trying to sound calm even as I don't feel it.

Another look. "Not right away," Luc says after a moment. "He had information we needed, and then—he owed us more than a pound of flesh." *Torture*, I realize dimly. *He's talking about torture.*

But he's talking about torturing and killing a man who tortured little boys. Maybe this is just the universe's way of getting justice.

Some part of me is squeamish about the torture, but most of me just looks at these men and remembers they are just a small representative of the kids that Alexander tortured. He deserved to die.

"We think these people want him back," Max continues. "I recognized one of their scents, and while he'd never act on his own, I can only assume they're being stupid enough to target Luc because someone is pulling the strings and wants Alexander."

"But he's dead," I conclude, seeing where this is going now.

"But they don't know that."

"Can you tell them?"

That makes them both pause. "Might not be a bad idea," Max ventures.

Luc nods. "Get the word out. The sorcerer Alexander is dead. No sense in going after him." He looks at me, giving me a soft smile. "It might work. It might not, though; the problem with shifters is we're not part of either world, not really. We're not human anymore, but the supernatural creatures don't want us either. So, this will depend on how connected whoever is pulling their strings is to the gossip. But it's a good idea."

I glow with pride, and my hand finally stops shaking.

I can do this. I can hear about a dead man who definitely deserved to be murdered, and I can offer useful, relevant suggestions to their little war room.

Luc watches me for a moment, eyes soft and almost dewy, before he turns to Max, straightening his posture entirely. "Go make some calls." Luc turns back to me like that's the end of it, but Max clears his throat. "What?"

"Calls are your area, not mine. If people hear me calling, they're assuming they'll die tonight."

"You're acting like they don't think the same when I call," Luc grouches, but he doesn't argue, just sighing. "Love, would you be okay by yourself for a bit while I sort this out?"

I nod. "Go; I'll be fine."

He stands and kisses the crown of my head. "Finish your eggs," he orders gently, then retreats into our bedroom, shutting the door behind him.

I stick my fork back in the eggs, but they've gone cold now and the idea of eating them makes my stomach revolt.

Max seems to get it without pressing, because he just smiles in a way that softens his whole face, saying, "So. What do you like to do for fun?"

We're on the floor by the fire, and Max is texting while gently rolling a crumpled up piece of tinfoil at Jinx, trying to convince her that he's not a threat with limited success. Luc finally emerges from the bedroom, eyes beelining straight to me.

He stops and stares at us for just a second, but seems to decide me sitting next to Max and trying to coax Jinx closer is a normal enough activity, because he just slips into the armchair behind me, tugging me gently until I'm sitting between his legs. He takes out his phone, presumably finishing up business, and moves his leg a little closer to my shoulder, pressing just enough that I know he's there.

I lean back, absorbing his heat, and continue to try to get Jinx to come closer.

Of course, with two werewolves right here, there's no hope for that. Even with Luc feeding her regularly now, she hasn't exactly been won over yet, but that's okay. We have time.

She gives me a mournful little meow and meanders over toward the window, lying on the floor and rolling onto her back.

"That's wild," Max breathes, staring at her, then looking at me. "You have any idea how hard it is for us to get close to animals like that? I think the hardest part of becoming a werewolf for my wife was accepting we'd never have a pet."

"Jinx let Luc touch her yesterday," I tell him, thinking of him holding me while I stroked our entwined hands through her fur. "So, there's still hope."

Luc snickers. "You'll be pet shopping before New Years," he predicts.

"Adopt, don't shop," I say automatically, then shake my head. Am I really giving immortal werewolves pet parenting advice?

We watch Jinx roll around for a moment, and then Luc hands me his phone.

Oh, fuck. Just because I offered a slightly helpful suggestion to this whole "controlling all the supernatural creatures in the world" thing he has going does not mean I'm ready to participate any further. I don't want to see any pictures that could in any way be related to what we've been talking about. I've never seen a dead body outside of a funeral home, and I'd like to keep that streak for as long as possible, and—

It's Zillow. He's showing me Zillow, open to a page of houses not horribly far from Stephanie, although these houses are much nicer. My eyes bug out when I see the price tag on some of these places.

"What's this?" I ask, proud of how even my voice comes out.

He shrugs. "I'm leaving the governor's mansion in a matter of weeks, and I don't have another home to take you to. We need to pick one. These are by no means your only options, but I thought it'd be nice to start getting an idea of what to look for."

Holy shit. He's talking about moving in together, and while I objectively knew that was the plan eventually, he's talking about a matter of weeks. He's talking about buying a giant house just because I say I like it.

I have to stop being surprised by these things. Luc is nothing if not consistently shocking.

I glance down at the phone in my hand. "No one needs this many bedrooms." There's two of us. Unless Luc has a secret family he hasn't told me about, six bedrooms is far too many.

He shrugs. "Wasn't sure if you needed room for your family to come visit."

My heart starts beating faster. I want to kiss the shit out of this man for thinking of that. That is so incredibly sweet, even if he says it like it's just a matter-of-fact thing. "They'd live twenty minutes away. I think we'll be fine." I don't want to live in a place that feels like a museum again.

"So, set an upper limit on the number of bedrooms then. There's a setting for that."

I set it to two, which already feels more than generous for two people, given that I doubt either of us will be interested in sleeping separately, but Luc will probably need an office or something.

Then I set an upper limit on the price, and scroll through for a minute. "Just favorite any of the ones you like," Luc says quietly, and then he starts playing with my hair.

I left it down this morning, which I don't usually do. It's not conducive to working at the restaurant. But for head scratches like this? I'll never tie it up again.

Max leans over. I startle at having such a big guy suddenly in my space, but he doesn't get any closer, just looking at the phone. "Make him buy you a pool," he says. "Get your money's worth."

"I can't swim," I say, swiping out of yet another house when I realize how big the yard is and how much effort that's going to take to maintain.

"You can't?" Max asks, shock coloring his voice. Luc kicks him with the tip of his shoe, which I doubt hurts someone Max's size, but he backs off immediately anyway.

"Do you want to learn?" Luc asks quietly.

I shrug. Sure, the same way I want to learn a lot of things. There's just never enough hours in the day. "Things like that take time," I say.

"You have time," Luc says. "Not to put too fine a point on it, but you never need to work again. And I'm hoping you'll agree to being made like me. Immortality is a long time, Penny."

It takes me a second to catch my breath, unsure which point to tackle first. But no, immortality is simply too big. There's too much to unpack there, like the fact that I'll outlive my entire family, and I can't deal with that at this point. I just have to pretend he didn't say that for now. That can get packed away in a little box of *things we don't think about* that I can open at a more convenient time.

"I'm not becoming your housewife, Luc," I manage to say. I turn so I'm fully facing him. I'm looking up at him from the floor and I don't like that, so I move to stand, but Luc just tugs me into his lap.

This makes me taller than him, but it puts us mere inches away from each other, and I'm not sure I can argue with him like this.

Luc doesn't seem to want an argument, though. "Alright. What do you want to do? Is the restaurant important to you?"

I appreciate that he manages to say it without judgment, just open curiosity. That restaurant is great. It's a labor of love through four generations of Louise's family, and Stephanie loves it with her whole heart now. The two of them dream about the boys working there someday. I love that it feels like family, even if I sometimes feel like an interloper in that family.

None of that means I love my actual job.

"A job is a job," I tell him. "I like that it pays my rent and buys my food. And I like working with family. And it's so far from what things were like before, and that's important to me."

He tilts my chin down so I'm looking at him. I'm getting used to him doing that and used to the flutter of butterflies in my stomach it inspires every time. "You'll never be back there," he says seriously. "You'll never worry about a roof or food again. And as for your family, you'll never be far away, not unless you want to be. So... what else?"

That's the thing, isn't it? I have no clue. No earthly idea what else. In high school I'd idly thought about going to college, but I'd already known that wouldn't happen. Greg offered it to me once, but then there were all the excuses, all the things of *his* that we needed to prioritize first, and I'd never gone.

Stephanie got a business degree, and Louise went to culinary school. And I have my high school diploma and no idea where to go next.

Luc must be able to read that on my face, because he murmurs, "You'll figure it out. But in the meantime—you don't have to worry, love. Pick a house you like because you like it—don't worry about costs or bedrooms or other people. If you want to take up macrame or fencing or car racing, just let me know."

I blink, the incredibly sweet moment broken. "*That's* what you think of when you think of hobbies?"

"I'm open to suggestions." When I can't come up with any, he smiles slightly. "Right. So that's a no to the macrame then?"

"I will take up macrame if you can tell me what it actually is."

His mouth opens and closes. "It's like knitting," he decides.

"I'm pretty sure you're wrong."

"You are," Max confirms, reminding me once again that there is absolutely no privacy around werewolves. We turn to look at him, and he holds up his phone, showing a picture that is apparently macrame. It seems like it has to do with knots.

"I like knots," Luc says mildly, but I flush, only able to think about him talking about tying me up this morning.

"I'm going to pretend you're not subjecting me to even more of this," Max says, taking his phone back and typing. "Last night was enough." He looks at us, setting his phone aside. "No judgment, but this house smells like sex."

I'm flushing and turning to hide my face, but Luc looks supremely unbothered. "I've been to your house too, you know," he says mildly. "You're welcome to go back outside at any time."

"A *snowbank* is more welcoming than you," Max grumps, but he doesn't get up to move.

"If you like snow so much, you can go out to get more firewood."

I expect Max to argue, to get one more joke in, but he just gets up and finds his boots, giving Luc and I a moment in the glow of the fire.

# CHAPTER 21

# Luc

Max doesn't come back for a while. I doubt that the admittedly still heavy snow managed to take him out, so I'm assuming he's giving us some time alone. I'm choosing to believe it's a mark of respect and not petulance.

It doesn't really matter if it *is* petulance, though, because the result is the same. I have Penny in my arms, warm and soft. I don't even want alone time to have sex, just to hold her.

Today—and yesterday, and the day before—has been a lot for her. I can see it in her eyes every time something new is brought in, every time I'm forced to remind her what's out there. If it was up to me, Penny could live securely in her own little bubble, in a safe house much better than this one, and never have to worry about any of those things again.

But it's not up to me, and Penny doesn't want that. She might be overwhelmed, but she's still choosing to be involved.

The cat eventually wanders back over. Cautiously at first, she sniffs where Max sat, then the chair we're in. Apparently deeming it acceptable, she jumps up, landing on the back of the chair and lying down, her tail whacking me in the head once before she settles in.

I'll take any and all progress with the cat. Getting her to like me is going to be a herculean effort and simultaneously one of the more important things I've done recently.

I don't dare risk reaching out and touching her, but she's here. She might even be sleeping, right next to my head. That's a sign of trust.

Penny shifts in my arms. "We never cleaned up from breakfast."

I couldn't give less of a fuck. It'll presumably get cleaned up whenever we go to make lunch, and right now, her being here, relaxed and in my arms, is much more important. "I'll get it later," I tell her, running my nose along her hair. She washed her hair with the shampoo here—a three in one that's serviceable for getting blood off me—and I wonder what her hair smells like with her own shampoo. Even under the three in one, though, I can smell her cinnamon scent that makes me want to lick every inch of her.

*Restraint.* I've been famous for it; when I snap, it's because I've chosen to let go. But with Penny it's like she's constantly pushing me toward the edge, making me a little wilder, a little more hungry.

But right now, I want to be calm for her. Soft. Be the man who can hold her like this and give her peace after a stressful few days. The man who lets her relax in front of a fire with her cat, knowing everything is alright.

"What's one thing you always wanted to do, but weren't able to?" I ask her a few minutes later. It seems like a safe enough question, but I'm conscious of how overwhelmed the houses and hobbies seemed to make her, so I'm prepared to back off at a moment's notice.

She doesn't answer for a long minute, but then says, "Travel." I think she's going to leave it there, but then she continues. "After my mom left, it helped to think she was on these great adventures, you know? And I know that's probably not true, but it was still a nice dream. I wanted to see all the things I imagined she was seeing. Eiffel Tower, Great Wall of China, Leaning Tower of Pisa, Machu Picchu—everything I could see in a book, basically."

I kiss her temple again. "Then let's go," I say. "When this is over, we'll book flights."

"It's that easy for you, huh?"

"It is." I move so I can see her. "Penny, if it's something you want—it's done." I need her to understand how serious I am about this.

"What do you want to do?" she asks. "Once you resign, I mean. What would make you happy?"

Ah. *That* is a good question. I have no idea; I've only ever sought more. More power, more control. And while I'm not giving up my power entirely, I'm no longer chasing more.

What am I without all of that?

I'm Penny's. It's that simple.

"Make friends with your cat," I tell her. "Buy you a house that'll make you happy. Take you to see the world."

"I meant for you."

"That is all for me. I told you from the start, love, I'm selfish and I'm obsessed. Believe me, that is just as much for me as it is for you." Earning her smile is really all I want in life.

Penny snuggles closer into me, and I close my eyes, basking in it. Her breathing evens out. "Falling asleep there, love?"

"Mhm. Jesus, I just woke up."

"You've had a long few days." A long life, really. Penny rarely takes days off, and while I want to make her life easier, I can't pretend I've done that yet. "You can rest."

She's asleep on my shoulder within minutes.

Max eventually shows back up, but I don't move, daring him to make a comment. He doesn't. He just cleans the kitchen, moving quietly so Penny can continue to sleep.

I should probably be nicer to him.

Max is my best friend in the entire world. My brother, really—we may even share blood, although no one can say for sure.

He's known me for two thousand years, through thick and thin, but I know I haven't been a good friend.

When he wanted to have a chance with Casey forever, I didn't tell him what I knew about Alexander, about the spell that made us. I strung him along, extracted a promise of continued loyalty, and ensured I always held the reins.

I did everything to give him the forever he dreamed of, but I did in on my terms, and I remember how pissed he was when he realized I'd known more than I let on.

I can't let go entirely. It's not in my nature, and the world would go to shit if I gave him up. He's my enforcer, and his name strikes fear into the hearts of creatures who might otherwise break my laws. There are others who work for me now, but Max was always the greatest weapon I had.

I can't set him free, not entirely. But maybe I can loosen up a bit.

"You should take your wife on a vacation," I murmur, quiet enough to not disturb Penny. Max can definitely hear me though. "Somewhere nice, to make up for missing your anniversary."

He plops the dishrag he's using to clean on the counter with extra force. "This isn't our actual anniversary. I'll have you know I went all out for that. Impressed the hell out of her. This is the day I proposed. It's different."

I pause for a second, wondering if he's referring to their wedding anniversary, which I officiated a little less than two years ago, or the anniversary of the day they started dating, or the anniversary of the day he started stalking her. Are Penny and I going to have the same amount of convoluted dates to keep track of? "Well, whatever you call it then."

"Casey understands what I do for you. Not all the details, maybe, but she knows. She's not hurt that I left, because she's too good for me and better than both of us. She knows that if I'm not coming home, it's because something real is going on." He darts a glance toward Penny. "And this one matters. You're an asshole, Luc, but I won't forget that you gave me Casey. And I'm going to do the same for you. Casey'll let me make it up to her later."

"So make it up to her. Somewhere nice." I've always kept Max close, but maybe it's time. "Unless she wouldn't like to travel?" Casey has terrible anxiety, so maybe travel would be overwhelming for her.

Max is staring at me. "You mean it."

"I do."

"Fuck, what's she *done* to you?" he asks. "Brain transplant? Sucked your personality out through your dick?" I growl at that, but Max seems undeterred. "I'm just saying. You never would have suggested that before yesterday."

No, I wouldn't have. "When I told her earlier I was leaving the governor's mansion, that wasn't a line," I tell him. "She wants me out, so I'm out."

He stops moving entirely, still as a statue in my kitchen. "Entirely?"

"I think we both know a power vacuum would be the worst possible outcome. No, not entirely; the humans can fill my spot, but the supernatural creatures can't. You and I are still needed. We can't just give up and fuck off to Tahiti. But if we're halving our workload... a break might be in order."

Max stares at me, but nods slowly. "I've always wanted to take her on vacation."

"You should."

He smiles like he knows some great secret. "You've gone soft."

If he says it in front of anyone else I'll deny it, but we both know it's true. I look at Penny, getting a faceful of her hair, and hold her tighter. I can live with being soft—even if it's only among the three of us—if it means I get these moments with her.

Penny wakes up after a while, muttering about needing to pee, so I let her go and get up to make us lunch.

Considering he was driving through a snowstorm and had to walk the last half mile or so, Max did a decent job at stocking up the fridge. There's bread, milk, eggs, cheese, pasta sauce—enough to feed us for hopefully as long as we'll be here.

None of which solves the problem of me having no idea what to do with any of it. I stare into the depths of the fridge, hoping an answer will magically occur, but nothing happens.

Max snickers from where he's been sitting at the table texting for nearly an hour now. "Need some help?"

"It was much easier when we would just put a rabbit on a stick." I admit I've let a lot of my survivalist skills fall by the wayside over the years.

"Pasta and sauce. Or grilled cheese. Can't go wrong with either," Max advises, attention already back on his phone.

Right. A grilled cheese. I can do that.

This place doesn't have fire alarms—after they'd gone off the third time I'd lit a controlled fire in the basement, I'd deemed them unnecessary—and right now, that seems like an oversight. The bread smokes up while I'm cooking it, but the cheese won't melt fast enough.

"So—I'm guessing cooking is not a strong suit of yours," Penny says, resting her hip on the counter when she walks over to investigate what the issue is.

"Not so much," I admit. "I think it's edible?"

"Lucky for you, I'll eat just about anything. And I like my grilled cheese a little burned."

I can't tell if that's true or if she's just saying it to placate me, but she pulls some plates from the cabinet and then nudges me out of the way, taking over the cooking until there's a stack of five grilled cheese sandwiches.

"Two for each of you," she says, setting the burned one on her own plate. "Anything to drink?"

I take her plate from her and walk it to the table. "Have a seat; I can handle drinks." It's not her job to serve us food here, and I need her to realize it.

Penny sits facing the window this time, which leaves me the seat where I ate her out. I take it eagerly, half tempted to kick Max out so we can repeat the experience. The noises she makes when my mouth is on her—

"I can't believe it's still snowing," Penny says, interrupting my train of thought. "We're going to be *buried* out here."

Max clears his throat, setting aside his second sandwich that he's already half done with. "Good news; when your boyfriend kicked me out today, I went and dug out the car and pushed it up the ditch. It's fully right-side up now, too."

"Will it still run?" I ask.

"Guess we'll find out in the spring. I'm assuming we're taking yours out of here. Good thing it's under the car park."

Penny blinks at us. "I guess I didn't process that you *flipped* a car."

"Not fully flipped; just on its side a bit. Trust me; that's not that big a deal for us. We bounce."

"I'm a better driver than he is," I add, just so she knows I won't flip a car with her in it.

"I resent that." Max considers, then shrugs. "It's called defensive driving."

"It is definitely not."

Penny laughs, the sound coming out as an adorable little snort, her whole face scrunched up with it. I stare at her, enthralled.

She's radiant as the fucking sun, and I want to give her reasons to laugh like that every damned day.

# Chapter 22
# Penny

After lunch, we all settle back around the living room. Luc pulls me directly into his side, but he ends up on his phone, tongue poking between his teeth as he types furiously.

I pull out my own phone, which I've barely touched since I made that 911 call, and I check for messages from Stephanie. There's a picture of the boys decorating cookies, so I send back a heart and tell her I hope they're having a good day. She doesn't respond, but that's fine. I'm sure she will later; she's busy with her family and I don't begrudge her that.

I don't have any other friends. It sounds pathetic, but there's no one else to text, no one to distract me except the two guys here, both absorbed in their own phones. This place desperately needs board games. A deck of cards, at the very least.

I end up downloading Heads Up onto my phone out of sheer desperation, then force Max and Luc to play with me. It doesn't go great, because apparently even though they've been alive through literally every decade of pop culture ever, they don't pay nearly enough attention to it.

We're halfway through our third or fourth game when Max's head jerks to the left. He's staring at the door, head tilted, listening for something.

"What?" Luc asks, all gentleness gone from his voice. "Tell me." Then his head turns too, and I'm the only one out of the loop.

"Eight of them," Max says. "Maybe ten. Maybe more—the snow isn't helping."

"What?" I ask, pulling my legs up under me on the couch, looking back and forth between the two of them rapidly. My heart starts beating faster; whatever this is, I know it's bad news.

"You said this place was secure," Max snaps.

"It should be. No one knows it's here, and there's magic..." Luc freezes. "You went out on foot. And came back on foot."

"*Fuck*. They fucking lured us," Max spits, and I don't think it's my imagination that he suddenly looks even bigger.

Luc shakes his head. "It doesn't matter. I can kill the sorcerer later. Right now—what's the plan?"

I'm still processing the casual way he says *kill* when Max jumps up, moving toward the door. "Unless you have a way to lock this place down, we need to get out of here," Max says. His voice is deeper now, more growly, and I shiver. It makes my hair stand on end and my skin prickle; it's unnatural in some way.

Whatever Jinx feels when she's close to these men, I think I'm getting a taste of it.

Luc turns to me, grabbing my knee to get my attention. "Love, we have to go. Right now," he says. "I have to get you somewhere safe."

"The snow—"

"I know, but we don't have a choice. Get up, Penny."

I stand on autopilot, shoving my phone in my pocket. "Jinx—" I look around frantically for her, but she's nowhere to be seen. The bedroom, probably, hiding from Max and Luc. I start moving to get her, trying to remember where we stashed the carrier.

"We have to leave the cat," Max interrupts. "She'll freak out and slow us down."

I open my mouth to argue, but Luc says, "They won't hurt her, love. They'll be too busy following after us. We'll come back for her soon."

That shouldn't be reassuring—people want to kill me—but it somehow is. My heart twists, guilt settling heavy in me, but they're right. "Okay," I whisper, my voice wobbling and so quiet I'm almost surprised they can hear it. "Let's go."

Luc looks directly at Max. "Penny is your priority," he says, voice heavy with some weight I don't understand. "Your only priority."

Max nods. "Understood. We have to move."

I shove my feet in my sneakers at Luc's prompting. The sneakers won't do shit against the cold and snow. Both Max and Luc have boots, but neither bothers to put them on. "What—"

Luc grabs my shoulders and turns me to face him, staring into my eyes like he can see my soul. "Penny. Humans have it in their DNA somewhere to be afraid of large animals like us. But I need you to remember who we are, to see past those instincts. You can't shy away from us; I need you to trust us."

"I do trust you," I say, confused why he'd bring it up now. Haven't I made it clear by now?

Then, as if some hidden signal's been given, Max and Luc both turn toward the door, their bodies bending and changing, twisting in a way my eyes can't quite believe. Their skin rips, their bones bend, and fur sprouts out as they transition to four legs.

*Werewolves.* There are two werewolves in front of me, the largest of whom is nearly as tall as my shoulder.

I step back, unable to help myself, my heart beating so fast it feels like it might explode right out of my chest.

The closest one nudges my arm with his nose. This is *Luc*. I saw him like this the other day, and it feels just as trippy now. But there's no time for panic. I fight for control, taking a few deep breaths until I can master this. I can do this. I can keep calm for them. I won't be any more of a hindrance than a human who doesn't know how to fight has to be.

The wolf looks me in the eye, seeming to stare into my soul for a second before it makes a little yipping sound. I have no idea what that means, but Max must, because he knocks the door right off its hinges and charges outside.

There's a bear standing right on the edge of the porch. I fall back a step, but Max doesn't hesitate, lunging at him. There's a roar, and then there's blood. Luc steps in front of me, ears pinned low. He nudges my hand with his shoulder, but I don't know what that means. He does it again.

Oh. He wants me to hold his fur. I can't see more than five feet in this storm, but he presumably can. He needs me to stay close.

I weave my hand through his fur, stepping up beside him. He has to walk slowly so he doesn't lose me, and I fight to make it through the knee-high snow faster, unwilling to be the one who gets us all killed.

Max crosses the path in front of us, a dark-gray blur of fur against all the white, and then there's another growl and a ripping sound I don't want to think too much about. We have to be near the car now.

Luc whines, deep in his throat, stopping suddenly.

"What's wrong?" I whisper, even though I know that everything out here can probably hear my heartbeat.

Another hesitant step, and then I can see the car. It's mostly clear of snow, considering it's been parked under the car park, so at first I can't figure out what's wrong.

I take another step. The tires, I realize belatedly. They're flat. No, not just flat—someone shredded them.

We're trapped here. I can't get enough air into my lungs as the realization hits me. We're stuck and we're being hunted, and I'm going to die and so are Luc and Max.

Luc nudges my side again, then points his snout out toward where the road presumably is. It's indistinguishable from anywhere else except there are no trees there, and I'm trying to figure out what he thinks is going to happen. Does he think we can run out of here? Maybe he and Max can, but me—

Max. The car he left out there, the one he dragged back onto the road earlier. The one we're not even sure runs, but hopefully it's far enough away that these shifters didn't feel the need to disable it.

Luc howls, and there's a howl in return, lonely and piercing the snowy air. I hope that's Max talking back to him, but I don't have time to ask, because Luc starts urging me down the road.

I can't fight through the knee-high snow drifts quickly enough, so Luc untangles himself from my grip and walks in front of me, using the wolf's frame like a snow plow. I try to stay right on his tail, worried about losing him in the whiteout.

My shoes are too heavy, weighed down with snow and water, and I'm half a second away from deciding they're more trouble than they're worth when Luc stops in front of me.

There's a growl to our left, just outside of my range of vision, and my hair stands on end. My heart in my throat, I turn to look. I don't know how I've already figured this out, but I know that's not a wolf.

Some sort of big cat lurks out of the shadows. I wait for Max to appear, but he doesn't come.

*Shit.* I let out an involuntary yelp, unable to keep quiet with that big cat staring at me, lips pulled back to reveal deadly teeth.

Luc turns to glance at me, then looks away and lunges at the cat with a growl so low it makes my organs shake. When the cat turns to intercept the strike, Luc changes directions, swiping claws along his exposed side. There's a yelp, a howl, and then I need to look away, unable to breathe.

I'm standing here in the middle of a snow-covered road, soaked to the bone, holding stock-still between at least two supernatural fights that I can't possibly hope to survive. If anyone gets past Max and Luc and gets to me, I'm dead. I look around for something to defend myself with, anything—a tree branch, a rock, *anything*—but there's nothing under all the snow.

There's a weird sort of serenity that comes with accepting that, with knowing that it's out of my hands. I'll either live or die, but there's nothing I can do this time. There's no stiletto shoe conveniently nearby. There's no use panicking, because I can't control the outcome.

I am so, *so* far out of my league with all this supernatural bullshit.

But I can get to the car. I know Max and Luc can easily get through this snow, that I'm the one holding us up. The least I can do is keep moving. If I stay in a straight line and don't veer off into the trees, we should be fine. Surely I'll see the car when I get close enough; Max said he put it back on the road just a few hours ago, and there's not enough snow to bury a car.

There's a yip behind me, a pained noise, and I can't tell if it's wolf or cat. I hesitate, but I have to know. If Luc got hurt because of me—

I can't see. I can't see if Luc is alright, if he got killed defending me, if—

He's running toward me, blood on his muzzle and things I don't want to identify sticking to his fur. Once he's in touching distance, I sink my hands into his fur, barely resisting the urge to go to my knees and wrap him up in a hug. He's alright.

Not entirely, I realize once I get a better look. Some of that blood is his. He has a gash on his shoulder, jagged and deep. "Oh my god, does that hurt?" I gasp, trying to get a better look, wary of hurting him more. There's so much blood.

He nudges me with his snout like he's pushing me toward the car. I resist for a moment, but I'll be able to better check him over once we're safe, so I let him get in front of me again, pushing snow out of my path so we can make the last of the trek.

I can hear growls and the sound of a fight not far behind us. But there's a red blur appearing at the horizon now, and yes—that's a car. We did it.

I jump back when another creature appears, my heart ready to beat out of my chest, but it's just Max, far bloodier than even Luc. He's so covered in blood that I can't tell if he has any injuries, although he's moving like he's completely unhurt.

With Max clearing the path, Luc falls back into my side. His head swivels, watching every shadow we pass like danger might jump out, but nothing comes.

As soon as we reach the car, both men turn back to humans, their bones and muscle and skin warping again until two very naked men stand in front of me. I avert my eyes, fumbling for the door to the backseat.

Luc is there, reaching across to open it with smooth, confident moves. "Are you hurt?" I whisper.

"Nothing that won't heal. Get in, love." I do, sliding into the back seat, and it's like my body takes sitting as permission to fall apart. Every muscle starts shaking, tears bud up behind my eyes, and I'm genuinely worried I might puke on Luc.

"You drive," Max says tightly. "I need to be ready."

*Ready for what*? I don't get to ask, half-hysterical, picturing Max pulling out a machine gun from somewhere or, I don't know, jumping out of the car and turning into a wolf to fight our enemies while we're driving. But I don't get to ask, because they both turn in unison back the way we came.

I don't have to wait long to know what they sensed, because even my mediocre human eyes can see it. *Fire*.

Luc's whole body looks tense enough to break. "They found out the basement is empty."

"Jinx…" I murmur, my brain stalled out in disbelief, unable to put a thought together. "Jinx…"

*She'll be fine*, I try to tell myself, the part of my brain that got me through hungry nights and Greg's worst days and the trial, the part that looks on the bright side so I can just keep going. *Cats survive fires all the time, they're famous for it. Remember that news story about the wildfires? Jinx is smart, and scrappy, and —*

I'm crying, big, ugly wet tears tracking down my face and practically freezing to my skin, and I can't get a deep breath, and—

Luc reaches down to cup my face. "Everything will be fine," he says seriously, and then looks over at Max. "Protect her with your life."

And then he lets go of my face and turns to run even while he's shifting back into the wolf, and it's like my heart splits in two as he runs off into the snow.

# Chapter 23

# Luc

I 'm about to risk my life for a cat, and I don't even hesitate. Penny's tears wrenched my heart, and I can't leave her precious pet to die in a fire.

Nevermind buying fancy cat food; this better win me the cat's loyalty.

I cut through the snow, moving as fast as I can now that I no longer need to keep pace with a human. Something lunges at me, but I don't even bother to check who they are, swiping them down and moving on. If they get up to chase me, I'm faster, and no further attack comes.

I don't know how long cats can survive in fires, but I refuse to be the one who has to bring Penny the corpse of her pet.

The heat knocks me back long before I reach the house, but I keep pushing forward. The snow is melting away close to the house, and the flames have jumped to a nearby tree. It better keep snowing, or else they're going to burn the whole forest down.

Gritting my teeth, I burst through the front door Max broke. A cursory glance tells me that they did indeed find the basement, the heavy door off the kitchen hanging off its hinges. I sincerely hope they follow the scent and find the bones in the woods. I want to crush all their dreams before I rip their heads from their necks.

The heavy, acrid smell of the cabin burning nearly drowns out Jinx's scent, but I find it. She's in the bedroom, under the bed.

*Stupid cat.* The door was wide open; she could have been up a tree by now.

I shift back into my human form, because the cat is going to be freaked out enough and I need opposable thumbs to operate the pet carrier door.

I immediately find the flaw in that plan; the coat closet I shoved it in is too close to the basement, where they clearly started the fire. I can barely get the door open, and when I do I find the carrier half melted.

Right. Can't shove the cat in that. Carrying her out by hand it is.

It's easier said than done, because she's going to hate every second of it. But failure isn't an option.

Jinx is hiding under the bed. The smoke isn't too bad in here yet; I can almost get a full breath, but my vision is obscured by the haze of smoke.

"Hey, cat," I murmur, hoping my voice is soothing. "Time to go."

To my immense surprise, she practically jumps into my arms. Before she can change her mind, I pull her close to my chest, standing and looking around the room. There.

Shoving a cat in a pillowcase is undignified, but it's the only way I can carry her while in my wolf form without hurting her. She yowls indignantly when I push her in, but I tie the pillowcase shut and put it on the floor before letting my wolf out again. I pick up the pillowcase with my teeth, and set off at a run.

The smoke is getting thicker, but I burst through it into the snowy forest air, moving away from the cabin as fast as I can. The car. I just need to get to the car.

If I strain my ears and ignore the sound of the complaining cat, I can hear people in two different directions. One is Penny and Max, still in the car. The other is six, maybe seven others, moving deeper into the forest.

*The bones.* They're about to find Alexander's bones.

If his remains can give us two more minutes to get away, then they can have them. They can treat them like holy relics, for all I care; I have much more important things to worry about than Alexander's corpse and revenge.

I shift back into my human form before I get to the car but don't dare to release the cat; I have no time to chase her through the damn forest tonight. When I reach the car, I wrench the back door open, shove the pillowcase at Penny, and slide in beside her before she even processes what's in her hand.

"Drive," I snap at Max, And he nods once, sharp and sure, and turns the key in the ignition.

The car turns on. Max's disastrous driving apparently hadn't done too much damage, and I don't believe in a higher power, but I'm feeling like something genuinely is looking out for us tonight.

We're going to get away. The shifters are distracted and Max is pushing through the snow. We're not fast but we're steady. I can only hope that the main roads have been at least partially cleared of snow; we should connect with the main highway in twelve or so miles.

I turn to Penny, pulling her into my arms. I'm naked and covered in blood and soot, but I think she needs comfort more than she needs clean clothes. She's not crying anymore, although I can see the tear tracks on her face. Her hands won't stop shaking long enough to untie the bag, so I reach over and do it for her, releasing the cat into the car.

I brace for her to panic and try to run, but she lets out the most plaintive, panicked meow, then tries to burrow herself between the two of us, trusting us to save her from the threat.

It's unexpected but not unwelcome, but I don't have any time to wonder about it. Penny's still shaking under my arm, and I rub her shoulder, trying to reassure her and push warmth into her skin. "You're alright," I murmur, doing my absolute best to be comforting. It's not something I'm especially known for.

She pets the cat with shaky fingers, just the lightest touch like she doesn't believe she's real. Jinx chirps, and Penny starts crying again.

"Shh, shh," I say, turning her head into my shoulder, trying to hold her without squishing the cat. "We're all okay. It's okay."

My injuries are already starting to heal. The car works. We're all going to make it, even the damn cat. "Penny, love, listen; I know this was a lot. Too much, and unfair to ask of you. But I swear, no one is going to hurt you."

She makes an indignant sort of growl. "You think it's *me* I'm worried about right now? No one tried to take a bite out of me."

That really depends on how she defines *tried*, because from where I'm standing, this whole attack qualifies as them trying. It's why every one of them has signed their death warrants just by being there.

I doubt explaining that would make her feel better, though. "I'm going to be just fine," I assure her. "It's already healing, look." And I take the hand not on her cat to touch my torn up shoulder, only to stop when I feel her frigid skin.

"Fuck, love, you're an icicle." I start tugging at her wet clothes, needing to get them off her. I run hot and can bring her core temperature back up, but I can't fight the effect of the soaked fabric.

"There's a blanket back there somewhere," Max says, eyes firmly on the road as I strip Penny's clothes off of her. Her underwear is damp but not soaked, so I leave it on, then dig around for the blanket and wrap it around her before I wrap myself around her too. The cat, dislodged by my attempt to take Penny's clothes off, settles back into her side under the blanket.

She struggles against me for a moment. "You're naked. You must be freezing."

I take one of her icy hands and put it on my chest. "We run hot."

Her frozen fingers flex against my skin and I drop her wrist so I can wrap my arms tighter around her. I need to give her some of my warmth.

Max clears his throat from the front seat, eyes still on the road. "Where to?"

"Your house." It's the closest place we have; we can't exactly take this to the governor's mansion.

Max growls at me. "You'd risk my home, again? I was already bait for you once, Luc."

"And now your wife can handle it. It's the closest, and it should be temporary. Just until we regroup."

There's a tense silence in the car for a moment, but then Max inclines his head slightly. "Let me call her."

"And while you're at it, you need to call your dragon friend."

"Marcus? Why Marcus?"

Because most creatures are smart enough to think twice before crossing a dragon. Solitary and not especially inclined to involve themselves in others' business, the dragons are nevertheless the ultimate predator. And the shifters might be too stupid, too brainwashed, to think in their own best interest, but hopefully Marcus' presence will make whoever is pulling their strings hesitate.

"You realize we're not friends, right?" Max continues. "Marcus doesn't have friends. He tolerates me because Elise likes Casey."

"And you saved Elise's life. Call in your favor. If he flies, he should beat us to your house."

"Who's Marcus?" Penny murmurs, turning her head further into my neck.

I kiss the top of her head. "A dragon, love."

"A *dragon*? Those exist?"

"Yup," Max says crisply, poking at the center console's display so he can make the call. It doesn't seem to work great, although I don't know if that's because of his huge fingers or damage to the car. "And he's an asshole."

Penny peeks up enough to look at me, and I shrug. I'm also an asshole, and so is Max usually, and she seems to like us well enough, so this should work out just fine.

# CHAPTER 24
# Penny

W hen we pull up on a perfectly normal suburban street lined with well-maintained brick houses twice the size of the one I currently live in, there's three people already standing outside.

The shorter, curvier woman with wild black curls throws herself at Max the second he steps out of the car. He lifts her off her feet, swinging her into a hug that crushes them together enough that it's hard to tell where one person ends and the other begins.

"What're you doing out in the cold, baby?" he asks.

She laughs. "You're going to have to remember someday that I'm not that breakable anymore."

He pulls away from her, giving me a glimpse of his face that says he'll never stop worrying about her, regardless of how breakable she may be.

I stand up on shaky legs, clutching the blanket around me with one hand and holding Jinx with the other. She's unusually still; in any other circumstances, she'd have squirmed loose by now. But she stayed pressed into my and Luc's side the entire drive, regardless of how we moved or jostled her. Clearly, her experience today shook her up. It might have even convinced her that Luc isn't evil.

"I'm Elise," one of the women says, looking at me and my blanket and my cat with kind eyes. "This is my husband Marcus, and the one glued to Max is Casey."

Casey flushes, pulling back a little more from her husband. "Hi," she murmurs, looking at the ground.

"Penny," I manage to say, overwhelmed now that I'm looking at another werewolf, a dragon, and... I'm not even sure what Elise is. They're probably going to tell me *vampire* or *mermaid* or something equally unbelievable, and I can't handle that right now. "I—hi."

"Nice to meet you," Marcus, *the dragon*, says. I somehow doubt his sincerity. I look at him, mind still stuck on the idea of *dragons*. Taller than Luc but smaller than Max, Marcus is lean, has slightly reddish hair, and looks like most boring business-men who come into the restaurant. Even so, there's something vaguely threatening about him.

"You too."

Luc steps beside me, and that's when I realize he's still naked, Max is still naked, and I'm in my underwear and a blanket. No one here reacts like this is in any way strange. Thankfully it's well after nine by now, and no neighbors seem to be peeking out their windows.

213

"Inside," Luc orders, despite the fact that this isn't even his house. "Let's go." He starts to steer me toward the door. He stops for a second when we're in front of Max and Casey, looking at her and saying, "I apologize for taking over your home."

"Please don't do as much damage as last time. The blood took a long time to get out." Then, when I'm reeling from whatever *that* might mean, she turns to me. "C'mon, Penny. Let's get you dressed."

"Luc's naked," I say asininely, like she can't see that on her own.

She waves a hand. "I'm sure they'll figure it out. Max has clothes in the trunk if it comes to that."

I look to Luc, who nods. "Go," he says. "I won't be far."

Elise steps away from Marcus, and she and Casey escort me and Jinx into the house.

My first thought is *damn, this is a nice house.* It's actually not dissimilar to a few of the ones Luc showed me on Zillow earlier. One of those houses might have even been on the same street, not that I was paying much attention to directions when we drove in.

Casey escorts me upstairs. She's gone quiet, but Elise takes over the talking. "Are you okay?" she asks. "Not injured, are you?"

I shake my head. "Just cold. But both Max and Luc, they were injured."

"They'll heal fast," Elise dismisses. "We can deal with the cold. Let's find you something warm."

"In here," Casey says, gesturing to a heavy door. "You can let the cat explore," Casey says once we're in the bedroom. "She'll be fine. I don't think there's anything she can get into."

I doubt she'll go far, and I'm quickly proven right when I kneel down to let her go, but all she does is rub against my legs, purring. "I know," I croon at her. "You had a rough night, hm? It's okay now."

Elise clears her throat. "What happened?" she asks gently. "Max wasn't clear on the phone. Unless he told you?" she asks Casey, who shakes her head.

"He just told me who was coming."

"I'm Penny," I say, looking up at them from where I'm still crouched on the floor. "Luc, uh—this sounds worse than it is, but he was kind of stalking me. But it's not that bad, I promise."

Whatever reaction I expected, I don't get it. They look at each other and shrug. "Max admitted after we got married that he followed me around for a few weeks between the first time he saw me and the first time I officially met him," Casey says.

"Marcus did a full background check on me. Like, the type of stuff it should take the FBI to dig up. And then followed me home. You get used to it. Not that I'm an expert, but it seems to me that these supernatural guys are all like that."

"Territorial," Casey clarifies.

Elise nods. "Yeah, that's a great word. So, he stalked you. But you said it's not that bad, so I'm guessing you don't really mind?"

"It's fine. We worked it out. But now there are shifters who apparently want someone he doesn't have anymore, and they want to kill me to get him. They chased us out of the cabin we've been staying in, and then burned it to the ground. They almost killed my cat."

I still can't really believe Luc went back for her. He's so controlled, so practical. He would never risk himself unnecessarily, and there's no doubt he sees the cat as unnecessary. But he went back for her—I didn't even ask him, and he did it anyway. I reach out and dig my hand into her fur, needing to feel her warmth and softness to assure me she's still here.

Honestly, Jinx is my only proof that this is all real right now.

"I'm so sorry," Elise says sincerely. And not in the way you say *sorry* to someone superficially; she's sorry and means it.

"This world can be violent," Casey murmurs. "*Really* violent."

I gulp. I've thrown my lot in with these people before I even fully knew what I was doing. I'm not saying I want to back out; I'm not sure I could back away from Luc now. But I can't deny that I'm scared.

"It's not all bad," Elise counters. "This is the first really dangerous thing I've seen since Ethan."

"Once a year isn't terrible odds," Casey muses. She looks at me, then moves to a dresser. "I don't know how well my stuff will fit you, but..."

"I appreciate it." I'm probably four inches taller than her, but I'm over walking around in just a blanket, and putting my cold, wet clothes back on sounds like torture. These people are far more comfortable with nudity than I'll probably ever be.

The sweatpants are too short, but they fit through the hips and thighs, and that's plenty good enough for me. The sweatshirt she gives me covers everything it needs to, so we'll call that good enough.

"So... you're a werewolf?" I ask Casey.

She nods, sitting on the edge of the bed. I pick the armchair in the corner, because Jinx is so clearly stressed out and I want to give her some space. She curls up in my lap.

"For almost two years now. Well. More like eighteen months."

"You started as a human?"

"Mhm. The same spell that made Luc and Max made me. I just, you know, got to consent to it."

"And you are..." I ask, hesitating when I look at Elise, leaning against the wall. I don't know if it's rude to ask, but at this point I honestly need to know.

"Human," she says.

"Really?" I can't quite believe that. The dragon with the human? Can humans hold their own in this world? Luc's talked about changing me already, but would it be possible to be with him and stay human?

"That's not fully true," Casey objects quietly.

Elise shrugs, walking over to sit on the other side of the bed. "I don't have a better word. I'm fully human, just—with some extras now."

"Extras?"

"I get some benefits for being mated to Marcus. I'll live as long as him supposedly. I won't age any further. I'm a little hardier when it comes to injuries, although not invulnerable. But—still human."

"You can do that? It's possible?"

"It's a dragon thing," Elise says apologetically.

"Well, could he share it with Luc? Help us out?"

Casey sniggers. "Yeah, Elise. Could you help her out?"

Elise flushes. "Yeah, I wouldn't bring it up with Luc—not if he's as possessive as Max and Marcus are. It involves, uh, come. Lots of it. Like, I get dragon come inside me, and I become whatever the hell it is I am. And it takes repeated doses. Near as I can tell, it's a biological device so a dragon can hoard humans they really like."

Holy shit. Alright, definitely not something to suggest to Luc then. He doesn't seem like someone who shares—and I'm not, either. "Got it." I look away, because I just met this woman and now I know more than I want to about her getting dicked down by her husband on a regular basis.

"Yeah. Sorry to burst your bubble, but if you want this to be forever, you're going to have to go Casey's route," Elise says. "But you don't have to choose it. It sounds like you've only known about all of this for a few days?"

"Yeah."

"That's fast to make these types of decisions. No judgment if you are, though. I moved faster than I *ever* thought I'd be comfortable with Marcus. Sometimes, when you know, you know."

*When you know, you know.* Yeah, and I definitely know. I don't know how I know it so quickly, but I do. Luc is a part of my life forever.

Even if that means becoming a werewolf. I pick up Jinx, holding her so I can look her in the eye. "Will you still like me if I become a werewolf?" I ask her softly.

Jinx can't answer, but I wish she could. It's a legitimate concern; I don't know what I'd do if my cat hated me.

"What's it like?" I ask Casey.

"The change? It isn't that bad," she says.

"I mean, being a werewolf."

"Oh." She shrugs. "Tell the truth, it's not so different. I kind of forget about it sometimes—I don't feel different unless I'm literally turned into a wolf. Honestly, the things that make Luc and Max and all the others like they are isn't so much the *animal*. It's the childhood."

"The whole death-cult, child soldier thing?" Everything I've heard sounds horrific, and I'm not sure I want to know more.

"Yeah. That. Things are complicated between shifters and the other supernatural creatures," she says, darting a look at Elise. "So honestly, being a shifter like they are—it's a separate culture, basically. I've been thinking about this kind of like someone who converts religions when they get married. Like, I believe in being a werewolf. I'm convinced being a werewolf is real and right and true and all that. But I don't have the childhood, the cultural background that comes with it, you know?"

I consider that, then nod. I can see that. When Max and Luc talked about Alexander, their childhood, when Luc talks about how he bends the world to his will because he can't be out of control again—that's something I'm never going to get. I can be there and I can listen—and I can even do it as a werewolf—but I'll never fully get it.

"For what it's worth," Elise says, "I think the general attitude about shifters in the supernatural community has changed. Marcus never has anything negative to say about those two because they're shifters. Just grumbles about having to share my time and attention when I make him come here."

"Marcus isn't a fair representation," Casey points out. "He's... you know, kind of anti-social."

"Fair point," Elise concedes.

"Someone's trying to kill them," I remind them both. "Someone tried tonight."

Casey bites her lip and seems to get smaller for a second, but then she looks at me. "They always make it," she whispers. "I have to keep believing that. I don't usually know all the details of what Max gets up to until after, but I keep telling myself that. He always comes home to me. They know what they're doing."

I think of all the blood, the easy way they moved, the way they jumped into fights without a second of hesitation.

Elise leans in. "There's not a lot of people like us," she says. "You know, who came into this world after being human for most of their life. We're kind of a small circle. Meeting Casey really helped me."

"Elise helped me too," Casey says.

"We got to stick together," Elise nods.

"Is this an invitation?" I ask, petting my cat while I watch these women who have seemingly already navigated the situation I find myself in.

"Welcome to the former human club," Elise says.

"I'm not former," I point out.

"Even if you stayed human forever, which I don't think you'll do, your life will always be different," Elise explains. "You know too much now."

She's not wrong. "So, this is an official meeting of the former human club?" I ask.

"Welcome," Elise says. "We're happy to have you."

# Chapter 25

## Luc

**M**ax's clothes dwarf me. If we had my car, there'd be a change of clothes in the trunk, but I doubt my car survived the fire at the cabin.

I look ridiculous, but I won't let that stop me from taking care of this situation. Someone tried to kill us tonight. Someone put *Penny* in the line of fire. It has to be dealt with, and rapidly.

We stand around in the kitchen, acting like this is a war room. Max is washing the blood off of himself in the sink, despite the fact that Casey's already seen it and *hugged* him when he was covered in it. Something tells me she's not squeamish about blood anymore, if she ever was to begin with.

Penny didn't seem to mind, either. She didn't complain, at least. But maybe that was the shock. I'm debating if I should wash off in the sink next when Max turns to me. "Did any of your research into Alexander turn up someone working with him?"

"No." But Alexander had always been particularly elusive, like he knew I was doggedly one step behind him. I'd get scraps of information here and there, most of it coming from shifters we'd found after Alexander had discarded them.

"So, you have nothing," Marcus summarizes. He stands a little way apart from us, and I'm irritated that he has clothes that actually fit him, looking like he just came from the office.

"I have a dead ancient sorcerer, about five or so dead shifters from tonight, and the knowledge that they're working with *someone*," I offer tersely. I'm not going to be spoken down to by this dragon.

"That sounds like nothing. And if you have nothing, then I'll take Elise and go home. I'm not your bodyguard, Luc."

"You are if I say you are," I tell him, voice cold and weighty. "We saved your mate, Marcus. You can pay your debt by protecting mine."

He goes very, *very* still. He's not the first dragon I've looked in the eye, but it's been a long time, and I'd nearly forgotten the deeply unsettled feeling his gaze brings. I'm not used to being the prey, but in his stare, some deep, instinctive part of me knows I am.

Dragons as a species take almost no effort for me to rule. For one thing, there are very few of them left. For another, they're largely solitary, don't talk much to humans, and don't make messes that I have to clean up. The worst they do is accumulate too much wealth, and, considering the way some humans act these days, that's not triggering much suspicion.

Marcus' mate being stolen from him had been the single most demanding interaction I've ever had with a dragon. If he'd given into his instincts trying to get her back, there was a real chance we could have had a fully transformed dragon rampaging down the streets of Manhattan, burning everything in his path. A quick intervention had been just as much for my benefit as his.

But he doesn't need to know that. I straighten under his gaze, and force myself to hold eye contact.

"Mates aren't bargaining chips," he growls.

No, but they're chess pieces on this board as much as any of the rest of us are. Just because Penny is my queen doesn't negate that. She's a piece in play, and so are Elise and Casey if I need them, too. That's how the world works.

I know it's a cold way to view the world and I don't need their judgment, so I don't say it. Max chimes in to save the day. "Marcus, you know Elise likes hanging out with Casey. She'll probably like Penny too—you know there's not a lot of people like them. They need each other."

Marcus keeps glaring at me for a moment before he looks away. "Fine," he says. "For Elise, we'll stay a little longer."

I fight to not let my confusion show on my face. Max has stepped in to save me from physical attack immeasurable times, but never from a social situation. Max has always been a *hit first, someone else can ask questions later* kind of person.

Hm. Interesting.

"And while you stay, you could help us," Max offers. "Since your wife is here too."

Max might be pushing it, but I'm not going to be the one to show fear first. We stare each other down.

I don't know what does it; our persistence, the real threat looming, or the soft sound of voices filtering down from upstairs. Regardless, Marcus nods. "Get some of your people here," he tells me. "If I'm going to help, then someone else is going to protect my mate."

I nod. That'd been the next step anyway, so I reach for the phone and begin dialing.

When I have a dozen shifters on my payroll on their way to Max's house, Marcus looks at me from the seat he's taken at the kitchen table. "If you can just make calls and have people jump to do your bidding, then you can surely find your man."

My lips press into a thin line, not wanting to be forced to explain this to him, but he's not going to let it go. "Shifters answer my call every time. The amount of work I put into keeping the rest of you all in line—it doesn't lead to easy phone calls."

"I'm usually in the background breaking skulls," Max supplies.

Marcus looks at us and then nods. "I don't give a shit about your so-called crown. I don't care about these issues between born and made supernaturals. But you're right; my wife is upstairs, and she's happy. And in her own way, she's made, so I'm going to protect a place for her here. Even if that means making some asinine phone calls."

This man ran a business for the better part of a century. He was socially savvy enough to know when to change names, move, and reinvent himself. He could get investors and customers and employees to like him. So I shouldn't be shocked that he thinks he can do this.

"This sorcerer, they sell shifters?" he checks.

"I don't know if that's the current business model," Max says. "But it was the old one."

"I have more money than anyone could ever hope to spend; hopefully it draws the right people," he says, and begins dialing.

Marcus knows some of the same gossip hounds who try to move black-market items through our world that I do, and he knows some others besides. I make a mental note to check into them when this is over, when I have time to purge the world of people who think they're above my laws.

Marcus is unflappably calm and in command when he talks to these people, acting like ordering a small, brainwashed militia and being willing to pay top dollar for it is a perfectly normal thing. If I didn't know better, I might have to kill him just on principle.

It takes hours. A quick glance at the microwave clock tells me it's almost one in the morning, and while shifters can go longer than humans, I'm starting to fade a bit; we need a break soon.

Then Marcus' voice picks up, becoming more firm, more pressing. "Tell me more."

I lean in, listening to the shady contact tell him about a guy he's heard of. He seems unsure, but after waffling around for a moment, he spits out a name.

*Alaric Vane. I'm coming for you.*

"How do I find him?" Marcus asks. Then, "He's a fucking lawyer? Really?"

A lot of us have day-jobs. But picturing an ancient sorcerer working as a lawyer surpasses believability a bit.

Marcus snaps his fingers and I hand him my phone. He opens up a new tab and types in *Parsons, Vane & West*.

It brings us to a sleek website for a high-end law firm, and the answer of why an ancient sorcerer is working as a lawyer becomes immediately obvious; this is the type of firm that hides money and crimes for the insanely wealthy. Surely if Vane can do it for them, then he can hide his own ill-gotten gains from trading shifters.

I take my phone back and click forward to the partners' page, which should have a bio and, if I'm lucky, a picture of Vane.

There're giggles, and then feet on the stairs, and then the three women join us in the kitchen. I look Penny over; she looks good, although the clothes don't fit her right at all. Maybe I can send one of the shifters I have hiding in trees and parked on the street to buy her some clothes that will actually fit her.

But regardless of her clothes, she looks happier. I expected a little more tension after she came so close to death tonight, but there's an ease to her shoulders, a calm look in her eyes. Maybe there's something to this after all; Max has told me more than once how good it's been that Casey and Elise met, and it looks like it's true for Penny too.

"What can I do for you, love?" I murmur, setting my phone on the table.

"Nothing. We just came down because we got hungry."

The last time she ate anything was lunch. *Fuck*. I should have had someone bring her something here. "I'm sorry, Penny."

Casey is already going to her fridge, her movement impeded when Max grabs her around the middle to kiss the crown of her head. She laughs, letting him, and then tries to squirm away, but he doesn't let her go.

"I got it, Casey," Elise says, smartly side-stepping Marcus' chair as she moves to the fridge, looking over their ingredients and frowning. "You don't have much."

"Yeah, I... Max was supposed to go the store with me, but—well—"

It's my fault, then. Max's face shifts into an expression of abject guilt, and he turns Casey in his arms, pulling her close so she can rest her head on his chest. "I'm sorry, baby."

"It's okay. You had things to do." He opens his mouth to protest, but she interrupts and says, "Keeping Penny alive is important. I didn't starve. I *could* go shopping if I had to."

Maybe, but Casey's relaxing her full weight into Max, letting him hold her. With his big frame, it must feel like he's shutting the world out a bit, because four guests in her house is already a lot for her. Shopping on her own must be deeply unpleasant.

But she's right. Protecting Penny was paramount.

Elise pulls out eggs, wilted spinach, and an almost-full sleeve of bagels. "This'll work," she mutters, although she side-eyes the bagels for a second.

A few minutes later, there's a stack of bagels topped with scrambled eggs. Marcus' face creases, looking more and more grumpy as Elise puts the platter on the table. But he lightens up when she slides one onto a smaller plate, handing it directly to him.

Penny steps in to help, clearing debris off the table so we can all sit. She picks up the phone and turns to hand it to me, then freezes. "Why do you have a picture of this guy?"

I'm always watching her, but before it was with a sort of passive admiration. Now, I'm laser-focused on her. "Do you know him?"

She shrugs. "He's eaten at the restaurant a few times. He's the type of guy who stares. Seems like he never blinks, just stares at women the whole time. It's gotten so bad that most of the other servers trip over themselves to avoid him being sat in their section. And he's a shit tipper, too."

"He's been at your *work*?" I ask, my voice suddenly sounding far away behind the roaring in my ears, my wolf fighting to get out and protect our mate. "More than once?"

"Yeah. Like once a week for a few months, I'd guess."

Max and Marcus exchange a look with me, all three of us putting the pieces together.

He's been able to get close to Penny for ages. He could have hurt her. I'd left her too vulnerable for too long.

"Luc, what is it? Who is he?"

"A sorcerer," Marcus says when I can't, finishing off his bagel. "Probably the one trying to kill you."

The phone falls from Penny's hand, landing on the table. I move to her, tugging her into my arms, letting her collapse a bit against me. "He... why?" she asks, voice barely coming out a croak.

"Because of me." Because it's all my fault. Because I fell for her, and I justified just watching as *protecting* her, as keeping her out of my world. In reality, I was just leaving her vulnerable. "You said he stared?"

"Mhm. It was creepy."

I make a mental note to pluck his eyes out. "My best guess is that the restaurant smelled like me. And he was trying to figure out who in there was connected to me."

She shakes her head. "He's only been coming in for four, maybe five months. You visited three years ago. I know you all have good noses, but that's unbelievable."

When I don't answer fast enough, she pulls back to look at me. "Luc?"

I take a deep breath. "I might have hung around the restaurant a few times."

"You said you didn't follow me."

"Does the restaurant really count? I already knew you worked there. And it was just a few times, when I had more time to myself than expected."

She shoves at my chest slightly, although not hard enough to say she's truly mad at me. "Considering it's basically the only place I go, yes it counts, you asshole."

"Love—"

"How many times is a few times?"

Eight. I'd had eight free afternoons where I'd followed her to work. "A handful."

"What, you just spied on me?"

"The restaurant windows really aren't big enough for that. It was more like I'd be near and I could smell you. On bad days, it kept me calm. I could hear you talking to customers. And sometimes, yes, catch a glimpse of you."

"Why didn't you just come in?" she demands. "It wouldn't have been weird, you know. We serve food. People come there to eat."

"You don't understand." I pull her close enough that I can press a kiss to her mouth, which she doesn't fight. "If I'd seen you in person, that would have been it. You'd have been over my shoulder and out of the restaurant before anyone knew what happened."

Her breath catches and her eyes dilate. "Caveman," she accuses, but it sounds half-hearted. I can smell how the idea of it turns her on.

Everyone here but Elise probably can, and if they comment on it I'll kill them. Thankfully, they all choose to stay alive. "You watch from your car?" Max asks shrewdly.

The asshole knows I didn't. He's spent enough time railing against how bad automobiles are for trackers. He has middling luck with them, and he's the best tracker I know; if I'd stayed in the damn car, I likely never would have been caught.

"No," I admit. "It would be too obvious if I just sat in my car in the parking lot for hours in broad daylight. There're some big trees behind the restaurant."

Penny's mouth drops. "You *sat in a tree*?"

"Let's get one thing straight," I tell her, pushing her back into the table so I can box her in. I don't pin her like I want, but this'll do while we have an audience. "I will do literally anything in the world to be near you. Everything you think is too much, a step too far—I'd do it, Penny, if that's what it took."

Penny looks around like she expects reinforcements, but no one here gives it to her. Everyone here is aware of just how deep this kind of obsession goes.

"It's not worse than sitting outside your house almost every night," I point out. "Or the two nights I broke in."

"You broke in?"

Right. I hadn't exactly told her that yet. "I thought we were over the stalking thing."

She sighs, one hand coming up to fist in my shirt, leveraging herself closer to me and giving herself a little more control. Not that she didn't always have it; I'd kneel at her feet if she asked. But if being able to physically steer me makes her feel better, then I'm not going to stop her. "You are insane," she tells me.

I kiss her again. "You have no idea."

"Alright," Marcus says, sounding bored of the whole thing. He's grabbed Elise and pulled her into his lap and is trying to feed her bites of a second bagel with little success. "So, you stalked your mate, and the shifters tracked the scent. The sorcerer showed up to decide which human was of interest to you. Then they followed you to her house—"

"No, we saw a shifter in a restaurant," I say. "Shortly after I'd been inside her house for the first time." *Fuck*. I can see it now; I left my scent all over her life, a giant advertisement of how to hurt me.

"Okay then. Then they tried to kidnap her, and you interrupted. And they're still after you."

"You know who it is now," Casey says. "That has to count for something."

Maybe, but the sorcerer isn't going to just hold still while we go after him. One wrong move and he'll disappear, ready to attack us from a new angle.

And in the meantime, there's still an unknown number of shifter soldiers out there, all after Penny, aiming to capture her at best and kill her at the worst.

My throat tightens. My own army standing around outside, the three shifters and a dragon inside—none of us are enough. There are too many ways Penny can get hurt.

"Let me change you," I tell her. "Let me make you like us. We could do it; it could be done by tomorrow. You'll be safer. Harder for them to kill, faster—they won't be able to sneak up on you as easily."

I don't know if this is the right course of action. I always thought I'd be more measured in my approach to changing humans, but right now, I can't think of anything beyond her safety. I need to change her, damn what it means, damn the consequences. I need her to be safe.

Penny opens and closes her mouth, completely at a loss for words.

"Luc—I'm like you guys now, but that doesn't give me the training you had. I can't magically fight an army," Casey points out, evidently trying to be a voice of reason.

I growl. I don't need the audience here when we discuss this. "You'll be harder to hurt. You won't have to fight; you'll have me for that. But I need to know I gave you every means possible to stay safe."

"Are you out of your mind?" Penny asks, voice sounding small.

She's only just now realizing that? When it comes to her, I'm completely unhinged. "Keeping you safe is my only priority, love."

"You want me to change my *species* for someone I met three days ago?"

I want *everything* with her—her laughter, her smiles, the moans she makes, her entire future. I'll give her everything she could ever want, and I'll lay my life down for hers. Surely this isn't too much to ask for in return.

I pick her up and throw her over my shoulder, and I go upstairs to find a place to talk.

# CHAPTER 26
# Penny

"**P**ut. Me. Down," I growl, pounding on his back. I might as well be tapping him for all it does.

"You like when I manhandle you, don't lie," Luc drawls. He carries me up the stairs like a sack of potatoes, then turns down the hallway, thankfully away from Max and Casey's bedroom.

Because I do like when he manhandles me. I like it a bit too much. And I have a feeling I know how this will end, and I'd die if it was in my new friend's bedroom.

He opens a door to a small office, then tosses me on the couch before shutting the door. There's no lock, but then again. I think everyone downstairs knows not to interrupt us.

Oh, *fuck*. They can hear us, can't they?

Luc is on top of me before I even know what's happened, spreading my legs with his knees and pinning my wrists above my head, looming over me. "Let's get one thing straight," he growls. "I will never prioritize anything above you. And that includes your safety, Penny. Your ability to take care of yourself."

I squirm, but I already know I'm not breaking his grip. "I do take care of myself, asshole."

"I know you do in the human world, love. A stiletto to the neck is an inspired move. But you're in my world now, and I'll do my best to protect you, but things are bigger than you, meaner than you, faster than you here."

"*You* brought me into this," I growl right back.

Luc stops moving entirely, pulling back slightly. "Do you wish I didn't?"

"Yes. Maybe," I admit, even though I know it's not true. Thinking about Luc driving me home and leaving me there, disappearing from my life again, is like thinking about scooping out my heart. I could no sooner cut him out than I could the rest of my family. I know we're intertwined now, but this is all just a lot. "You're asking me to change when it's only been a few days, Luc. It's too soon."

"It's not," he disagrees. "You think I'm going to leave you? Change my mind? Love, I will burn the world down for you—this isn't ever ending."

"Relationships can go bad," I whisper, getting to the heart of the problem that I didn't even know I was still worried about.

His hands release my wrists, and I almost protest at that. Then he takes one of my hands and draws it to his own throat, wrapping my fingers around it. "If I ever treat you like he did, then you rip out my throat, no questions asked, no second chances given. And it'd be a lot easier if you had claws to do it with."

He's not wrong, is the thing. Luc is offering me a way to protect myself on a level I never even imagined. He's offering me access to his world. No—he's already brought me into his world. He's offering me a way to navigate it safely. I have no doubt he'll do his best to protect me, but the ability to protect myself is priceless, and not something to give up.

But he's asking me to make what sounds like a lifelong commitment after a few days. Not only that, but he's asking me to change my species, to put another barrier between my family and myself. I'll live and they'll die, and I've been trying so hard not to think about to, but now he's forcing me to confront this head-on.

It's not the changing after a few days. Elise was right when she told me I'd know when I know, and I definitely do. Luc is it for me, and it might be a little twisted, but it's mine. Changing gives me access to his world, but it'll also take so much from me.

It's too much. It's all too much, and I need a moment, need to think. But what comes out of my mouth is, "Convince me."

Luc's grin is feral, and he rasps, "Gladly," before taking my hand off his throat and pinning it back to the couch. "You need me to show you how much I fucking want you, hm? How much I need you? That you're mine and I'm never letting you go?" He shifts my wrists into one hand, then slowly pulls my borrowed shirt up with the other, until it's stopped by my pinned wrists.

"Perfect," he mutters, and then, to my shock, uses the shirt to tie my wrists together. I test the knot, tugging lightly. I can move my arms if I want, but I can't separate my wrists from each other.

"Luc..." I begin.

He holds still. "Are you saying stop?"

Am I? No, I don't think so. Just the reminder that I can is enough. We talked about this, and he told me he wanted to tie me up so he can take his time on me. I said yes because the idea made me drip, and it still does. "No."

"Then be a good girl for me and let me fucking show you how important you are to me." My bra has a front clasp, and he flicks it open, exposing me to his roving, hungry eyes. "Gorgeous girl," he murmurs, the praise enough to make me shiver. "You are so fucking important to me, you know that?"

I do, logically. Luc's desperate obsession is clear in every move, in every action. But I shake my head anyway, just to see what he'll do.

What he does is growl, pull Casey's pants off me so fast I'm worried a seam popped, taking my panties down with them until I'm completely bare to him. His hands are on me immediately, running up the inside of my thighs, then over my hips and up my stomach to my breasts, skipping over where I want him entirely. "Luc..."

"No," he rumbles, fingers teasing at the underside of my breast. "If you're going to tell me you *don't know*, then you're going to lie there and let me show you. Because I'm fucking obsessed with you, and I'm going to teach you this lesson until you never forget it again."

I'm not scared of him, but my heart is beating double-time regardless. "Luc..." I whisper, "what are you planning for me?"

He pinches my nipple hard enough I bite my lip, staring up at him. "I'm planning on making you make that face until there's nothing else you can think about," he informs me, voice rough and low, sending shivers down my spine. "You're going to come again and again and again until all you can remember is that I fucking love you, Penny. That I am obsessed with you and only want good things for you. That I'll take care of you, and this is forever."

And then his mouth is on my nipple, replacing his fingers with biting, bruising kisses and firm tugs with his lips and teeth. He's not being gentle with me; I don't want him to. I need to be covered in bruises, in proof this is real.

*We're crazy,* I think deliriously, arching up into his touch. We're both perfect for each other because we're both head-over-heels already, and there's nothing left to stop this runaway train. It won't be me, I know that much.

His hands are busy, trailing down my stomach, then shoving my thighs further apart, making room for himself between my legs. His touch is self-assured, confident that he can play my body like a fiddle, and he's right about it, too; I'm teetering on the edge, ready to fall over before I can even process it.

I don't know how, but Luc knows my body as well as I do, and he pulls back, hovering above me, sliding his fingers out of my pussy to just watch me. I whine, trying to move, but I can't go anywhere, can't get any relief.

"Are you convinced?" he rumbles, and my nipples, already sore and bruised from his mouth, grow harder as a shiver rolls through me. *Jesus.*

"Getting there," I manage to gasp. I don't know why I'm being contrary. I don't know why I don't just tell him *yes*, because we both know where this is heading. I'll say yes to him, and I'll deal with the consequences later.

Maybe I really do need him to prove it to me.

"Then I'm not doing a good enough job." I'm flipped onto my knees before I know what's happening, chest pressed into the couch, hands still bound over my head. Luc slows down for a second, running his hand up my arm, then lightly tugging at my t-shirt restraint.

"You're not going anywhere," he tells me conversationally. "You're going to come your brains out until all you can think about is *me*. It's only fair; you're all I've been able to think about for three years."

And, with no further warning, he thrusts his fingers back inside me.

It's like my body is already primed to go off. Luc is the maestro and I'm his instrument, and he crooks his fingers just right to get me falling over the edge. I bury my face in the couch, trying to muffle my groans, my body spasming around his fingers.

When I calm down, Luc still has his fingers inside me. I hesitantly lift my head, turning so I can see him, and he's just sitting there watching me, an inscrutable look on his face. "That's one," he says calmly.

"One?" *Oh, Jesus.* "How many are we going for?"

His free hand gropes at my ass, molding and squeezing the flesh like I'm his stress ball, and why does that feel so fucking good? "How many do you think you can take before passing out, love?"

I have *no idea*. Is it wrong that I want to find out?

He pulls his fingers out and I whine, but he ignores me, lining his cock up and thrusting inside, merciless and immediate. I yelp, burying my face in the couch again, and Luc freezes.

He works a hand into my hair, tugging at the roots—not enough to pull, but just enough so I turn to look at him again. "Too much?"

I shake my head, hard to do with him holding me, but he gets the picture. It feels good. I'm stretching now, accommodating him, and he feels so fucking good inside of me.

"Fucking perfect for me," he mutters, and it's his first slip of composure. Don't get me wrong; I know Luc is wild for me, is near feral. Every action shows it. But his mask is slipping, and when he pulls out to fuck back into me, I can feel his desperation that matches my own.

I take his thrusts, allowing them to shove me up the couch. He uses one hand to anchor me in place, a firm grip on my hip that he uses to pull my ass higher in the air. "I did a bad job the other night," he says, voice giving no indication that he's in the middle of fucking me, and I almost hate him a bit for it. "Got plenty of bruises all over your pretty front—but I left your back unmarked. We'll need to rectify that as soon as possible; can't have a single inch of you not thinking it's mine."

*Fuck.* I try to squeeze around him, try to push him over the edge. He grunts, and his hips stutter for a second, but he doesn't stop driving into me.

My movements do more to push *me* closer to the edge than him, and this time I doubt the couch will properly muffle my scream. He doesn't stop, pushing into me again and again and again, and I have my eyes closed, watching spots dance behind them—

His thumb rubs over my asshole, and I freeze, opening my eyes and turning my head slightly. He's waiting for me, watching me right back. "I told you," he says, still with that infuriating almost-calm, "*Every single inch of you*. You're all mine. I'm obsessed with all of you, and I'm greedy enough to take it."

Fuck, I—I've never been fucked there. I had thought about it conceptually, but not in practice. Would it hurt? Do I want it?

With Luc? The answer is a resounding *yes.*

Like he can read that on my face, he pushes all the way into my pussy, grinding his hips but not pulling out. Then he leans down and slides his middle and index finger into my mouth. "Suck, love."

I do, and it's almost good to have something else to hold onto, something else to ground me here while his careful, controlled movements seem to grind right against my g-spot every time. I whine, but the fingers in my mouth muffle most of the sound.

"Keep sucking," he croons. "Get my fingers nice and soaked for me, love." I obey, sucking harder, rolling my tongue over his fingers, turning into a wet, slobbering mess as he continues to fuck into me, somehow setting the perfect pace to drive me closer, closer—

I come, only his fingers silencing me from screaming out with it. He pets my back with his free hand, whispering sweet nothings while I come down from the high, and I continue to suck on his fingers, desperate for something to ground me.

All too soon, he's pulling them out. "Good girl," he murmurs. "Doing what you're asked because you know I'm going to make you feel *so. Damned. Good.*"

I do know it. He traces his wet fingers around my asshole, not pushing in, just stroking over the muscle. "It won't be tonight," he tells me, "but someday, I'm going to have every inch of you, and you'll know when I do that every single damned thing about you is perfect for me." He applies more pressure then, just a little, just enough for me to know he's serious.

"You're going to come for me one more time. And when you do, you'll probably be a little rung out, maybe even sore—but you're going to remember this. Remember I'm obsessed with you, that I fucking adore you, and that I'm never going to give you up."

Do I have a thing for voices? Obedience? Or is it just Luc? Because I'm ready to follow his order already. I am sore, but it's a good sore right now; it's me being wet and open and hot and wanting, *needing* him to fill every inch of me.

And when he does, when his strokes are firm and his fingers slide into my ass just the tiniest bit, I can't help myself—I come again.

Before I'm even done, Luc's untied my hands and removed his fingers from my ass, but his cock is still inside me. "That's it. Good fucking girl," he growls. "Can you hold still for me, just a little longer?"

I give him a tired nod, so he starts fucking me again, deep and steady, groaning my name while he takes care of himself.

His come floods me, and I momentarily wonder what it'd be like to be dripping with it, to have him plug me after he fills me and leave me like that, to walk around with him inside me, and—no. I *cannot* go again. I can barely keep my eyes open now.

Luc pulls out when he's done, turning me on my side and using two fingers to tilt my face, which he studies like there'll be a test. "You alright, love?"

I'm sore, and exhausted, and somehow, inexplicably, still a little horny. But what I tell him is, "Luc? I'll do it."

# CHAPTER 27

# Luc

S he passes out less than five minutes after saying it. If I were a better man, I'd make her wait and say it again when she's fully conscious and alert and not dick-drunk. I'd do it about anything else.

But I can't take risks with this. I need Penny to be able to protect herself in this mess. If she ends up hating me for it—which I doubt she will—then that's just the price of keeping her safe.

Max's rather pathetic home office doesn't have anything that'd be useful for cleaning up, so I use her borrowed shirt, shrug my clothes back on, and kiss her forehead before going back downstairs.

"I'm going to fucking kill you," Max informs me, his words serious but his tone barely paying attention to me, too focused on his wife in his lap.

Everyone is doing their best to avoid eye contact with me. "I'll buy you a new couch," I say, waving it away. There are much bigger things to be worried about.

"It's not about the couch."

I don't have time for this. If it's not about the couch, then it's really not about anything. It's not like he was unaware that Penny and I fuck. "She said yes," I tell him. "So, we have a spell to prepare. As soon as possible, ideally—I want her protected as quickly as we can arrange it."

Marcus stretches out. "What do you need?"

Max and I look at each other. For all that I'm trusting him to be here and be another body between Penny and danger, I won't trust him with this spell. I won't trust anyone with it—the last thing the world needs is more people out there who know how to create shifters.

If we get incredibly lucky, we'll kill Vane, and he'll be the last survivor with the secret outside of the two of us. Then, any more shifters who are made will be made by choice. What a novel concept.

We stare at each other until he finally gives in, as I knew he would. "I'll go," Max says, moving to stand, which requires him to dislodge Casey from where she's on his lap. He presses a kiss to her hairline. "Will you be okay?"

"Between me, Marcus, Luc, and the dozen or so shifters hanging around outside—yeah. I think I'll be fine," she sasses, and he just rolls his eyes and kisses her again.

When he stands, he walks over to me, and I think he's about to make another comment about the sex, but instead he says, "Feed your fucking cat."

I glance around, but I know full well she's not in here. I can hear her little heartbeat in the closet off the kitchen. "What's she doing over there?"

"Being fucking terrified. The only person she trusts here is Elise, and even that is with a healthy dose of skepticism."

Marcus flashes a predatory grin. "She smells like dragon."

"Gross." Elise swats his arm, then turns to me. "I tried to get her to come out, but no luck. We made her a litter box with potting soil and an old box—probably not ideal, but whatever—but she won't come out. Can you make sure the poor thing doesn't have a heart attack or something?"

I'm about to say the cat doesn't like me, either, but then again, she did sit pressed into my lap for the entire car ride here. Maybe she'll tolerate me now.

"You have cat food?"

"Canned tuna should work, right?" Casey asks, shrugging. "It's what we were going to try, anyway."

I turn. "Max—"

He waves me down dismissively. "Yeah, yeah. Cat food and cat litter. I'm on it. Sure it'll be easy to find an open store at—" he glances at the clock, "—four in the morning."

"Be careful in the snow!" Casey calls after him. It's less bad here than it was further north, and if Max managed to drive out of that unscathed, I have confidence in his abilities to drive down plowed roads. But he gives her the biggest smile regardless, like her concern is touching to him.

When he gets his boots and coat on and disappears, I go to lure out the cat. The can of tuna has been helpfully left on the counter, so I crack it open, set it on the floor outside the closet, and sit back a few feet to wait.

Waiting on a ball of fluff that probably weighs less than ten pounds. How has this become my life?

But I can hear Penny's heartbeat upstairs, even and easy in sleep. That's why. Making peace with a cat is a low ask to have her.

Eventually, Jinx slinks out of the closet, her belly practically dragging on the ground in her fear. She gives me a mistrustful look, but ventures toward the food.

"I hope you know that you and I are spending the rest of your life together," I tell her. "Since there's no way in hell I'm giving up your mom. So, get used to me. I'm not so bad."

She licks delicately into the can of tuna. Then she must realize it's real fish, and dives in with absolute abandon. I take the chance to slide a little closer, using just two fingers to pet down her back.

She lets me, focused more on the food than me.

"That's it," I murmur. "You know you're safe, right?" I rescued this cat from a burning building; she better know she's safe.

When she licks the can clean, she turns around and swats my hand. Her little claws don't really hurt me, of course, but they do sting. "What the fuck?" I ask.

She turns primly, runs her entire body along my still-out-stretched hand, and retreats back into the closet.

Ungrateful cat now fed, I go back upstairs to Penny. Casey looks for a moment like she wants to say something, but decides against it.

And there she is, still asleep on the couch. Still undressed too, and I momentarily feel guilty that I didn't re-dress her before I left. I should have.

Then again—there's something to be said for access. And all I can think is a little request she made of me barely twenty-four hours ago.

My love needs me to wake her up with my cock because I'm just so obsessed with her? I'm more than on board.

My cock is, too. I thought I came harder than I ever have earlier, but here I am, ready to go again. Penny just does that to me. I quickly shed my clothes, leaving them in a pile on the floor with hers, and contemplate how best to do this.

This would be easier in a bed. There's a bed down the hall, but—no. That's crossing a line, even for me.

That's fine. I can be creative. And perhaps there's a benefit to not being some great, hulking brute. I can slip in right behind her, then tease her legs open, careful to move slow enough that I won't wake her. Not yet, at least.

She's still wet, my come leaking out of her. I slide a finger inside, but I really had no need to worry; she's still open for me.

When I fill her with my cock, she groans a bit, shuffling around. I wait a second, then push the rest of the way inside, bottoming out in her hot cunt.

She somehow feels even better like this, hot and wet with her own slick and my come. *Fuck.*

I lean forward, bending in half so I'm right by her ear. "Penny, love—time to wake up." Then I pull almost all the way out before slamming back inside.

I can hear the second she wakes; her heart rate picks up, her breathing changes, and she gasps my name.

"That's right, love," I growl, pleased to hear my name on her lips. "I couldn't resist you a second longer."

I slow down for a second, waiting to see if she's going to decide that the fantasy of this is better than reality. But all she does is groan my name again and try to rock her hips back for more, so I thrust into her, setting a brutal, desperate pace that's going to send us both to the edge.

She whines my name, and I decide I can't fucking stand not being able to see her face, so I pull out long enough to flip her, then push back into her before she can really register that I'm gone. "That's it," I encourage her, watching my cock disappear inside her. "Oh, fuck, beautiful girl—are you going to come for me again?"

She nods, biting her lip. To think she thought she couldn't come twice the first time I fucked her. This'll be her fifth in the last few hours. And someday, I plan on showing her how much more she can do.

I stroke her clit, murmuring, "Then come for me, my good girl."

She squeezes me like a vise when she comes, all hot and tight and irresistible. Someday, I'm going to have to ensure I still have tolerable stamina and she hasn't destroyed me entirely—making her come eight or nine times while edging myself seems like a good test. But it won't be today, because I can't resist her for a moment longer.

Her eyes are still glazed with orgasm and sleep, but her smile is decidedly wicked as she takes me in, completely wrecked by her, barely able to recover from my orgasm. Nothing in the world has been able to kill me in two thousand years, but I think Penny's perfect pussy might just do the job.

"Good morning," she teases, trailing one hand up my chest before she pauses. "Is it morning?"

"Close enough." It's time to start our day, at any rate, as loathe as I am to get up from here.

We need our own house, somewhere I can fuck her all day long. As soon as Vane is dead, burned, and buried, I'll make that my top priority.

"Did you like that, love? Was it everything you wanted?" It's not an idle question; if Penny is going to be mine forever—and we're just hours away from making *forever* a reality—then I need to know exactly what she likes. Sometimes fantasies are just fantasies, and I need to know if this is something I should do again, or if she's changed her mind.

She stretches under me, and her movement feels both incredibly good and incredibly over-stimulating. I pull out of her slowly. "It was great," she murmurs, voice still a little sleepy. "Exactly what I thought it'd be—did you like it?"

I spread my hand over her warm belly, pressing for a second before I stroke her skin. "I always want you," I tell her, voice husky. "Not having to wait is just a bonus."

I'm debating if asking her for another round is the right move, or if I should make sure she gets fed, when my cell phone rings.

"Fuck," I mutter, fishing it out of my pants. It's Max, of course. His terrible timing is going to make me strangle him. "What?"

There's silence on the other end, and I can just *feel* him deciding if he's going to give me shit or not. Thankfully for both our continued existences, he gets straight to business. "The shopkeeper is being less than helpful. And I'm debating if it would draw more attention just to kill him and get it done, or to have you come out here and scare the shit out of him. Thoughts?"

Max isn't one to wait on things like this. His life philosophy has been one of kill first, ask questions later. I can't judge him for that; it's definitely something I encouraged in him. It helps to have a mad dog off his leash.

But I know what he's asking; we need to do this in a way that draws the least amount of attention to what we're doing. The last thing we need is someone digging into why we were interested in this particular shop, with these particular ingredients.

The spell Alexander, and now Vane, used to make shifters is disturbingly uncomplicated. Not easy, perhaps, but far less complicated than I'd want something of such magnitude to be.

If the ingredients to create a loyal, trainable, practically un-killable army of child soldiers can be picked up at a particularly well-supplied magic store, what would the world do?

I don't want to find out.

Max kills all sorts of people for me, although I admit not as much anymore. The average person is just too scared to cross us these days, so Max only comes out for the most dire of situations. Sending him after a random magic shop owner likely won't qualify, raising too much suspicion.

I heave a put upon sigh. "I'll be there in twenty minutes. Don't let him leave. Don't let him call anyone. Hold him there."

I can hear Max's eye-roll through the phone. "Got it, boss," he quips, and then hangs up the line.

I look at the phone before turning to Penny. "Will you be okay here for a bit if I go help Max out?"

"I'm sure the dozen werewolves and the actual, real-life *dragon* will keep me safe," she says.

I'm sure they will too, if they value their lives. But that wasn't what I was referring to. Penny seemed to get along with Casey and Elise yesterday, but she doesn't know them. Is it arrogant to assume that I comfort her? Whatever; I know I'm arrogant, and I accept it.

"Where's your phone?" I ask her. She points to the pile of clothes, so I pull out her phone and put my number in it. It's wild that I was just inside of her and she didn't even have my phone number. I know phones are obviously a much more modern device, and I've fucked plenty of people before they were even invented. But Penny is different. Penny should know she always gets front of the line, instant access to me.

"Call me if you need me."

"I will. Can you hand me my clothes?"

I grab them, then remember I used her shirt to clean us up earlier. She groans when she sees it. "That's borrowed, Luc!"

"Laundry detergent exists. And I'll buy her a new shirt; it'll be fine. Here." I lift my shirt off the floor, but it's borrowed too, and it still smells more like Max than it does me. And I simply can't abide by that. "I'll ask Casey to bring you something." And maybe I'll stop at a clothing store and get some clothes for both of us on my way back; Max's borrowed clothes dwarf me, and I'd like Penny to smell like just the two of us.

She sighs and scoots off the couch, putting on her under-wear, the borrowed sweats, and her bra. "You'll be safe out there? You're worried about me, but remember, he only wants me because of you."

He only wants her because he's—correctly—ascertained that I'll do just about anything to keep her alive. He could get to me on a regular basis; I'm a public figure, after all. My location is rarely a secret. But he knows he'd die in the attempt. Maybe Alexander's untimely demise taught Vane caution, or maybe he just learned from all the people Max and I killed over the years. Regardless, he won't come directly at me.

"I will," I promise her. I have the utmost confidence I'll return to her unscathed in a few hours. "Get something to eat, yeah? You barely ate dinner last night."

She smiles shyly, clearly flattered that I noticed and worried, and I need to raise her standards, and fast. Me noticing when she's not being taken care of properly should be a bottom-rung expectation.

She leans in and kisses me, one hand on my chest for balance that I swear brands me straight through my clothes.

"I'll tell Casey you need her," I murmur as I'm forced to pull away. The sooner I go, the sooner she can be safe, so with a last, lingering look, I head out the door.

# CHAPTER 28
# Penny

When Casey knocks on the door, I have my apology ready. "I am so sorry, this was so disrespectful, and I'll replace the shirt—" I should offer to replace the damn couch too, I know. That's a little out of my price range, though.

Casey sighs. "It's not entirely your fault. Luc is—Luc. I've known him five or six years now, and I know what he's like." She gives me an appraising look. "Have to say, you're the first person to ever find him charming, though."

"People voted for him," I point out.

"Yeah, but I almost think it's because he's not charming—people trust that he means what he says, in a fucked up sort of way." She shakes her head. "But yeah. I don't want that shirt back. Just toss it in the trash." Then she holds out another one, which I accept gratefully, shrugging it on quickly.

"You don't like Luc much," I say once I get the shirt on. I try to say it without any judgment, try not to let how I feel about him cloud my mind.

She tilts her head, thinking. "It's not that I *don't* like him. Luc and Max are intertwined on some deep level and I can't resent that; Max wouldn't be alive without Luc, and that obviously means the world to me. And Luc was the one who married us, and fucking in my house aside, he's never been anything but respectful to me, in a reserved kind of way. He's just... cold, I guess?"

I can understand that. It's the complete opposite of how he is with me, but I can see how other people might see that.

I want Luc to have relationships, not just pawns to move around. I don't know how to help him with that yet, but I will. Maybe I'm already starting.

"How's everyone doing?" I ask. "Sorry I... left like that."

"You mean, got dragged off?"

I nod, feeling the blush heat my cheeks. Yes, and it'd been fucking hot. The absolute wrong place, but hot nonetheless. Not that I'm sharing that thought with Casey.

"We're fine. Elise and Marcus are downstairs. It's almost five, so Elise is thinking about breakfast."

"Oh, nice." Luc wasn't wrong when he said I didn't eat enough last night.

"Yeah. She's a chef, you know, so every time she comes over here, we eat better than we ever have before." There's almost a dreamy look in her eyes, and then she blushes. "Max and I aren't exactly great cooks."

"Well, let's see what she's making, then."

259

But when we get downstairs, Elise is dictating a list of ingredients to Marcus, who's nodding seriously as he notes each one in his phone.

"And you're sure you three will be okay for an hour?" he checks.

"How many shifters are outside, again?" Elise asks.

It's Casey who answers. "Like a dozen."

"I think we'll be just fine."

"Alright." The kiss he gives her is practically indecent, bending her backward and leaving her a little dazed when he pulls back. "I'll be back soon."

Elise grins when he leaves, cheeks still flushed. "When I met him a little over a year ago, he didn't know how to grocery shop. Look at him now."

"You didn't have to take care of the shopping," Casey murmurs, staring at the floor.

"Why not? It's not going to hurt him to do it, trust me."

"I should have—"

"He can handle it. You don't have to worry about it, Casey. You're letting all of us stay in your home. That's more than enough."

"That's because of me," I point out. "And I definitely feel like I'm not pulling my weight, so put me to work."

"There's not much to do until we get groceries," Elise says. "Unless you have something, Casey?"

"No, nothing," she says, then considers. "And it's not because of you. The things these guys got up to—it's not their fault, because they didn't ask for this. But grudges from thousands of years before you were born are coming up now. That doesn't make them your fault, either."

I open my mouth to say something back, but then my phone rings. I fish it out of the borrowed sweatpants, expecting to see Luc already calling me, but instead, my caller ID reads STEPHANIE.

"Oh shit," I mutter, but I'm already fumbling to pick up the call before either of the other two women can ask about it. I wander back to the living room. "Hey, Steph. What's up?"

"MERRY CHRISTMAS!" A chorus of voices shouts at me, the two high-pitched little boys' voices nearly drowning out my sister and who I assume is Louise. There may be more voices, too, honestly; Will and Manny are loud.

I pull the phone away from my ear slightly, drowning in the cacophony of it all, but it warms me from the inside out. "Merry Christmas, all," I say, already inexplicably a little choked up. "How're things there?"

There's a rustling noise, and then it's just Stephanie. "Did we wake you? Sorry; the boys have been up for thirty minutes, and they really wanted to call, and I assumed you'd be up, but if you slept in for once and we woke you—"

"You didn't wake me," I tell her, plopping down onto Max and Casey's couch. As soon as I sit, Jinx slinks into the room, then, when she sees I'm alone, makes a beeline for me, jumping up on the couch to settle on my lap. I pet through her white fur, no doubt getting it everywhere on this dark red couch. Max and Casey will remember us long after we leave. "I'm up. How's Christmas going?"

There's the sound of a door closing, and then the background noise gets even quieter. "Lovely," she deadpans.

"That bad?"

"Louise's dad is handling retirement about as well as is to be expected."

Ah. "So, he's bugging the shit out of you?" When Paul and Camila had still lived locally and run the restaurant alongside Stephanie and Louise, there'd been some head-butting by the end. Stephanie and Louise were ready to take over, but Paul wasn't quite willing to let go.

Honestly, he might never have let go if Camila didn't put her foot down and insist she'd like to see the ocean sometime in this lifetime, just like he'd promised her decades ago. Now they're retired and living all the way in Virginia.

"They had an argument about how to properly cook steak last night. So, you know. About par for the course," Stephanie sighs. "How's your quiet Christmas? Are you alright on your own?"

*On my own.* I almost tell her that I'm not, but I stop myself. I can't tell her any of this, especially not over the phone. Not when she's so far away and it'll just freak her out. "Yeah, it's been nice," I tell her. "Did the boys like their Christmas gifts?"

"They haven't opened them yet," she says with another heavy sigh.

"They've been up for half an hour and they haven't opened their gifts?"

"Oh, no," she informs me, all fake seriousness now. "Christmas morning breakfast comes before gifts."

That sounds kind of counterproductive with little kids around, but what do I know? I know nothing about raising kids and I know even less about appeasing in-laws.

Well, at least I won't have to worry about in-laws with Luc.

Stephanie might hate it when her father-in-law argues with her wife, or some of their outdated opinions, but I know she loves them. Considering how we grew up, how could she not? Having a family that cares about each other and is proud enough to pass down a legacy is a damn miracle, really.

"You sure you're okay? You're quiet," Stephanie murmurs.

I can't lie to my sister. Well, not entirely, anyway—I'm just coming around to accepting that I'll never be able to fully tell her the truth about my life again, and that's a gut-punch. I'll have to talk out with Luc how much is safe to tell her. But I have to give her something.

Stephanie picked me up when I was broken. I might have spent a lot of time trying to shield her when we were teenagers, but she's grown into a remarkable woman, and she's not stupid. I need to tell her something.

"Steph, I—I met someone," I admit.

She's silent for a minute. "What, in the few days I've been gone?"

Yeah, basically. But that'll sound like I've completely lost it, and Stephanie is already worried about my ability to spot a healthy relationship. "No, I've known him longer than that." It's technically true, at least, so I'm not entirely lying to my sister. "It's just—I didn't want to make a big deal out of it until I was sure."

"And you're sure now?" She sounds skeptical, and I try not to let that hurt. She has good reason to be.

"I'm sure about him," I tell her quietly. "We're going to spend today together." Another partial-truth. "And someday soon, I'd like you to meet him." I don't know how exactly I'm going to explain that he's the governor. That's a problem for later-me to solve.

"Well, I hope I will. He should be doing the whole gentleman thing, picking you up for dates at the front door."

"Steph... I think I'm going to move out."

She's silent so long I worry the call dropped. "*What*?"

I wince. "C'mon, Steph. You can't want me crashing your space forever. This way, the boys can have their own rooms. You deserve your life back."

"You're part of my life, you idiot," she scolds, but it doesn't sound that harsh. "Is this to move in with him?"

"Maybe?" Definitely, but even I know that sounds too fast.

She's quiet again, but then asks. "Is he good to you, Pen? Treats you good?"

Luc put himself between me and danger multiple times. He rescued Jinx from a burning building when he had no obligation to do so. He heard my whole past and, rather than being freaked out, he made me feel safe.

He is obsessive and he is a stalker, and I know there's violence lingering under his skin. But I also know the violence isn't directed at me, and that he will bend over backward to give me whatever I want.

I'll never feel like I'm begging for attention again.

"Yeah. He treats me great."

"Good." She exhales slowly. "We'll talk about this more when I get back. You'll bring him to dinner so Louise and I can meet him—will he treat the boys okay?"

I have no idea if Luc has ever spent any time with kids outside of a child-soldier death-camp situation, but he'll be polite to the boys if I ask him to.

"Yeah. We'll do that."

There's voices in the background of the call, and then I hear the high-pitched shriek of one of the boys. "Time to go," she says. "Merry Christmas, Penny. We'll talk when I get home."

"Love you, Steph."

"Love you too." She's already shouting for Will before the call ends.

I don't wish I was there. I don't really wish she was here, either; I don't want her anywhere near this mess.

But I want her all the same.

Jinx rolls so she's flipped upside down in my lap, and I smile and pet her fluffy belly.

Casey pokes her head around the corner, looking even more shy than normal. "Do you want company, or...?"

"Sure." It's her house, after all.

Elise follows her in, and the two of them sit on the other couch.

"Family?" Elise asks.

"My sister. My only family, so yeah." My throat gets a little tight. "How do you two deal with that, with all this? You both started as human, so you must have human families."

They're quiet for a moment, but then Casey says, "My family sucks. Even before I was this, Max was my family. I like to think I'll try to mend bridges with them again someday, but it might not ever happen."

"It's just my mom," Elise says. "We visited her a couple months ago. I don't see her that often. That's not just because of who Marcus is; it's been like that since I turned eighteen. I haven't decided what I'm going to do about the not growing older thing yet. I'm hoping I have a little while before it's obvious enough to be an issue."

"Stephanie is amazing," I tell them. "And she picked me up when I was at my lowest. I can get why telling her all of this would be dangerous, but I can't cut her out."

"Then don't."

"Aren't there rules?"

Casey shrugs. "Penny, you're about to marry the guy who *makes* the rules. Tell him to make an exception for you."

My stomach lurches unpleasantly. "Isn't that unfair? Wouldn't that put them in danger?"

"Talk it over with Luc," Elise suggests. "Maybe you two can come up with a plan."

Would he? For me, would Luc change the rules?

What would it even look like? If I tell Stephanie, what would that mean for her? Would she have to keep it a secret from Louise? What about when she gets old and I stay this age forever?

Every bit of this is unpleasant to think about. I don't have answers, and I'm not sure I'm ready to find them yet. This all should make me doubt going forward with this plan, but I know it won't. I've made my decision. The rest is just living with the consequences.

Elise uses her hands on her thighs to push herself up. "I made coffee, if anyone wants some. And Marcus will be back with food in half an hour or so."

I carefully remove the cat from my lap, grateful for any distraction, and follow her to the kitchen.

# CHAPTER 29

# Luc

I arrive back at the house with Max in tow, the two of us carrying armfuls of shopping bags, to hear the women laughing in the kitchen.

It took longer than we thought, between the magic shop and the clothes shopping and the series of texts I got halfway through. More shifter sightings. It runs counter to everything I know, but I force myself to ignore them. I'm not going to get lured into a trap again.

Still, they're getting closer and dangerously bold. If we don't take down Vane soon, then the shifters truly are going to do something we can't come back from.

Elise is at the stove, standing over something that smells amazing. Casey and Penny aren't that far away, laughing at something Elise said. Marcus is sitting at the table, watching them—watching Elise, really—with a fond look in his eye.

Max drops his bags on the floor and pulls Casey into a hug, just making her laugh louder. "You're back."

"Mhm. Missed you."

I scoop up the bags. I hate to pull Penny away from what seems to be a good time, but this can't wait. "Penny, can I borrow you?"

She bites her lip and nods, turning away to follow me. "Don't have sex on my couch again," Max calls after us.

"Why? I already said I'd replace it."

"Luc—" Penny whispers, flushed and clearly mortified.

"Alright, alright." I wrap an arm around her, then lean in so I can kiss her forehead. "Let's get this done."

There's no real reason why we couldn't do this right in the kitchen. It's essentially just a drink. But it feels private, somehow. I convinced her to do this, but that doesn't mean that her concerns about this being a big deal were invalid. She's changing her species.

This feels almost like a marriage proposal. I should have picked up a diamond ring before I came home. It's only eight in the morning—there probably aren't a lot of open jewelry stores right now. It'll have to be something for later.

But if I'm proposing forever with her, I want it to be just us. I want to make her feel as comfortable and at ease as I can—even if it's only Max's office.

"So," she says when we reach the upstairs landing, jarring me out of my thoughts. "Is it a bite? I'm realizing I don't know how this works."

I blink at her. "You know it's not a bite. I've bitten you plenty." I trail one finger down her chest, hidden by her bor-

269

rowed shirt, but we both know she has plenty of bruises from my mouth under there.

She flushes. "Those didn't break skin."

"Werewolf bites are a movie thing, love. It'd do nothing but hurt you. It's a spell."

"What, you stand over me, wave a magic wand, chant some words?"

The idea is beyond ridiculous. I shut the office door behind us, steering us back over to the couch. The smell of the two of us is strong here, and I concede that I might have to offer to re-do all the fixtures in this room instead of just replacing the couch. That delicious scent isn't going to fade for a while.

"I'm not a street corner performer, Penny. In fact, I don't have any magical ability at all."

"You turn into a giant wolf."

Fair point, because I can't quite argue that it's *not* magic, but it doesn't change what I'm saying. "No magic words here. Think of it like an elixir. You drink it."

She looks at me skeptically. "What, you just mix some juice, and, bam, werewolf? Why aren't there a thousand werewolves running around?"

"It's not grocery store ingredients, love." That's putting it mildly. The reason Max was having trouble is the pure rarity and expense of some of these ingredients. The magic shop owner didn't even want to admit he *had* some of them in his possession.

I set my bags on Max's desk, careful to keep the ingredients off to one side. "What're all of these?"

"Clothes, mostly. And cat things—I guess I should have left those downstairs." I peer into the bags, find the one with a disposable litter box and cat food in it, and leave it outside the door for someone else to deal with.

"Why so many clothes? Are we moving in here forever?"

"No, but when you first change, it can be hard to control the shift at first," I admit. "I didn't want you tearing through your only clothes."

Her mouth falls open slightly, a soft *o* that I want to kiss. "That's sweet of you," she murmurs, digging into the bag.

"I had to guess your sizes. Which I didn't like, by the way. Tell me all your sizes so I can have them memorized."

"Planning on doing my shopping for me?" Planning on buying her plenty of gifts, and I won't be texting her to remind me of her bra size before I do. "You didn't do too bad. They're not far off." Then, without any warning, she pulls off her borrowed clothes and starts changing, and I completely lose track of the ingredients I planned to measure out and just watch her body move.

*Fuck*. She's facing away from me, her whole back on display, and I'm reminded of my promise to mark it up like I did her front. Then she bends down to pull fresh underwear on, and I nearly start salivating,

If only I could turn her into a shifter by biting her. I'd sink my teeth right into that plump, perfect ass.

When she pulls out new socks, the gift I'd added tumbles out and onto the floor. "What's this?"

"An anklet," I tell her, grinning now. I pick it up, then kneel in front of her, lifting her foot onto my thigh. "Something pretty to dangle by my ears when I'm eating you out, remember?"

"Oh, Jesus..." she whispers, and it turns into a moan when I stroke gently over her ankle bone. "Luc, we promised we *wouldn't* have sex up here again..."

"I didn't make any promises." But I let her go with a kiss to her knee, gold anklet now in place. It came from the same twenty-four hour box store the clothes did, so it's not quite as nice as I'd like for her. "I'll replace that with real gold sometime soon."

"You kidding?" she asks, withdrawing her ankle further away from me like she thinks I'm going to snatch it off her. "You gave it to me as a gift. Because you saw it and thought of me. Even if you were thinking with your dick, it's still a gift, and you'll have to take it from my cold, dead hands."

I frown, although I don't know if it's the characterization of *thinking with my dick*—always a little true when I'm thinking of Penny, admittedly, although I like to think it's in a giving, loving way—or the idea that she won't let me replace it. "It'll be a lot nicer," I try. "Diamonds, maybe?"

She bends down to pull her socks on, hiding the damned piece of jewelry. "It's mine. You gave it to me and it's mine now. You thought of me and brought me something just because. You can't take it back."

Well, when she puts it like that... I can see why it matters to her. It'll just have to be one hell of an engagement ring, then.

She starts carefully folding Casey's clothes and setting them aside, and I turn to the ingredients in the last bag. It'd taken months to beat this secret out of Alexander. He'd always loomed large in my mind, a terrifying bogeyman from my childhood. When I finally got my hands on him, though, it became clear quickly that, without his magic and his army, he's a particularly breakable man. Still, even when I'd been especially creative in my torture, he'd held out for months. This secret had been worth it to him.

I mix things together quickly but carefully, putting it all in the metal cocktail shaker I picked up. "Should I do it like a shot?" she asks, coming to stand beside me and watch me work.

"If you want. Max says it tastes terrible."

"Max says? But not you?"

I focus on the shaker, making sure all the ingredients are combined. "I don't remember having this given to me, Penny. Neither does Max. Our best guess is it was dripped into our mouths shortly after we were born. Max only knows because Casey. As far as we know, she's the first shifter to ever be turned as an adult, and the first to choose it."

"Jesus," she breathes, and then her hands trace over my back, coming up to rest on my shoulder. "I'm sorry, Luc."

I know what she's apologizing for—the lost childhood, the pain, the fear—but honestly, at this point, all I can think about is what happened since.

I'm no one's favorite person, but I've made a difference in the world. I've freed shifters from under Alexander. I've kept the supernatural creatures in line to preserve our secrets and our ways of life. And I was even a decent governor for the humans.

And now there's Penny. Beautiful, brilliant, funny Penny. I'm going to spend the rest of my life with her, and I would have missed that entirely if I'd lived and died two thousand years ago.

"It's ready," I tell her instead of explaining that. "Want to sit down?"

"What's going to happen?"

I'd asked Max that same question. I need to know what to expect so I know how to look after her. "It'll taste terrible, and you'll get a little woozy. Might pass out. And when you wake up, you'll probably feel the need to shift. The animal will just be there. It'll take a little bit of time to get acquainted with them."

"Animal..." she murmurs, like somehow this is the first time she's thinking about that part. "You mean wolf."

"Not necessarily. We still don't know what makes a shifter one type of animal or another."

She makes a face. "I'm going to get something really lame."

"Maybe you'll get a big cat, since you're such a cat person."

She nudges my side. "I am equally a cat and a dog person, thank you."

That is oddly flattering in a way I don't want to examine too closely. "C'mon. It's not going to taste better if you wait."

I lead her over to the couch, pulling her to sit on my lap and wrapping both arms around her, proffering the shaker to her. "Drink, love."

She takes it but hesitates. "You're never going to change your mind about me, right?"

My heart aches for her. "Never," I promise, and I hope she can hear my sincerity. This is never ending, and this is only the first step for us.

This is the right thing to do. She needs to be stronger, *safer* in my world. I know that in my bones. This is always where we were going to end up. Even so, her hesitation makes my heart twist.

She studies the shaker for a second, then throws the mixture back like a shot, just like she said she would.

"Whoa." The shaker tumbles from her hand as she latches onto my arms around her, seemingly using them to stay grounded.

"Penny, love? You okay?"

"Spinning," she mutters, and then passes out in my arms.

# CHAPTER 30
# Penny

When I wake up, the world looks weird. Everything's at a strange angle, the colors are wrong, and I can't figure out where the hell I am.

Why is Luc above me? He's sitting on a couch, which must mean I'm on the ground, but that doesn't make any sense, and—

Oh. I try to move, but that's a *paw*.

I blink a few times, trying to make sure I'm not hallucinating it, but no, that's definitely a paw. I have paws.

Which means that I'm some sort of animal now. That looks like a big dog paw, but what do I know?

It's a light brown, not too dissimilar to my hair color. Long and kind of shaggy, I probably look like some sort of unkempt, bedraggled animal, which seems about par for the course.

"Penny?" I realize Luc's been trying to talk to me the whole time. I try to respond to him, but all that comes out is a *yip*. It's startling enough that I fall backward.

"Shh, shh, love," he soothes, getting off the couch and down onto his knees. "You're okay. You're *beautiful*, actually. Just need to get your feet under you." Then he reaches out to touch me, hands feathering through my new fur, and *oh*, that feels *good*.

Luc chuckles. "Nice to know that you like it when I touch you in both forms."

I roll my eyes at him, and he laughs louder, so I suppose it's gratifying to know that rolling my eyes translates into both forms, too.

This is all well and good, but I'd really like to turn back now. I'd like to be able to talk this out and plan our next steps. Unfortunately, I have no idea how to do that.

I turn in a circle, feeling more and more like a damned dog, except I'm chasing some elusive magical transformation instead of my tail. I want to snap at Luc to *help me*, but he sucks in a breath.

"Your anklet survived," he murmurs. "Your clothes most certainly did not. Good thing I bought you multiple changes, hm?"

I turn around to see my back leg, and, sure enough, there's that golden anklet around my hind leg. It's too big but not entirely slipping off.

I kind of like how it looks, I decide. He's *definitely* not taking it away from me. But I really want to be able to turn back now.

"Can you focus, love?" he asks. "I'd like to ask you some questions. You went right to this form, so I have no idea if anything hurts, or how you're feeling. Can you come back to me?"

*I'm trying, asshole*, I try to say. It comes out as a little growl.

Luc has the gall to laugh at me. "Alright, Penny. I get it. Focus on your human body. Toes, fingers, walking upright. The way your leg muscles move when you walk. The way you use your arms to reach for something."

I try to do what he says. I imagine balancing a full tray while I bring out plates at work. I imagine the way it feels to hold a coffee mug in my hands.

Suddenly, like no time at all passed, I'm sitting on the floor as a naked, largely confused, human. My legs are sprawled out in front of me, making me look like I just fell here.

"Is it always so hard to turn back?" It's almost a shock to hear my own voice.

"No," Luc says absently, leaning in to look over every inch of me. I thought the point of this was to make me less vulnerable to harm, but Luc's acting like he's going to find some gaping wound. "It's downright easy most of the time. Sometimes when you spend too long as the wolf, your mind starts to shift, and it helps to think about those human things."

"Glad to know it gets easier. How long will that take?" I push him away gently. I feel disoriented, a little fuzzy, but I know I'm not injured.

"No idea. Ask Casey."

"You don't remember?"

"When we were children, no one cared what form we were in. Wolf or human were all the same to them."

Right. Just another piece of his horrific childhood.

"You're a beautiful wolf," he says, sitting back and smiling at me, seemingly satisfied with his observation.

"How do I turn back?" I ask him. If he's so insistent that this will keep me safe, then I should probably know how to do it. "Think of running through the woods? Chasing my tail? Sniffing butts?"

"More or less. But stay away from butts that aren't mine."

I roll my eyes at him but otherwise ignore him. Obviously. Like I want to be sniffing around butts.

Alright, four legs. Big, sturdy paws. The way the world looked ever so slightly different—colors were wrong, but the world was sharper. The way that I could practically see smells.

I remember watching Luc transform and thinking it looked brutal, like a horrific tearing of the body. But it doesn't feel like that. It's like jumping into a cool pool, a slightly disorienting rush, and then I acclimate.

And now, I'm looking at Luc with wolf eyes again.

This time, I'm calmer. I'm relatively sure I can turn back to a human, so I take a moment to explore what it means to be a wolf. I lean closer to Luc, sniffing around his neck. Spicy. Louise would probably be able to tell me the exact mix of spices, but

I bristle at the idea of my sister-in-law sniffing him. So I'll just settle for *spicy*, in a warm sort of way.

What he doesn't smell like is *me*, and there's something in my brain now that's decided that is unacceptable. I lean into him, rubbing against his exposed neck.

His fingers latch into my fur, pulling slightly. But he's not pulling like he wants me to leave him alone, I don't think. It feels more like he's anchoring himself.

"Hello, love," he rasps. "Marking me as yours?"

Fucking right, I am. It feels both ridiculous and inescapable, and I make sure I rub my scent all over him.

"Thank you," he murmurs with far more sincerity than I expected. He has much more grace than I would when being accosted by a wolf. "Can you change back again?"

That is a good question. I think of human things—eating with silverware, coffee, and the way Luc touches me—and I'm sitting on the floor with two legs again.

"Alright?" he checks.

"Just fine. It's going to take some getting used to."

He nods, biting his lip. "As much as I don't like admitting that there's something I can't give you, you should talk to Casey. She's gone through this much more recently."

And in a way far more similar to what I did. I remember what she said when she talked about converting to werewolf-ism. We believe in it, but we don't have any of the cultural background. Neither of us were tortured in a death cult as children.

"We should go downstairs," I mumble. "Assure the others we're alive. Or—" I realize I can hear them as clearly as if they're in the next room "—can they *hear* us?"

"You get decent at tuning it out, if you want," he tells me, which isn't an answer, but tells me all I need to know.

We really had sex, *more than once*, in a house full of people who can hear a pin drop a whole floor away.

And now I have to face them while knowing it. I push myself to shaky feet, and Luc stands to support me. "It'll go away," he assures me. "Your body is just adjusting. Here. You sit."

He steers me toward the couch, so I sit and let him hand me yet another outfit.

I have to admit, he did a good job with all of it. The sizes are close when they're not right-on, and all of the pieces are things I'd genuinely wear. Once I'm dressed again, Luc opens the door, only to almost trip over a bag.

"Fuck. Someone was supposed to grab this," he says, the last part pitched just a tiny bit louder, no doubt to scold someone downstairs.

"I've done enough errands for you." It's as clear as if Max was talking right next to me, but I know he's all the way downstairs. Bizarre. "Besides, the cat hates me."

Oh, god. "Jinx," I gasp. Oh, my baby. Is she going to hate me now?

281

Luc looks at me like he can read my mind. "She'll come around. C'mon. We'll go see her now."

I understand the logic of getting it over with, like pulling off a band-aid, but I balk. I don't know how I'm going to handle it if she hates me.

"Penny," Luc says firmly, "that cat adores you. She stood between you and danger and has spent every day of her life with you. She's learned to tolerate *me* because of you. She'll be fine. You'll be the first shifter with a pet."

Alright. Sure. I have to hope that's true, so I hold my head high and walk downstairs. Luc follows me, carrying the bag down.

"She's in the closet again," Elise tells me as soon as she sees me. "She won't even come out for me."

I swallow, because that doesn't bode well, but I nod again. "Here," Luc says, handing me an unopened bag of cat treats.

*This man*. He didn't have to buy these; a basic litter box so she doesn't make a mess and some cat food would have been more than enough. But I've turned him into a cat dad.

Well, only if Jinx still wants us to be her pet parents. I'm not sure if that's currently true, but I take the treats, sit down outside the closet, and shake the bag.

I hear a little scuffing sound. She's moving in there. There's also a little thumping sound, and it takes me a second to realize that's her *heartbeat*. Because I can hear heartbeats now. Jesus.

I can hear her breathing too, faster than I think is right, but then again, what do I know? The only time before today that I could hear her breathe is when she fell asleep on my chest, and she was always calm and breathing slowly then.

"Jinx?" I murmur, shaking the bag of treats again. "Can you come here, baby?"

She pokes her head out but doesn't come any closer.

I lay a treat down in front of her, then another closer to me. Then I sit back and wait.

I can hear my own damn heartbeat. That's going to get annoying.

She inches a little closer, then snatches the treat. I half expect her to dart back into her closet, but she just sits there, watching me.

"It's okay, baby," I tell her, carefully extending my hand. "It's just me."

She takes another step closer. Then another. Then, in a rush, she's beside me, rubbing her scent into my outstretched hand.

"I know," I croon at her. "This is a lot. But we're going to be fine, hm? You're going to be just fine."

I don't think Jinx is ready for me to run around in my wolf form—we're going to be keeping those far away from her—but I do think she trusts me again.

"I want a cat," I hear Casey say behind me. Max sighs and Luc sniggers at him.

I've known Max for two days and I know he'll be doing his absolute best to convince a shelter cat he's not a threat within the week.

# CHAPTER 31
# Luc

I don't believe in a higher power, but I need to thank *someone* that the cat still likes her.

I think Penny can forgive me a lot of things—including being the reason her damned life is in danger—but I doubt she'd ever have truly forgiven me if I ruined her relationship with her cat.

Once I'm sure movement won't startle Jinx, I set up the damned litter box. Once again, I'm a servant to a ten-pound tiny dictator. And I have a feeling it'll be the same for the rest of Jinx's life.

"Love, you should eat," I tell her, looking over to see her still petting the cat. Jinx is mostly walking circles around her, no doubt re-scenting her, but she's consistently letting Penny touch her, so it's progress. "That took a lot out of you."

"We have food," Elise assures her, getting up to walk over to the fridge. Jinx watches her for a second, but ultimately, she decides to stay with Penny.

Elise re-heats a plate and hands it to Penny, right there on the floor. Some part of me hates my woman eating on the damned floor, but I know without even trying that she's not moving, so I sit down on the floor with her. Not right next to her, since I don't want to upset the cat, but close enough that I could reach out and touch her.

"So," Marcus says as soon as Penny starts to eat, "I've been thinking. Vane isn't going to poke his head out with four shifters and a dragon inside the house, and a dozen more shifters outside."

"Right," I agree slowly, already sensing that I won't like whatever he has to say. "That's why we're all here."

"Even if we never get anywhere? Even if Vane just goes to ground and you never find him?"

"He works at a fucking law office," Max points out. "I can be standing outside of it in like two hours and grab him when he walks in."

"And he'll disappear at the first sign of you. You already said he could magically hide his scent."

That's true; Max had lost the shifters living near Penny. We're definitely working at a disadvantage here. Not that that'll stop us; we've certainly done more with less.

"So, that's why I've been thinking—the best thing to do is lay a trap," Marcus continues.

Every muscle in my body snaps to readiness. My mind screams *threat* and *kill*, seeing this dragon as a direct threat to

286

my mate. "Penny is not fucking *bait*," I growl, fighting the shift as the wolf pushes to come out and handle the threat.

"She'd be perfectly safe—"

"She's not bait!" My heart is beating like a jackhammer and I'm sweating at just the thought. I've made Penny safe; there's no way in hell I'll throw her right back into danger.

Elise turns on her husband, giving him an unimpressed look. "Marcus."

He shrugs. "I'm not suggesting we give her to Vane, angel. Just set a trap."

Penny reaches out and puts a hand on my leg. "Listen to him."

Her touch calms me slightly, but that doesn't mean I suddenly think this is a good idea. Why she's listening to him, I have no idea, but I'm going to have to teach her to regard her own safety more highly. "We are not going to put you in danger, love."

"It'd be pretty safe," Max muses, like this is a thought exercise. "We'd all be right there, watching."

"What would I have to do?" Penny asks before I can tell Max to go fuck himself.

"Go home," Max says, like he's just thinking out loud. "Just go home and we'll stay nearby, ready. I'd assume if you're left supposedly unprotected, Vane would show up. He'll have to; he's found Alexander's bones at this point. If he wants to keep playing this game, then you're the only piece left."

Penny's actually considering this. I feel like the last sane person left. "Penny—"

"It'll have to be tonight," she says, ignoring me completely. My whole world feels like it's unravelling. "My sister and her wife and kids come back the day after tomorrow. I'm not putting them in danger."

"We can make that work," Marcus agrees. "The sooner the better, really. End this whole thing."

"Penny—" I need her to hear me.

She shakes her head, finally turning to look at me. The cat, no doubt sensing the tension in the room, disappears back into the closet. "I won't have this following us around forever, Luc. And when my family gets home—something could happen to them. I won't allow it. Besides—you wanted me to be able to protect myself. This is what you get."

I growl. "This is *not* what I meant."

She shrugs. "Tough. It's what you're getting. Now, work with us to plan, please. I think it'll be stronger with all of us, but if you want to risk it—"

She's cornered me. I'm a sucker and I walked right into this one; I backed her into letting me change her, and now she's exacting her price for it.

I'd admire it if her price was literally anything else. Money? I'd hand her my wallet. Eternal favors? I'm at her damned service. But allowing her life to be put in danger?

She's not going to back down, though. She's going to insist on this course of action, and the only thing I can do is try to minimize the damage.

"Never seen you give in to another person before. Ever," Max muses as we sit in a car a block away from Penny's house.

"Penny's different." Much to my chagrin. It'd be so much easier if I could intimidate her like everyone else.

"I get it. And it's good for you."

"Good for me?" I ask disbelievingly. "My future wife is in there alone, waiting for an attack. Don't call this good for me." I'm holding on by a thread right now, and don't want to even contemplate who I'll become if this all goes wrong. This isn't just bad for me; it's potentially bad for the world.

"Your future wife checked your ass in a way no one else can," he points out. "You should be excited about that."

I'm so fucking excited. There's just a thousand things I'd wish for Penny to demand of me first.

"She's going to be just fine," Max tells me.

"You don't know that."

"I know there's a fucking dragon circling the sky. And we're here. And you have another twelve shifters within a quarter of a mile. Everything is going to be fine."

It better be.

"That reminds me," I say, keeping my eyes intent on the house. "When this is over—" when Penny is safe, when Vane is dead and I'm not worried about a threat to my heart as it walks around outside my chest "—you and I are going to pay a visit to a prison." I haven't even had time to look up Patton yet, but I haven't forgotten him or the death sentence he has hanging over his head. People who hurt Penny don't survive, whether they're a powerful sorcerer or a run-of-the-mill human criminal.

"What? Why?" I can feel his eyes turn to me even when I don't look away.

"Watch the fucking house," I say sharply. "And because there's a man there who we're going to kill, that's why."

He seems to consider for a moment, then shrugs. "Any particular reason, or...?"

"He hurt Penny."

"Is this a wedding present, then?"

I stop to consider that. Would she like that? She handled the news that I murdered Alexander and have every intention of killing Vane just fine. Maybe offering to slay her demons will be appealing to her.

Once Vane is dead, I can sort out what I should do from her reaction. Greg is going to die either way; that's not negotiable. No one hurts my woman and lives.

Speaking of... I stare intently at the house, waiting. Before I can plan what to do about Greg, Vane has to die first.

# CHAPTER 32
# Penny

I keep looking over my shoulder.

The house is too quiet. The shadows are too long. I know a lot of that is from being so used to having three adults and two toddlers in the house, and the absence of the boys running around makes the place feel empty. But it's not just that.

Something sinister is lurking in every shadow. It's like the whole house feels hostile now, and I hate it. This place has been home for six years, and I've always felt safe here.

I know I won't live here much longer. I can hardly live here when I turn into a giant wolf sometimes; I felt in complete control when I was at Max and Casey's house, but the last thing I ever want is to put my family in any danger. But still. It's my home.

Maybe it's Jinx not being here that makes it feel so threatening. We agreed leaving her behind at Casey's house was the best course of action, considering we're planning on someone trying to break into mine in the next few hours. I'm sure Jinx isn't thrilled about that, and I'd much rather have her here; she keeps me calm. But right now, that's the safest place for her.

> How're you doing?

It's my sixth text from Luc so far. He seems to be checking in every thirty minutes exactly, and I've been blowing him off a bit, but I decide to be honest.

> I don't like how quiet it is here.

His response is immediate.

> Want me to come get you?

> No. We're going to see this through, Luc.

> I was afraid you'd say that. You don't have to put yourself in danger, love.

I do, though. It'll get this all over with sooner and give us an actual chance. I can protect my family, and Luc will sleep easier when he knows Vane isn't out there anymore.

Vane is going to die at the end of this. I've been trying to make my peace with that over the last few hours and found it disturbingly easier than I expected. Then again, every time Luc or Max open their mouths about their childhoods is a sharp reminder why. Vane can die screaming, for all I care. He'd deserve it.

> When this is over, I want to suck your cock.

I almost don't send it, but I decide I need to, because I've been thinking about that too, and because I think he needs something to distract him a bit.

He waits a whole ten seconds to respond.

> Whatever you want. Whenever you want it.

> Been thinking about me?

> Mhm.

> Want to get on your knees and suck me while I tell you how fucking perfect you are?

I bite my lip.

> You'd like that?

> You'd look so fucking pretty on your knees for me.

I sink onto the couch, the cold, lonely, emptiness of the house having been successfully chased away. It's not as good as him being next to me, but it's enough for right now. I'll take it.

> But I don't want to come in your mouth, love. I want to fill up that perfect cunt of yours. Make you full of me.

Oh, *Jesus Christ*. I'm going to have to go upstairs to my room and get myself off if this keeps going. I was playing with fire, but I should have known Luc was better at it than me. Now it's like I'm burning.

> Keep talking.

Apparently I'm a glutton for punishment here. I pull my legs up under me, pressing my thighs together.

> The second this is over, I'm taking you somewhere private. I don't think I'm going to have the patience to give you your fantasy, love. Not at first. I need you. Need to be in you. Need to feel you around me and make you moan. Your cunt is home, Penny, and I never want to leave again. Let's never be apart again.

I moan, one hand trailing down like I'm going to slide it into my jeans. I pull back. Not now. This might be a good distraction, but I can't *actually* let all situational awareness go. I'm technically under imminent threat of attack. It doesn't matter that Luc, Max, and Marcus all promised they'd kill Vane long before he ever gets to me; being caught masturbating while my life is in danger would just be embarrassing.

> I shouldn't be this turned on right now.

> I like when you're turned on.

Yeah, no shit. That's a hell of an understatement.

Rolling my eyes, I stand up and walk to the kitchen, determined to distract myself before I really do go upstairs and let Luc sext me for the rest of the afternoon.

The rotisserie chicken I planned as Jinx and my Christmas dinner is still in the fridge. I suppose it *is* Christmas, so I should eat it today, even if it feels a bit weird and sad to be celebrating.

If it weren't for Vane, I could be celebrating with Luc and all the people I met over the last few days. I could have actually had a proper Christmas, the first one I've truly looked forward to... ever, maybe.

It's not that I don't love Christmas with Stephanie and her family, but before Louise's parents moved away, they always came here to see the kids open their toys, and I'd always been the hanger-on. I've been a dead weight in Stephanie's life for too long now; I know she would never see it that way, would be heartbroken if I described myself that way, but that's what it has been. It really is time for me to start over.

I grab a chicken wing and some white meat. No sides, but I don't have the energy to make a good Christmas meal. I sit down at the lonely table, and pull out my phone to see if Luc texted me again.

The back door creaks open.

I freeze. Stephanie and Louise never fix the creak on that door; they say they want to hear if the boys are messing with it. And that might be saving my life.

I turn slowly, trying to text one-handed.

"I wouldn't."

Vane's voice is chilling. He rarely talked at the restaurant, but he'd always been soft-spoken. He's not loud now, but he's speaking with a self-assured coldness that makes my bones rattle.

He's staring at me, but not the same too-observant stare that made all the waitresses nervous around him. No, I feel like a rabbit, locked in his sight.

"I'm well aware your boyfriend is nearby," he continues, like we're having a conversation. "This couldn't be a more obvious trap if they hung a sign on your front door." He takes a step further inside, letting the kitchen door close behind him. I swallow, forced to look up at him now. My hand is still on my phone, but I don't dare look at it. I try to hit send. Even if my message doesn't make any sense, Luc will surely know something is wrong if he gets a nonsensical message from me.

"What those brutes failed to consider is *magic*," he says. "Perhaps Maximus can rip off a head, but they never stop to think about what I can do with magic. And they're not getting in here now." He smiles, and it's a thousand times worse than anything else he's done.

"What do you want?" I whisper, clutching the back of my chair with my free hand. "They didn't care about you. They didn't know you existed. You could have gotten away if you didn't come for me."

"It's refreshing to see the great Lucius Lawson fail at something," he muses, taking a step closer. "He likes to think he runs the world, that we all live in fear of him, but there are plenty of people pulling one over on him. Drop the phone; it's tedious."

I debate for a minute, but under his stare I don't really have a choice. I drop it onto the floor, letting it fall beneath the table, and pray I got to send a message before I did.

But what could it even do? Vane says that his magic will prevent them from getting in here. Luc might know something's wrong, but that doesn't mean he can do anything about it.

"No matter what you do to me, they won't give you what you want," I say, hoping I sound braver than I feel. My heart is ready to beat right out of my chest. I don't think a sorcerer will have as good of hearing as a wolf, so maybe he doesn't notice. I try to keep my face composed and my voice steady, but I don't know how well I succeed. "You wanted Alexander, right? He's dead."

"I know." The cold mask breaks, revealing the burning fury in his eyes as he steps even closer. "My shifters found his bones, just outside of that cozy little cabin they were keeping you in. Did it feel good to sleep over a graveyard? I imagine your little boyfriend killed plenty of people there."

I try to keep my face impassive, but I had no idea they'd killed and buried him there. Was that what his supposed "safe house" was for?

Well, I'm glad I didn't know that when I was staying there. Thinking of someone as awful as that being anywhere near me is disgusting.

"So you know he's dead," I say. "What could you possibly still want? There's still time to run—" He'll never get away, not now that he put me in his crosshairs. Luc won't allow it; I know he'll hunt Vane to the ends of the earth. But maybe Vane doesn't know that.

"Because Lucius Lawson doesn't get to bite the hand that *made* him and just get away with it," Vane snarls. He's standing practically right on top of me now, forcing me to tilt my head all the way back to see him. "There are *consequences* to the type of meddling he does. Just because they took a while to catch up doesn't mean they don't exist. He needs to lose something, and, unfortunately for you, you might just be the only thing he cares about."

I'm not leverage. I'm not his hostage. I'm the sacrificial lamb.

My heart is in my throat, my body feels like lead. *No.* I can't do this. I can't let this happen. Vane isn't wrong; Luc cares about me. It might be conceited to say, but I don't think he'd do well if I was gone.

Luc would *burn down the world* if I was taken from him, actually. Getting my shit together won't just save me, here.

I take a deep breath, then another. Then I force myself to look into his eyes, to see the cold hatred there.

I had someone loom over me with hatred in their eyes before, but Greg is in federal prison and I'm here. I can do this.

"So you're, what, going to kill me because you're pissed off?" I ask, tilting my chin up and hoping I don't look as scared as I feel. "You know your friend killed children, right? I thought you all believed in the survival of the fittest. If he died, it sounds like he earned it."

I'm playing with fire and I know it, but Vane's nearly apoplectic reaction makes it worth it. I can practically see the steam coming out of his ears.

Good. In my experience, angry people make the stupidest mistakes.

I try to glance down at my phone, but it's hidden by the table now. I can't see if anything I typed made it through. Even if it did, if I believe Vane, it doesn't matter. I need to find a way out of here.

"Someone always dies," he seethes, voice low and deadly. "If Alexander died, that's his own fault. But I can't let your wolf get ahead of himself. Someone always pays the price."

"You didn't bring anyone with you," I point out. "You've always sent shifters after me before. Can't handle your own dirty work."

"I'll show you exactly what I can handle," he snarls, building some sort of ball of light in his hand. I don't know what it is—I don't know anything about magic—but I do know that I want that nowhere near me.

I don't have a stiletto handy, but I do have the knife I was using to cut my chicken. I scramble for it, then jump out of my chair and stab wildly at him. The knife glances off his skin, but I'm gratified to see that I hit him.

He looks at the blood seeping from his hand. "You really think that'll save you?"

No, but it made his hands stop glowing for a moment. I think of wolfish things—four legs, fur, blood and hunting and death—and let the shift take hold.

I growl at Vane, and he takes half a step back. Something primal in me preens at that—so he's not used to shifters not under his direct control. He doesn't know how to interact with people who aren't terrified to cross him.

The human part of me recognizes that I'm fucking terrified but going to do it anyway. In the wolf's body, though, that all feels distant; there's no room for fear when we're on the hunt. It's the strongest adrenaline rush I've ever felt, and everything not immediately connected to survival shuts down. All I can see, smell, and hear is Vane. My eyes seem to instinctively pick out weak spots, and I know exactly how much force I have to bite with to tear off that already-glowing hand.

I'm not faster than him, though, and he throws the glow at me. It burns with the pain of a thousand suns, blowing up like a firework around me, pulling a long, pained howl from me. I freeze in place, paralyzed by pain.

*If you stop now, you'll die and Luc will be alone.* The voice inside my head is cold and merciless, making me grit my teeth through the pain.

Fuck biting off his hand. I want the whole head.

I lunge for his neck, snarling as I jump through the air. My aim is off—mental note, practice leaping with four legs—but I still hit him square in the chest and knock him down to the floor, crashing into something as we go.

I look down at him as I loom over him, pinning him to the ground with my paws on his chest.

Last time I had a man bleeding on the floor at my mercy, I couldn't do it. I let him live. I don't think I'm going to have the same issue this time.

"Mutt," he grunts, and I see a light out of the corner of my eye. I don't think, just react, lunging at his throat and letting my teeth close around it.

There's a disgusting crunching sound, and a coppery taste in my mouth. Blood. My human brain screams that it's disgusting, but the wolf refuses to let go until he stops moving.

I bat at the limp body with one paw, and nothing happens. I do it again, just in case, but he doesn't so much as twitch. Which makes sense, because even with the human side of me trying to ignore it, I can see the way his throat is completely ripped open.

His head is hanging at an unnatural angle; I think I might have severed his spine.

I whimper and turn away from the corpse. That will haunt my nightmares long enough without continuing to stare at it, thank you very much.

My limbs don't move as fast as I'd like, and I can't tell if that's shock or the lingering spark-like pain from Vane's stupid spell. We broke the table and one of the chairs when I knocked him down, apparently, so I move to the other side of the room, then over into the living room, away from the body so I don't have to look at it anymore.

I start trying to think of human things, but my thoughts are too scattered for that. I don't want human things—I want Luc. I want his touch, the way he holds me, the way he comforts and loves me. Curling into a ball in front of the couch, I let out a plaintive howl, hoping I'm heard.

# CHAPTER 33

# Luc

When she stops texting me, my hackles immediately go up.

They shouldn't. There's a million reasons why she might not be texting me. She might be in the bathroom, or using both hands for a myriad of tasks. She could be texting her sister or just over the little game we were playing. Logically, I know these things.

But that doesn't matter. I know in my gut something is wrong, and I'm halfway out of the car before Max even knows what's going on.

"Do you want him to see us?" he hisses, grabbing on the back of my shirt.

"He's here." I say it with absolute authority; authority I don't have right now, but I *know* it. And I won't waste time when Penny's life could be in danger.

"I don't smell anything—"

"You couldn't smell those shifters, either," I interrupt. "Let's *move*."

Whether it's the desperation in my eyes or the centuries of following my commands, Max nods and follows me. When we get closer to the house, we both slip into our wolf forms, ready to take on any enemy. I don't smell any other shifters, but that doesn't mean they're not here.

All my soldiers see us moving and fall in behind us, closing in on the house. I should tell them to hold back, to keep their eyes peeled, considering I haven't even seen Vane yet. But something inside me tells me I need to get in that house right now. My heart is beating double-time, every beat sounding like *Pen-ny, Pen-ny, Pen-ny*. I need to get to her.

I'm thrown backward the second I reach the back gate. I blink, lying on my back, staring at it and unable to explain what the fuck just happened. Max growls and charges at the gate, and he's thrown even further back than I was, landing on his ass and making a mournful little howl.

Marcus lands in the street, and I know dragons have an innate magic to hide themselves from humans, but it's still disconcerting to see a giant lizard-like beast on a suburban street. He turns into his human form quickly enough, striding over to us. "What happened?"

I'm not leaving my wolf form to explain, not now that I'm even more sure that something is grossly wrong. I growl, then stand upright and charge the gate again, only to be thrown back once more.

"I'll just burn the damn thing down," Marcus murmurs, and before I can tell him it's a terrible idea, he's turned back into a dragon, taking up way more space than he has any right to, and is blowing fire toward the house my wife is in.

The flame blows right back, and I growl at him while dodging it. Honestly, he's lucky there's some sort of barrier. If he lit Penny's house on fire, I'd find a way to murder a dragon.

He turns back, evidently valuing thumbs over brawn, and shrugs. "Was worth a try. Magic?"

Obviously. I was right, and something has gone terribly wrong.

I start running. Fences can be replaced, and gates are just suggestions, anyway. But no matter where I try to breach the fence, it repels me backward, throwing me on my ass.

I can't get through. I can't get to Penny, to my love who's in danger. We promised her she'd be safe, and we already failed her, and I—

I burst through the fence near the front door. Not stopping to analyze why, I run for the door. If I changed back, I could open it, but that'll take too long—I need to get to Penny *now*. I break it down by forcing my way through it, and it folds like cardboard.

The front door opens into the living room, which looks exactly the same as the last time I saw it except for the trail of blood. Heart in my throat, terrified for what might have happened to

Penny, I follow the trail to find her in wolf form, curled up by the sofa, completely still.

My heart stops beating. Oh, fuck. Vane got to her—is she breathing? Is her heart still beating? I bound over there, nudging her with my nose, trying to get as close as possible.

She moves when I poke at her, making a rumbling noise and welcoming me into her cuddle pile. I haven't done this since I was small, and even then, only rarely—we weren't exactly encouraged to develop friendly bonds with each other. But I accept immediately, curling into her so our fur all blends together, and you can't tell where either of us begin or end. I rest my head on hers, trying to get a deep scent of her.

The blood isn't hers, or at least, not as far as I can tell. It doesn't smell like hers, and she doesn't smell like fresh blood. There's some drying blood matted into her fur, especially around her muzzle, but I don't think it's hers.

I want to turn back and ask her what happened, but the way she's leaning on me right now tells me that's a bad idea. If she needs comfort from me like this, then she'll get it.

The others burst in through the back door. I lift my head just enough to see them, but then lower it again, returning to a world of just my mate and I.

I listen as they pace the whole house, checking every inch of it. A part of me registers that I should be joining them, that I shouldn't let my guard down until I know for sure we're safe.

But I know that where I am is exactly where I'm meant to be right now.

Eventually, Max returns, crouching down in his human form a good yard or so away from us, making sure to give us space. "Penny," he asks, voice gentle, "did you kill him?"

I jolt at that. It shouldn't be a surprise, not with the blood around her muzzle, but my Penny, a killer?

I growl. She shouldn't have had to be. We failed her.

I expect her to turn back and answer Max, but all she does is bury her head deeper into my fur.

Max sighs, but doesn't seem to actually need an answer. "Vane is dead," he reports to both of us. "Penny tore his throat out and severed his spinal cord. Honestly, it's pretty impressive work."

I preen at that. Of course it was. My woman is pretty impressive all around.

"I'm assuming all his spells and not just the barrier fell when he died," he continues. "So I sent all our guys out to hunt for any of his shifters who might be nearby, now that they should be able to smell them. If we can turn them to our side, we will. Otherwise, we'll take care of the problem. Do you want me to join them, or watch the house?"

I'm torn. Max is my best soldier by far, and he's most useful out there, hunting down rogue shifters. But Penny was just attacked in her own home—again. I want to ensure she's perfectly safe.

Marcus strolls in, not bothering to get down to our level like Max did. "I am going to go and put the fear of the dragon into some shifters," he announces. "Let's see them immediately run to your boys for protection. And after that, I am going home. I've been away from my nest and my mate for too long. Don't call me again."

He turns to leave, and I guess that answers that. Max might be fierce, but even he can't inspire the fear of an angry dragon.

"I'll keep watch, then," Max says. "And move the corpse." He walks back over to the kitchen, and I hear a thud, no doubt him moving the corpse and not being particularly gentle about it.

If I were in my human form, I'd remind Max it's broad daylight on a holiday, and he can't just carry a corpse out the door. As it is, Penny is my priority, and I just trust that he knows.

I nudge Penny with my snout, hoping I can convince her that it's safe here and she can turn back. She doesn't respond.

Well, that's fine. I'll be whatever she needs, and if she needs a pillow right now, I'll be that. Penny's never killed anyone before, and while I don't truly remember a time before my first kill, I understand that this is probably stressful for her.

It takes a while, but Penny finally pulls back from me. I look into her wolfish eyes—brown, just like her human ones—and see her hurt there. I lean up to rub my face against hers, and she makes a sad little sound before turning back.

I turn back with her, and soon we're in a pile of naked limbs on her sister's living room floor.

Penny still has blood on her face, but now it's dried and scaly and no doubt itchy. My wolf form would lick that off of her, but I don't want to turn back when she might start talking. I'll get her a wet rag in a minute.

"How're you feeling?" I ask softly, taking her hand and stroking my thumb across the back of it.

She shivers. "He's dead, right?"

"He's dead," I assure her. "I'm sorry you had to deal with him. I promised you wouldn't be in danger, and you were. That was unacceptable."

She turns her hand in mine until she's interlaced our fingers, then squeezes. "Luc," she says firmly, "I made the decision to do this. I wanted—I *needed* it to be over. And now it is."

"You shouldn't have had to do that. I know killing isn't something you wanted to do." I'm a killer to my core; I can't separate who I am from the murderer. But I never wanted that for Penny.

"I just thought about you," she admits quietly. "About what you went through as a child, and all the other shifters he's probably done that to. And about how you'd feel if I let him hurt me."

"I'd destroy the world," I tell her immediately, and, bizarrely, she smiles. "There is no me if you're not here, love."

She leans in and kisses me, and I eagerly return it, blood be damned. What's a little blood between soul mates, anyway? "I know," she whispers when she pulls away. "I know you would. That's why I had to do it. So we can have forever together instead."

This woman is too good to me. I scoop her into my lap, hands a firm band on her hips, pulling her to me. It'd be so easy to rock up inside her, but this isn't about that. I just need to feel every inch of her pressed against every inch of me. I need to feel her alive and breathing.

I press our foreheads together and hold her there, breathing her air and sharing her space. Eventually, she pulls back and asks, "Do you need to help the others?"

Should I help them? Probably. Does anything take priority over Penny? Fuck no. "I'm here for you," I tell her, but that does mean I should probably start actually taking care of her. If she's well enough to suggest I leave, then she's well enough for me to move her. "Let's get you cleaned up."

Upstairs, I get Penny into the shower while I raid her room and pick out an outfit for her, more comfy jeans and another oversized sweatshirt, and yet another thong underneath. I need to take her shopping somewhere where underwear doesn't come in a pack, and add it to my to-do list.

Hell, I owe her some Christmas presents. Although that might be more of a present for me than for her.

She's out quickly, skin scrubbed pink from the too-hot shower. She lets me help her dress, which gives me the side benefit of triple-checking her for any missed wounds. She's completely clean, the only thing on her skin being that stupid fake-gold anklet that won't break.

"He burned me," she says, breaking the silence. "With some sort of magic. I half expected to see some of my skin blistering and falling off."

I hate imagining Penny like that and have to suppress a growl. I hate the fact that he hurt her even more, and have to remind myself he's already dead. He died far too easily, but there's nothing that can be done about that now. "The beauty of speedy healing," I manage to tell her. "Nothing lasts forever."

"Handy," she says, studying her skin like it's foreign to her.

I don't like the way she's looking at herself, and I kiss her hands before feeding them into her sweatshirt. "You're still you," I tell her. "Everything that makes you Penny is still there. You just hold up to the world a little better. Although I'm not going to ever let you be put in a position like that again."

She pokes her head out of her sweatshirt, and she's so damn cute I have to kiss her, pushing her wet hair out of her face so I can touch every inch of her skin.

"Alright," she murmurs, her lips an inch from mine but her tone far more serious than I'd like. "I think I broke the house. And Stephanie is coming home the day after tomorrow. So, what are we going to do?"

# CHAPTER 34
# Penny

L uc's people finish fixing everything just minutes before Stephanie and Louise pull up to the house.

Luc's monitored them the entire time, all cool and collected, while I've been slowly getting more and more stressed out. It's kind of twisted that I'm somehow less stressed about killing someone than I am about being forced to tell my sister about it because we didn't clean the damage well enough.

"I should get into crime scene clean up," Luc mutters. "I'd make a killing."

"You should," I agree. "Since you're so good at it. Plus, you'll have more free time now."

"No, I won't."

I stop pacing and face him. "Did you change your mind about resigning?"

He steps into my space, taking my face in his hands so I have to look at him. "Of course not, love. But I'm going to replace all that time with something far better: you."

I snort, trying to turn out of his hold. He doesn't let go. "Even I'm not so demanding I'd take up as much time as your full-time job did."

"You should be." He's still completely serious. "You should be that demanding, Penny. You deserve that." He leans in and kisses me softly. "I want a future with you, love. I want *everything*. I want to take you to see all the places you dreamed of, and I want to spend every waking moment reminding you how much I adore you. So yes, that's a full time job. And one I'm excited to take on." He stops for a moment, considering. "I don't think I've ever been happy to do something before. I know that sounds pathetic, but it's true. And here I am, happy. That's because of you."

My breath catches, and I almost tear up. I knew he felt all of that, because he won't stop telling me. But to hear the commitment, the final sign that this is all real— "I love you," I tell him, because I need him to know.

His smile is slow, perhaps a little surprised, but entirely happy. "I love you, too," he promises, then leans in for a kiss.

We're interrupted by the same man Luc brought to fix Stephanie's carpet and bar cart last time. I don't remember his name, and I frown. I should learn these people's names. They're all going to be a regular part of my life now.

"All done, boss," he says, wiping his hands off on a rag.

"And it looks perfect?" Luc presses.

He huffs. "You have any idea how hard it is to match worn flooring? It'd be easier if we could just replace it."

"I think it'd be hard to convince my sister she won a home makeover show when she didn't apply," I point out. "And I don't want to explain the dead body in her house."

He nods, acknowledging my point. "It's done. I mean, if they memorized every crack and speck of dirt, they'll notice. But it'll pass a casual inspection."

The nice thing about having two small kids running around is the house always seems to be chaotically changing. I'm sure Louise and Stephanie will put any changes they do notice down to the boys.

"And the table?"

"Replaced. And the old one is gone, all the splinters picked up." He eyes me speculatively. "You did a number on it there."

Luc growls and steps in front of me, some sort of warning to his friend, but I take it as the praise I know he meant it as. "Thank you," I say from around Luc. "I appreciate you getting all of it done."

He blinks at me, clearly unused to hearing *thank you*. "No problem. We'll get out of your hair before your sister gets home." He turns to Luc. "And Maximus said he's on his way."

"Max is coming?"

Luc nods at me, turning away from his friend, who apparently takes it as dismissal and walks away. "You need the cat back.

And I need a ride out of here. Unless you want to introduce me to your sister today?"

That seems like a recipe for disaster. We haven't come up with a story yet, and even if I wanted to ask him to let me tell my sister the truth someday, it can't be like this. Revealing that I'm a werewolf and I'm going to marry a werewolf is delicate.

*Marry*. Jesus. It's obviously going to happen at this point, and I've made a way bigger commitment to this man already. It's just jarring to think about. I honestly never thought I'd be married again.

But I'm not opposed to the idea. I'd marry Luc in a heartbeat. He told me before to name the time and place, and I wonder how long I'm going to last before I tell him I'm ready.

The front door opens, and I brace myself for the invasion of the toddlers, but it's just Max, holding a box that seems to contain the world's most indignant cat. "You'd think that if she likes you, she'd learn the rest of us don't mean her any harm," he grumbles, handing me the box.

"Hey, baby," I murmur, opening the box and sticking my hand in, careful to give Jinx enough space so she can choose to approach me. I'm worried the few days without me might have made her standoffish again.

But within a few seconds, she's rubbing against my hand and purring. Soon enough, she's physically climbing my arm, trying to get out of the box, so I scoop her up and let her perch on my shoulder, repeatedly rubbing her entire body against my head.

"We have to go," Max murmurs. "Unless you want to explain why we're here?"

Luc tugs me into a deep kiss, leaning me back until Jinx meows angrily and clings to me with claws through my sweatshirt. "I'll talk to you later," he promises lowly. "Don't miss me too much, alright?"

"My phone broke," I remind him, because we'd dug the crushed pieces of it from underneath the broken table. I'm going to need to replace that soon.

"Who said anything about calling?" Luc asks, and before I can even reply, he and Max are out the back door, just in time for the front door to open and little feet to run into the house.

After the boys have shown me their Christmas presents and tormented my cat with pets and shrill exclamations of how much they missed her, after Stephanie and Louise fall onto the couch, exhausted after bedtime, interrogating me about my plans to move out and the guy I'm involved with, after we all agree to go to bed, I close myself into my bedroom and nearly collapse.

I look around the place. The cat furniture takes up most of the space, and I bet Luc will help me get it out of here. Or tell someone else to do it, at any rate. It'll make a good bedroom for one of the boys. They're getting older; they really do deserve their own rooms.

Stephanie told me four or five times that I don't need to leave, that I'm welcome here for the rest of my life. It's sweet but not necessary. I can see it in the tension around her eyes; she's worried about me. I spent so much time worrying about her, but she's the one who had to pull me out of my spiral and keep me going. But I don't need that anymore. I've found my footing, finally.

Greg fucked me up, there's no denying it. But I've spent six years clawing my life back, and I'm not going to let him interrupt it anymore.

There's a knock on my window. My muscles go tense like they've been replaced with steel rods, rigid and ready. Not again. *Not again*. It was supposed to be done now.

I turn slowly toward the window. If I turn to a wolf and keep it contained to my room—

But it's Luc, giving me that look he gets. He's sitting on my roof at the end of December in New York, looking torn between patience and like he wants to eat me alive.

I crack the window open so fast I might damage the frame slightly. "Jesus," I hiss, looking around furtively, but no one seems to be out to notice a strange man climbing in my window. "What the hell are you doing here?"

"I told you we'd talk soon. What the hell did you think I meant?" he asks, shutting the window without taking his eyes off of me. As soon as it's shut, he wraps me in a hug so tight I'd think he's trying to meld our bodies together, so there's no space between where I start and he ends.

"What if they hear us?" I whisper.

"We can hear far better than they can. Just be quiet, love."

He's so calm about everything. Too calm, really.

One hand scrapes through my freshly washed hair. "They seemed happy to see you," he muses.

"They did, I—" I process what he said and pull back enough to put my hands on my hips. "Lucius Lawson, have you been stalking me again?"

"Why change perfection?" he quips, then shrugs. "I missed most of dinner. Had to run out for something. Speaking of—" He reaches into his pocket and hands me a cellphone. "For you. All set up."

I stare at it for a second, choked up a bit. "Thank you." This was thoughtful of him.

He tilts my chin up so I'm looking at him once more. "I want you to have everything you need," he tells me seriously, then sighs. "Plus, I'm going to assume you're not going to agree to move out of here yet, so it's in my best interests for you to have a working phone."

I laugh, clutching the phone a little tighter. "Soon," I promise him, because it will be soon. I don't think either of us will handle a long separation well.

"And speaking of that—do you want to sit down?" he asks me abruptly, and without waiting for a response, he moves us to the bed, sitting with his back against the wall and pulling me to sit between his spread thighs. I snuggle back into him, and am pleasantly surprised when the cat jumps up, settling at our side and curling up to go back to sleep.

"Speaking of what?" I prompt him.

"Did you watch the news at all this evening?"

"No. There was a lot going on here." The boys had taken all our energy. Honestly, I don't know how Stephanie and Louise are going to do it with only two adults in the house. It's not like I'm an extra parent to their boys, but I'm at least an adult who can take on a little of the load.

Luc and I will just have to live locally enough that I can help out whenever I can.

"Check your phone," he murmurs. "I texted you a news story."

I power on the phone, which looks like an exact backup of my old one, except on a much nicer model. I don't even want to know how he made that happen.

There's a text message. There are half a dozen, actually, but most of them are Stephanie reporting on the progress of their trip home earlier, blissfully unaware that my phone was in little pieces. The last one is from Luc, and I open it, eyes scanning past our last conversation that we still need to get back to to see the news article he sent me.

*Governor Lawson resigns for health reasons.*

I swallow, a lump forming in my throat as I click on it. It's like having an out-of-body experience, like I can't quite believe this is real. I feel a little bit like I'm dreaming.

"Health reasons?" I manage to ask once I read the press release he sent out a few hours ago.

His lips press into my hair. "It'd be bad for my health if I couldn't have you, love. And possibly some other people's health, too. This is a decision to benefit everyone, really."

"How long?" I ask.

He shrugs. "My lieutenant governor can handle it. I'll get her up to speed, and then in a week or two, it'll be done."

"Is she another shifter?"

"Nope. Completely human. Has no idea what I am, and will probably be happy to never have to deal with me again. I'm a little frustrating for her."

"Can't imagine why," I say dryly, leaning further back into his arms. "What will you do after?"

He's quiet for a moment. "You know I won't be entirely done, right? I can leave the humans to govern themselves. I'll stay out of the spotlight, and it'll probably take a few months of laying low. Too many people have seen my face on the news. But as for the rest—I am what I am, Penny. There's a whole world out there that legitimately functions better when I'm in charge of it."

"I know," I tell him right away. I never expected him to leave that behind. Frankly, I couldn't care less; if any of the supernatural creatures I met recognized my face, they didn't act like it. I've yet to hear about the supernatural gossip magazines, so I think I'm safe. I wouldn't want to take away what Luc worked so hard for. "And if I can do anything to help, you'll tell me? I mean, I'm obviously not able to, like, *help*. I can't get shifters to fall in line or kill sorcerers—"

"I think you're very good at both tasks, actually," he interrupts, and I elbow him.

"You know what I mean. But I'll be with you. When I'm not at work."

"Work." He repeats it like it's a foreign concept. "You mean you're going to keep working?"

I shrug. I haven't truly thought about it yet, to be honest, but right now I'm leaning toward yes. "Have an issue with me having a job?"

He sighs. "I'm going to spend a lot of time stalking you still, aren't I?" he asks rhetorically. "I got you to fall in love with me, but I *still* have to follow you around, unseen."

"Or you could get a hobby."

"That is my hobby."

This man is ridiculous. But as I snuggle back into him even more, I kind of get it. He told me my scent is soothing to him, and he's definitely soothing to me.

321

I'll always know where he is, at any rate. No more sneaking around completely undetected.

"I should let you rest," he murmurs, kissing the top of my head again. "You've had a long few days." He slips out from behind me. I'm not overly helpful; he's comfortable to cuddle with.

"Luc?"

He freezes by the window. "Yes, love?"

"You don't need to stalk me from the street anymore. Just come up."

He grins at me, sharp and a little dangerous. "Noted, love," he says, and then comes back to bed.

# CHAPTER 35

# Luc

## Two Months Later

I'm almost late to dinner.

In my defense, I have an excuse. But it's not an excuse I particularly want to share with anyone attending this dinner.

Greg Patton is dead. It had taken nearly two months to set up what I needed, but I'd been patient. I'd waited, because Penny deserved my best effort.

Max and I had faked his death in prison, removed him, and taken him to a new location just for this purpose, since Vane's shifters burned down my last dungeon for assholes who needed to die bloody and screaming. And then I'd spent the better part of two weeks making him regret every decision he's ever made.

Penny thinks I haven't been following her to work anymore because I got a hobby. I suppose I did, but probably not the one she expects.

Honestly, I could have kept going for months longer. Patton wasn't quite as durable as Alexander was, so I had to exercise caution and not kill him too fast, but I'm capable of being cautious when it gets me what I want. But I finished it an hour ago, then burned and buried his mangled corpse. It's time to move forward.

Penny thinks Patton died in prison, and she suspects I've had something to do with it. She hasn't asked me outright yet, but she probably will, and I'll tell her the truth if she wants to know.

She deserves to know that Patton will never so much as breathe the same air as her again, and equally importantly, that he's been punished for what he put her through. No one hurts my love and gets away with it.

We'll have plenty of time together in the next few weeks, and I'll have an answer ready for her if she asks.

Penny is waiting for me outside her sister's house, arms crossed and impatient. "Dinner is almost ready."

"And I'm here." Bearing gifts, too, because even a day filled with murder isn't an excuse to make a bad impression.

I've made enough of a bad impression already. First I was the man who Penny didn't tell them about in what Stephanie considers a timely manner. She's still leery that Penny has moved out of her house and into mine, and that's with her thinking we've been together a lot longer than we have. And there's the whole former governor thing, too. The story about resigning for my health didn't hold water in a lot of circles, and many speculated that this was my attempt to outrun a looming scandal.

Just because no scandal ever broke doesn't mean Stephanie ever decided to fully trust me.

I don't need her to like me, but I do need her to co-exist with me. Penny isn't going to give up her family until she absolutely has to, and I want her to have as many years with them as possible.

"Let's go," I mutter, but then contradict myself by pulling her into my arms so I can give her a kiss. "Did you have a good last day at work?"

She shoves lightly at my chest, but I know she's not trying to get away. "I keep telling you; it's not actually my last day."

"For a month, it is." Penny waited until the restaurant could hire and train a new server, then gave it two more weeks to be sure. But now, she's officially free of obligations, and tomorrow we're getting on a plane so I can take her away for a month.

She wrapped up her obligations to the restaurant, and I wrapped up my murderous urges today. We were both very productive.

She keeps insisting she'll go back, and maybe she will. I don't want to keep her from her family, after all. But I'm hoping she'll give me longer than a month.

I've already packed my luggage, and there's a diamond ring tucked neatly inside my bag.

That'll be another thing for Stephanie to resent me over. She'll say we're moving too fast. I like how she worries for her sister, and I know she has good reason to, considering what happened in Penny's last marriage; I just wish I could prove to her that I'm different.

Ah, well. Only time will tell.

We walk up the drive with her arm through mine, and I shift so I'm carrying my shopping bag in my free hand.

The older boy, Will, opens the door, with his mother running behind him. "I keep telling you, don't open the—oh, hey guys," Louise says, snatching her son up and throwing him over her shoulder, making him giggle hysterically as she carries him away.

"Charming," I mumble, but only so Penny can hear me.

She elbows me in the side. "You *like* it," she whispers.

The chaos of the children? Well, I like how Penny likes it. And I might have toys stuffed away in my bag of goodwill gifts. And Penny might have mocked me the other day when she found the paperwork from me setting up college funds for both boys. But none of that means I actually enjoy them.

"Don't hog my sister," Stephanie calls from the kitchen. "You have her all the time now."

"Clingy," I mutter, and Penny elbows me again.

"Like *you're* one to judge, Mr. Stalker."

True. For the two weeks she still lived in this house after Christmas, we hadn't spent a night apart. I'd gotten very familiar with climbing through her window. And now I have her in my bed every single night, and I plan to spend every moment I can get with her.

We walk into the kitchen, where I promptly present my gifts; a chocolate tart I'd picked up from a local bakery, a nice bottle of wine, and more pieces to the model train set I've been bribing the boys with every time I see them.

Stephanie sighs. "Now we'll never get them to sit and eat." She gives me a look and I just ignore it. We both know she just likes having something to complain about when it comes to me.

Truthfully, I think she reluctantly likes me. She may not want to, may be convinced hating me is the best way to keep Penny safe, but even she can see that I'm head over heels obsessed with her sister.

"I've got it," Penny promises, kissing my cheek before she runs after the boys, cajoling them to the table with promises of playing with them after.

"You'll take care of her when you're gone?" Stephanie asks me while Louise pours the wine.

Penny can take care of herself and she's proven it a thousand times over in her short life, but I know what Stephanie is asking. Penny will never have to take care of it alone again. "I will," I promise her.

"And don't come back married," she insists. "I know this is some romantic vacation, but Penny deserves to have her sister there for her wedding."

Penny absolutely does, but I'm floored that Stephanie even thought about it. Maybe she won't be as shocked and appalled by my plan to propose as I thought.

"We won't," I promise her. Maybe I should tell her about the engagement ring. But I don't ask anyone but Penny's permission for anything, so Stephanie will just have to find out when Penny decides to tell her.

She shoos me off with a wave of her hand. "Go get your girlfriend before my kids distract her all night. Tell her dinner is ready."

I take the excuse to leave her presence and find Penny, who's still urging the boys to set the trains aside. I short-cut the whole experience, telling them, "Go wash your hands and eat or the trains leave with me."

They both scramble to move, and Penny turns in my arms. "You can't threaten them."

"It worked fine." It always works fine. It's how I've gotten most everything in my life.

She turns toward the kitchen, but I stop her with a light grip on her wrist. She freezes like I expected, no doubt thinking of how I woke her up this morning. I fight back a smile.

"What?" she asks quietly, leaning subtly into my touch.

"Nothing." I lean in and steal a kiss. "Just really looking forward to starting forever with you."

She smiles softly, her eyes getting that shiny look they get when she has trouble believing things. I squeeze her wrist lightly so she knows this is real, and then take another kiss before leading her to the kitchen, steeling myself to be nice to my future in-laws for a few hours.

# Want More?

Get an exclusive bonus epilogue about Penny and Luc on my website, www.addyjameswriter.com.

# Also by Addison James

Crae Romance Series

Callum

Bryce

Heath

Celia

Silas

Estrid


Supernatural Christmas Series

A Werewolf for Christmas

A Recipe for Love


Standalones

Dragon's Treasure

The Heat Cure